# Mrs Morphett's Macaroons

Modern Women:
Entertaining Edwardians book 2

Patsy Trench

Prefab Publications

Published in 2021
by Prefab Publications, London



ISBN 978-0-9934537-8-6

§

As with my previous books, while *Mrs Morphett's
Macaroons* is a work of fiction one or two real and
recognisably famous people appear in it. Their lives and
their personalities have been researched carefully, but any
interaction they are supposed to have had with my
fictional characters is, of course, entirely invented.

'Let me explain about the theatre business.
The natural condition is one of insurmountable
obstacles on the road to imminent disaster.'
Philip Henslowe (from *Shakespeare in Love,* Tom Stoppard)

# Author's note

*Mrs Morphett's Macaroons* is the fourth in my series of novels about women who, against all the odds, break free from their allotted roles. Other books in the *Modern Women* series are *The Awakening of Claudia Faraday* and *The Purpose of Prudence de Vere*, set in the Roaring Twenties, and *The Makings of Violet Frogg,* book 3 in Entertaining Edwardians series.

The books are connected by the characters of Claudia, Prudence and Violet, yet each novel stands alone and can be read in any order. There are common themes running through them: women's independence, the suffrage movement, marriage and divorce, work, sexual liberation and the changing expectations of a woman's role according to the prevailing rules of society. The action moves from the late Victorian era to the reign of Edward VII and on to World War 1 and the Jazz Age of the 'bright young things' of the 1920s.

Despite the constraints, my three heroines all experience some form of awakening which leads them to find out who they truly are. The passing of a hundred years or more have seen important changes in the lives of women, and indeed men. But in our deepest selves perhaps we all have something of a Claudia, a Prue, a Violet, and even perhaps a Merry and a Gaye.

# Overture

How does the famous saying go? "Be nice to people on the way up because you'll meet them on the way down."

Nowhere, might one argue, does that saying apply more pertinently than to the entertainment business. Firstly, because as we come to the end of the nineteenth century and it has become acceptable for anyone to become an actor (*vide* the knighthood of Sir Henry Irving), so every Tom, Dick and Harriet wants to join the profession, rendering competition fiercer than ever. Secondly, because the theatre business is unlike any other in that today's call boy may be tomorrow's impresario; or more to the point, today's impresario may be tomorrow's call boy. The career of a person working in the theatre does not necessarily begin at the bottom of the ladder and proceed steadily upwards, rung by rung. Success is fickle and can strike, or not, at any time in an actor's professional life.

Miss Meredith Martin and Miss Gaye Worth, known to their friends and colleagues as Merry and Gaye, were unlikely chums. Miss Martin, tall and imperious, was the daughter of a brigadier, and Miss Worth, of medium height and sardonic, was the daughter of a low comedian. The one thing they had in common was an ambition to be other than where they were at the beginning of our story.

Unfortunately however, these two ladies had once made the mistake of insulting Mrs Violet Graham at a time when they considered their careers to be on their way up. This was a shame, because now that those same careers were on a downward slide Mrs Graham was in a position to advance them.

Violet Graham had once worked as assistant to the acting manager in Herbert Beerbohm Tree's theatre company. It being her first properly paid position she was ignorant of all things theatrical. She neither knew nor understood the ways of actors and how to treat them, and so she was mocked, at length, both separately and together, by Miss Worth and Miss Martin.

The circumstances were these:

Miss Martin and Miss Worth were appearing together on stage at the Haymarket Theatre in the late 1890s in one of those light-hearted yet forgettable plays so oddly beloved by Herbert Tree, the title of which was *Johnson's Retribution*. They were playing two women who were rivals for the favours of the play's hero, and in one particular scene each was given the opportunity to say her piece to prove she was the more deserving of the young man's attentions.

While Miss Martin was delivering her speech, which she had practised assiduously, her rival Miss Worth decided to partake in what's known as a bit of 'business'. Miss Martin, who was declaiming passionately to the audience, and oblivious of what was going on behind her, could not understand why she was getting laughs, especially from the gallery, for what was intended to be a serious moment in the play. On turning around she caught Miss Worth pulling faces and making elaborate mocking gestures which, while in itself was 'in character' – the two were playing rivals after all – was a blatant example of what is known in the theatre as upstaging. As a result of this transgression the moment the two actresses left the stage, and in full view of the stage manager, Miss Martin socked Miss Worth on the jaw so hard she fell to the floor.

The stage manager threatened to sack Miss Martin on the spot. So the following morning she appeared in the office of the newly-arrived assistant to the acting manager, Violet Graham, in order to vent her spleen.

A somewhat baffled and plainly frightened Mrs Graham listened quietly to Miss Martin's account of the event, and then asked to see Miss Worth to hear her side of the argument. Later on and having compared notes she summoned both ladies to her office together. On being invited in they proceeded to mock her, this time in unison, in a routine that a casual bystander might well have thought had been rehearsed. Thus, in their view, they had not only put Mrs Graham in her place, they had confounded her completely by presenting what appeared to be a united front.

To be fair to Miss Worth, and as aforesaid, the level of competition between actors at the time was fierce, and it was not unusual for an actor or an actress to resort to any means possible to draw attention to themselves and gain a round of applause at the end of a scene. This vulgar practice was widespread in the provinces but generally frowned upon by sophisticated West End audiences. Nonetheless in the cutthroat world of the theatre one thing no actress could afford to be was self-effacing.

So, moving forward to the new century and Mrs Graham, previously a very junior member of Herbert Tree's company, was now about to produce her first play in the West End: a light-hearted piece about women's suffrage entitled *Mrs Morphett's Macaroons*, written by newcomer Robbie Robinson. Featuring as it did suffragists and suffragettes the play contained a plethora of parts for actresses.

As our story begins all this is not yet known to Misses Martin and Worth, so the question as to whether or not Mrs Graham will have the magnanimity to put the women's bad behaviour behind her and offer one or other – or even both – of them a once-in-a-lifetime opportunity has yet to arise.

# 1 Mrs Morphett's Macaroons

'Do you mind if I make some suggestions?' asked Violet.

'Not at all,' said Robbie. He twitched.

They were seated on either side of a desk, the script spread out between them. Violet held a pencil between the second and third fingers of her right hand, which she was flicking back and forth. Robbie saw a bird of prey, waiting to swoop.

'First of all,' she said, 'a bit of pruning.'

Robbie nodded.

'Less of the slapstick I think.'

'Slapstick? What slapstick?'

'And the ending. Too much. Really. You will put people off – you will put the men off, in particular.'

'Isn't that the point?'

'Not to put them off wanting to see the play. To make them think, yes, and I understand what you're trying to do. Since we've been governed by men alone since time began and now . . .' She stopped suddenly. 'You know this is a strangely feminist play. Did you intend it to be?'

'Of course I did.' Robbie gave what he hoped was a disarming grin.

'To imagine a world governed by women alone. I understand the satire, I understand it *is* satire. *I* understand it's satire, but . . .'

'How many ways can one say a sentence and have it mean so many different things?' Robbie leaned back in his chair and crossed his legs. 'Kindly do me the favour of not flicking your pencil,' he said, with a smile.

It was the play that had brought the two would-be lovers together again after a ridiculously long separation. Written by Robbie and watched by Violet at its one performance on a Saturday afternoon the previous year at the Comedy Theatre, it was a farce called *Mrs Morphett's Macaroons*, about a humble kitchen maid who becomes involved in the suffragette movement and ends up in the House of Commons as the first female MP. It lampooned everyone from Government ministers to the suffragettes themselves. Coming from someone like the mild-mannered Robbie Robinson it was a revelation. And now Violet had been deputed to produce the piece for a full run in the West End.

The pencil froze between her fingers. 'So sorry,' she said. With studied precision she placed it down upon the desk before her and Robbie heaved an exaggerated sigh of relief.

'You made your point sufficiently,' said Violet. 'But to end up with a Government in which men are banned totally is . . .' she hunted for the word, 'too far-fetched. You carry the audience with you up until that point, or I believe you do. But to ask them to contemplate a world governed entirely by women is nothing short of terrifying. Don't you agree?'

'Not in the least,' said Robbie. 'I rather imagine it might be a better world than the one we have now, which is governed entirely by men.'

'That's as may be,' said Violet. '*You* may say that, though whether you truly believe it is another matter. Other men would not, I suggest. Other less enlightened men, which probably accounts for the majority of men in this country.'

'It's a farce,' said Robbie stubbornly.

'Nonetheless . . .'

'Farces are – well, how does one define a farce? – not to be taken literally. They're to make people laugh and, in this case, to make them think.'

'Which you do, admirably.'

'To have an audience leaving a theatre imagining a world in which everything is turned on its head. It is thought-provoking, or that's the intention. Otherwise, what are we left with? A kind of half-hearted ending, where women are allowed to become members of parliament.' Robbie shrugged. 'Where's the jeopardy in that? Where's the talking point? I want the audience to be flabbergasted. I want to see them leaving the theatre spluttering into their handkerchiefs in *outrage*.'

'And horror.'

'What's wrong with that?'

Violet did not immediately reply.

The two friends and business colleagues exchanged a look across the desk and the bone of contention that lay upon it.

They were in Robbie's study, a small and crowded room at the back of his bachelor apartment in Battersea, south of the River Thames. The desk was an ancient, much-worn affair he had inherited from the family home. The crowd was made up of piles of books and newspapers. For reasons unexplained there were no bookcases.

Robbie earned his 'bread and butter' as he put it in the newspaper business, but his love, his passion, was the theatre. The nearest he had got to it in the past was as a critic, and it was as a critic that he had attended the opening night of Her Majesty's Theatre back in 1897, the year of the late Queen's Diamond Jubilee. He had been introduced to the intoxicating Violet Graham under his critic's name of Algernon Lightly, and by none other than Herbert Tree himself. The assumed name was by Robbie's own confession an affectation, to avoid confusion between Robbie Robinson the critic and Robbie Robinson the writer and journalist.

Their 'romance', if it could be called such a thing, had for one reason or another been thwarted again and again over a period of months, and then years, as Violet disappeared completely, only to reappear some time later under a totally different name and guise. (The full story of which can be found in *The Makings of Violet Frogg*.)

*Mrs Morphett* was the first of Robbie's plays to be staged and he was fiercely protective of it. What he had not bargained for however was that now that there was a producer involved other hands might try to take his baby from him. He was yet to discover that once a play reaches the stage it no longer belongs to the playwright; that by the time it gets to see the inside of a theatre it will have been pawed over and mauled and pummelled until it barely resembles its original pure self. This Violet knew better than most people as she had once read plays for her former employer, the great Herbert Tree. She had witnessed these works of art being pulled through the mangle by any number of meddlers, from Tree himself down to the smallest supernumerary in the cast. As she smiled at her companion she felt a pang of sympathy for him and for what was to come.

'The theatre,' she began, doing her best not to sound patronising, 'is a collaboration. There was not one new play, or even an old one, that ever appeared on the Chief's stage in its original form. Except perhaps for Ibsen.'

'I am aware of that.'

'If we are to make this work, this . . .' she gestured across the desk, 'this partnership, we have to lay down some guidelines.'

The double meaning of her statement landed with a silent crash on the desk between them.

'What partnership is that, precisely?' he asked.

'Our partnership,' said Violet. 'This,' she indicated the playscript, 'all of this. This production.'

'I love you,' said Robbie.

'Oh.' It fell from Violet's lips like a sigh. Her hand went to somewhere near her heart. Then, 'That's what I meant by guidelines,' she said.

'What guidelines?'

'This is business, Robbie.'

'All I meant was . . .'

'I know what you meant,' said Violet. She cocked her head to one side and stared at him, rather like the schoolmistress with the dim-witted child.

He marvelled at the change in Violet since he had first met her. How she had evolved from a naïve, almost puritanical creature into the poised and assured young woman she was now. She was that wonderful mixture of a beautiful woman who was unaware of her beauty; or rather, who was not prepared to sit back and allow her beauty to do all the work for her. What a glorious being! Yet one to be wary of, nonetheless. There was a toughness in her he hadn't noticed before. She'd always been more concerned for her work than for her personal life, or so it appeared to Robbie.

'So?' She was looking at him enquiringly.

'So?'

'Were you listening to me?'

Robbie bowed in submission.

'I thought as much. What were you thinking about? No, don't answer that. I was going to suggest you sleep on it.'

'On what?' he asked, stupefied.

'The ending. Think about what I said.'

'I will,' he said, though he rather thought he wouldn't. Then, 'Can I ask you just one thing?' said.

'What?'

'May I please kiss your hand?'

She was still staring at him as he reached across to her and, rather like the schoolboy stealing a toffee from a tin, he took hold of the hand that lay passively in her lap, drew it to him and brushed the back of it ever so softly with his lips. And not till then did she allow herself the glimmer of what may just have been a smile.

# 2 Elizabeth Chester-Bolt

Miss Elizabeth Chester-Bolt: a name to conjure with, to have fun with. It was a name that had been made fun of fulsomely over the years. At school it was 'Chesty', or even 'Breasty'. Outside school she was known as 'Bosom', sometimes 'with body attached', or a number of other unkind nicknames to do with the prow of a ship. All of them by way of reference to Miss Chester-Bolt's prodigious *embonpoint*.

She was proud of her *embonpoint*. It was large but it was noble, and she wore it with panache. She drew attention to it with low-cut dresses that accentuated her cleavage. It was the first feature people looked at when she entered a room. It was quite often the only feature people looked at as Miss Chester-Bolt was otherwise not a beauty. Her face was somehow too big, her features too heavy, and her smile looked as if it was pasted on, never quite a part of her, and never quite reacting to the world around her as one might expect it to.

Fortunately Miss Chester-Bolt was extremely rich. If she could not make friends in the natural way she could buy them. She could invite young men to dine with her in smart restaurants, or accompany her on her regular outings to the races. Most importantly, she could offer them the best seats in the best theatres, and it was here where she felt most at home, for Miss Chester-Bolt was what was known as a patron of the arts.

She had contributed generously to almost every actor-manager and entrepreneur in the West End, including Herbert Tree. She was magnificently connected and universally respected, and that was the nearest Miss Chester-Bolt could get to being generally liked. She had almost single-handedly stumped up the money for Robbie to mount a single matinée of his play the previous year, and it was to her that he turned again when the chance arose to produce the play in a regular slot in a West End theatre.

~

Watching her now, sitting alone at a table at Romano's, one could mistake Miss Chester-Bolt for an aristocrat, or a minor member of royalty. She is dressed in bright emerald green with pendant and hat to match. She has the bearing, and the upwardly-tilted nose, which together give the impression she is looking down at her surroundings. Her habit of narrowing her eyes implies disapproval but in fact has more to do with her short sight. It only takes the slightest movement of a finger of one hand and waiters are dancing around her, smiling and bowing. Alone at her table in a crowded room she looks completely at home.

In due course she is joined by a young man with fair hair and spectacles. Tall, slender and loose-limbed, he could almost be a dancer. He takes her hand and kisses it lightly before seating himself opposite her. His manner is mildly deferential, not quite subservient. Watching them together you might take him to be her lover, even though she is a few years older than him, so what? Although on close inspection the effusiveness is more on her side than his. As they order, and drink wine, while they wait for their food he says something that makes her laugh: a

18

strange, high-pitched sound that turns the heads of their fellow lunchers. From time to time she taps him playfully on the wrist with her fan and flutters her eyelashes. He does not seem entirely comfortable with this, but he smiles nonetheless.

'I have a producer for my play,' says Robbie.

The food has arrived and Miss Chester-Bolt is attacking it greedily. 'Mm, yes?' she says, with her mouth full. 'Who is it?'

'Her name is Violet Graham, she is an old friend. She worked for Tree for many years, as his assistant. Read scripts for him. She has a fine mind, and excellent judgment of plays.'

Miss Chester-Bolt does not immediately respond to this. There are questions she would like to ask that might appear irrelevant. She thinks for a small moment and then asks them anyway.

'How old is she?'

'How *old* is she? I . . . well, I imagine she's in her early thirties.'

'Very young.'

'Not that young.'

'Has she produced plays before?'

'Not to my knowledge.'

'Hmm.'

Miss Chester-Bolt not only has the ability to talk and eat at the same time, she appears to swallow her food without chewing it. Robbie is momentarily distracted by this observation before he says, 'I have every faith in her. She is not one to, how should one say, mince her words. She is already having a go at my script.'

'That is not her prerogative.'

'Actually it is. And she may well be right. Every writer needs an outside eye.'

'Your play is perfect as it is.'

'That's very kind of you, Elizabeth. Nonetheless it does no harm to listen to other people. Especially someone with Violet's experience.'

'Violet.'

'I beg your pardon?'

'You call her Violet.'

'Of course. She's an old friend, I told you.'

There is another question Miss Chester-Bolt is burning to ask, and they both know it, which is why Robbie begins to gabble.

'She worked for Tree for some years, as assistant to his acting manager. She understands plays better than anyone I know. And she should be well-versed when it comes to casting, she knows so many actors, you see. She has a keen eye and a disinterested one, in the sense that she has never acted herself, nor wanted to, so there's no question of trying to write herself into a part. I have every confidence in her.' And then, before Miss Chester-Bolt can interrupt, which he can see she is dying to do, he changes the subject. 'Did you see any good plays recently? *The Voysey Inheritance* perhaps? A cracking piece, I do recommend it. At the Court.'

Miss Chester-Bolt pauses with her fork halfway to her mouth. 'I would not,' she pronounces, almost with a spit, 'touch a play like that with the proverbial barge-pole.'

'Oh. That's a shame. I thought you might have invested in it. Though on the other hand, perhaps not.' Robbie shifts a little in his chair and smiles to himself.

'It was sent to me,' says Miss Chester-Bolt. She wrinkles her nose in distaste. 'And I read it through, with care. You will not be surprised to hear I not only did not invest in it, I told Mr Granville-Barker I did not believe it should be produced in the first place. On any stage. Anywhere.'

'But didn't you think . . .'

'The level of ignorance, and misunderstanding, deliberate or otherwise, of some playwrights boggles the mind. It's one thing for the man on the street to know nothing of the affairs of business, but if you are going to stage a play that sets out to diminish, to mock, to . . .' she hunts for the word, 'to *vilify* business, just because it is business, then you should be held accountable. There should be redress.'

'I don't believe it sets out to vilify business,' Robbie remarks mildly. 'Its whole purpose is to expose the corruption of business.'

'The corruption of business – there, you said it yourself. As if the two words went together.' Miss C-B leans forwards and fixes Robbie with a steely stare. 'The world imagines that all businesses are corrupt. Playwrights encourage this thinking. It is not only ignorant it is naïve. They understand nothing about it. The ordinary man in the street distrusts business. He hates the rich because he envies them, which is why he has to believe they are corrupt.' She leans back in her chair again and her frown suddenly disappears. 'Do you not agree with me, Robbie?'

This is a tricky one. Here is a woman who, in many ways, Robbie admires. She is bright, she is sharp, she has an instinctive intelligence and she is not afraid to say what she thinks. She is the only surviving offspring of a man who made a fortune in coal, honestly or otherwise, and she uses that fortune to feed her passion, which is for the theatre. She spends her inheritance generously, and widely, and once she has committed herself to a project she is committed one hundred per cent. She believes in Robbie totally, he knows that. That he disagrees with almost every opinion she expresses should not matter. She has invested in his play because above all it espouses the cause of women, an issue very dear to the ample heart of Miss Chester-Bolt.

'Let's just agree to disagree,' he says finally. 'On certain points,' he adds, with a smile.

It is not as if his patroness were insisting on alterations to his script, unlike others he could name, or that by taking her money he is colluding in something he does not believe in. That he has no idea whether or not the money is tainted in any way – and there's a part of any artist that believes no fortune was ever obtained honestly – is irrelevant.

So it would seem to the interested bystander that the large woman in the green dress and her male companion are in total accord.

# 3 The Primrose Inn

The Primrose Inn was a little-known establishment situated in one of those tiny streets off the Embankment near the Strand. You wouldn't know it if you hadn't been told about it because there was really no need for anyone to venture down that particular street, which neither led anywhere in particular nor acted as a short cut. Therefore the pub attracted virtually no passing trade and was not a place one would come upon by accident.

This obscurity was one reason why the Primrose was frequented almost exclusively by actors, mostly unemployed. It was known as a place where you could buy a sausage roll for tuppence and sit throughout an entire afternoon or evening over a half pint of beer without being disturbed. The publican did not seem to mind that his clients were happy to occupy his stools for hours on end without spending any money.

It was somewhere even the most down-and-out, dispirited person (so long as he was an actor) could go and find company with like-minded people. Where he, or perhaps she, could spend all night complaining and find a sympathetic ear, or more importantly, someone who was worse off than himself. If he were not careful he might be tempted to exaggerate his grievances in order to prove he was suffering more than anyone around him: poorer, hungrier, and above all more devoid of all hope or optimism. In the unlikely event a person was feeling all right with the world when he entered the establishment, chances were he'd be feeling utterly wretched by the time he left.

The Primrose also served a genuinely useful purpose as a centre for Information and Gossip. It was a kind of unofficial Casting Office, where unemployed actors gathered to catch up on what was happening in the theatre world: who was mounting what play and where, and who was responsible for casting; the latest on who or which managers and agents were inclined to walk off with the takings or charge would-be clients a small fortune for promises not kept.

It was here that Miss Gaye Worth, otherwise known as Gigi, learned about a new play called *Mrs Morphett's Macaroons* that was about to be produced in the West End under a new and unknown management. The source of this information was a young actress called Lolly Mulligan who, so she claimed, was already cast in the leading role of Annie Addeley, the scullery maid who becomes a suffragette. It had received a single performance the previous year and was now to be re-produced, with a brand new cast. It featured parts for women of all ages and types, said Lolly, and the person to contact was someone by the name of Violet Graham.

The name rang a bell. A hollow one.

'Violet Graham?' said Gigi. 'She's not – no, she can't be.'

'What?'

'Never mind. It's just that once . . . What do you know about this Violet Graham?'

'A fair amount as it happens,' said Lolly.

A Bohemian before her time, Lolly Mulligan was a pale, slight young woman with bright red hair that was very obviously dyed and not yet quite fashionable. She wore deceptively simple peasant skirts that ended mid-calf, and layers of scarves and shawls knitted in bright and often clashing colours. Lolly was someone you noticed, and did not easily forget, and she was aware of it. She moved languidly and self-consciously, except at moments when she became excited and reverted to ten years old.

Right now she was the centre of attention and enjoying every moment. She was looking at Gigi with a mixture of mischief and suspicion. 'I knew Violet when she was a nobody, working for Herbert Tree,' she said. 'As a matter of fact it was me who found her the position in the first place.'

'She worked for Herbert Tree,' said Gigi. She nodded thoughtfully. 'And is she – was she – is she little and dark and . . .'

'Pretty, yes, exactly.'

'With a . . .' Gigi drew or tried to draw a picture in the air of a *retroussé* nose.

'The nose, yes, absolutely.'

'Oh.' Gigi studied her hands.

'Why?' Lolly looked closely at her companion. 'What did you say your name was?'

'I met her, that's all, when she was working for Tree. I worked with Tree too, you know.'

'You have a head start then,' said Lolly. She studied the other woman up and down. 'There are plenty of parts you could play.'

Gigi shook her head.

'Why not? Or have you had a better offer?'

Gigi just kept shaking her head, and muttering.

She remembered Violet clearly. She remembered even more clearly the way she and her fellow actress and rival Meredith Martin had treated her, laughing at her and making fun of her to their fellow thespians. More annoyingly she recalled, with some admiration, Mrs Graham's composure, her refusal to be riled, and the fact that those same fellow thespians did not join in with the mockery. Grudgingly, very grudgingly, she acknowledged there had been more to Mrs Violet Graham than she'd given her credit for. So it was not so surprising she had ended up as a producer, a clever woman like her.

'Anyway,' she said to Lolly, 'I'm already working.'

'You are?' Lolly arched her eyebrows. 'Then what are you doing in here?'

Gaye shrugged, and then turned her attention to someone else.

'Please yourself,' said Lolly.

~

No one would dispute that *Mrs Morphett's Macaroons* had placed Lolly Mulligan firmly on the theatrical map, and there was no one more aware of this than Lolly herself. Her performance was 'a *tour de force*' according to one theatre critic. She 'lit up the stage', said another. Yet another claimed that in a play that stretched ridicule to its limits, while making serious points, she was the undoubted highlight of the whole performance and brought the character of Annie Addeley so vividly to life it was hard to believe she was not a real person. (A response to this, written anonymously, declared that she was indeed based on a real person called Annie Kenney, who as a child worked in a cotton mill.) All this was unsurprising bearing in mind the part had been written specifically for her. Thus it was that Lolly refused all offers of engagements following the play's sole performance in the expectation of its – and her – imminent arrival in the West End. This opportunity was unfortunately hampered due to the withdrawal of one of the play's backers, a shipping industrialist by the name of Henry Poll-Perkins, who had until some days following the performance been

Lolly's lover.

For those unfamiliar with Lolly Mulligan it needs to be explained she was a woman of fickle feelings and short-lived relationships. She liked men very much but she preferred them married as, in her own words, 'they did not hang around'. The fact that Mr P-P was not married was a surprise to Lolly's closest friends, not least to Robbie himself, and it was not too far-fetched of Mr P-P to assume that once his usefulness so far as his lover's professional life was over and done with, so was he.

That was not quite the case however. Lolly was not like that. She didn't deliberately use men for material gain. But Henry was that unfortunate entity an unmarried man, and he did make the prime mistake of 'hanging around'.

So Lolly, feeling responsible for filling the gap left by her erstwhile lover, took it upon herself at the next suffragist meeting she attended to see if any of the ladies might be interested in investing in a regular West End run of the play. After all *Mrs Morphett's Macaroons* was nothing if not a call to action on their behalf, even if it did make fun of them as much as it did the stuffy members of parliament. The request for 'alms' as she put it, was greeted first with total silence and then with murmurings of, 'Well, I don't know about that,' 'I'm sure there are worthier causes,' and so on. But there was one elderly lady who approached Lolly once the meeting was over, quietly, and in private, and offered to put up some of the money in return for . . .

'Yes?' asked Lolly.

'In return for . . .' The lady coughed into her hand. 'Please don't laugh, and tell me to go away if I am being ridiculous.'

Lolly waited.

'In return for a small part in the play. Perhaps?' Then, when Lolly did not immediately reply she went on: 'Is that too silly for words? I expect it is. Never mind. It was just a thought. I always wanted to . . . you know.' She quivered with embarrassment.

'I don't see why that could not be arranged,' said Lolly. 'I can speak to the writer about it, certainly.'

'Oh, would you? Thank you so much. Did you mind my asking? You see, I love the theatre. I once saw Forbes-Robertson play Hamlet, did you ever see him? Sublime. A master. I will never forget it, I saw the play five times. "*Oh what a rogue and peasant slave am I.*" Oh, but you'll think I'm showing off, or even auditioning. Dear me. But I am thrilled. So thrilled. Thank you my dear. How shall I get in touch with you?'

She finally paused for breath.

'I will drop you a line if you'd care to give me your card,' said Lolly politely.

That was Lolly's introduction to Mrs Katherine Santenoy.

# 4 The fledgling producer

It was in the hours following the performance at the Comedy Theatre of *Mrs Morphett,* when excitement was at its height at the birth of what everyone involved was convinced was a hit, that Robbie and Violet felt that both their lives had suddenly, and gloriously, slotted into place.

Robbie had not seen Violet for a long time. Due to a mixture of circumstances their lives had diverged when Violet had left London to become housekeeper at the country residence of Lord and Lady Armstrong. When they met again, to Robbie's surprise, he asked Violet, on impulse, if she would produce his play in a regular slot in the West End; and she, on impulse, agreed. It was not until later that each of them had time to reflect on, respectively, whether or not the idea of a West End run was remotely feasible, and the fact that Violet knew nothing whatsoever about producing plays.

Robbie and Violet had only met a handful of times, and while the word 'love' had never actually been mentioned, until recently, there was no denying a strong attraction existed between them. However in the clearer light of the following days, having immediately given notice to her employers before she had time to think things over properly, Violet began to wonder at the reasons behind both Robbie's request and her agreement to it.

Her years working for Herbert Tree, or more precisely

for his acting manager Frank Sharp, had taught Violet a good deal about the theatre, but never in her wildest imaginings had she thought of herself as a producer. She had a rough idea of what a producer did: he – it was usually a he – was responsible for finding the money to produce the play, hiring a theatre, contacting agents and conducting casting sessions, engaging scene and costume designers, stage management and stage crew, and generally overseeing every aspect of the play's life from conception to full maturity.

These tasks had to be handled more or less simultaneously, and since each one depended on the other it was the producer's job to juggle them all in the air and keep them there until everything fell into place. Finding the money depended to a large extent on whether or not they could interest a 'name' to play Mrs Morphett; yet no name would agree to commit to anything that was not securely financed. Casting could not begin until the script had been 'licked into shape', as Tree liked to put it, and there was no point in hiring a theatre until they were ready to commit to firm dates. Rushing things was obviously a mistake, yet if there was too much of a delay for any reason – the non-availability of a designer or an actress for instance, or problems to do with the set or the costumes or the script itself – the backers might lose interest and turn their attention elsewhere.

Most important of all, a producer needed to show that he, or she, knew what they were doing. A producer could not be seen to have doubts, or to be indecisive or in any way confused. Like Mrs Beeton's lady of the house, as the boss Violet would set the tone for everyone working beneath her. One small hesitation could lead to gloom and despondency throughout the entire company.

So why, Violet asked herself, not once but over and over, had she accepted the offer to do something she didn't know how to do? Was it to get away from her not unhappy life as a housekeeper, which had always been a temporary stopgap anyway? Was it the opportunity to make a proper career in a profession she loved, to achieve the kind of undefined ambition that had all those years ago first spurred her into a hasty and unhappy marriage, and then urged her as hastily out of it?

Or was it perhaps the prospect of working alongside a man who both intrigued and at times infuriated her?

It is necessary here to explain that Violet, née Frogg, married name Turnip, professional name Graham, was still a married woman. It was many years since she'd walked out of her marital home. Divorce at that time was a tricky business that attracted quite the wrong sort of attention and entailed complicated conditions including, as far as women were concerned, proof of adultery with cruelty on top. While Violet had no particular desire for divorce and she cared not a hoot for whatever stigma might attach itself to the 'woman who deserted her husband', her current status did not feel altogether comfortable. She may well have been attracted to Robbie Robinson for a number of reasons but while she was still married anything more, such as – heaven forbid – an affair, was out of the question. About that she had no doubts whatsoever.

So as she prepared for yet another change of direction, and living back in London and with this huge venture before her, Violet felt in dire need of guidance.

There was one obvious person she could approach.

~

'Do you know how I first got to work with Tree?' asked Frank Sharp.

'I thought you said you couldn't remember,' said Violet.

'Oh, I remember all right.'

There was a pause while Sharp reached into first one pocket and then another, producing from one a pipe and from the other a pouch of tobacco which, while Violet looked on in silence, he proceeded to open and pack into the bowl of the pipe, with some deliberation.

'It was in a pub. In the West End somewhere. I always wanted to be a jockey.' He placed the pipe in his mouth, lit up, puffed, then withdrew it and glared at it with annoyance. 'But I got too tall,' he said. He tamped the tobacco down some more, replaced the pipe in his mouth and lit it again. 'So I thought I would become a bookmaker instead.' He puffed again, this time to his satisfaction. 'Do you know what a bookmaker is?'

'Of course I do,' said Violet.

'A bookmaker has to be able to do complicated sums in his head. So there I was in a pub somewhere in the West End with my bookmaker friend, and we were talking odds and each-way bets and all that sort of thing, and this tall fellow with ginger hair comes up to us and says something like, "I couldn't help overhearing, forgive me, but do you understand money?" Just like that.'

He paused.

'And that was Herbert Tree?'

'Turns out. He said he ran a theatre and he needed someone who understood how money worked, which he didn't, as we all know.' He tapped his pipe on the arm of his chair.

'And he hired you there and then?'

'He did. I told him I knew nothing about the theatre, never worked in it, never went to it, all I was interested in was the Turf. He said, "That's all to the good, you'll have no preconceptions. And if you're used to taking a punt on a horse, even better – they're not so very different you know. Horses or plays, they can both fall at the first fence. Or not."'

There was a pause while Violet waited to see where this conversation was leading.

She had written to Sharp a few days before, explaining she was about to produce a play in the West End and could she please visit and pick his brains? It was Frank who all those years ago had first hired Violet as his assistant, regardless of her total lack of experience, in order – as she quickly learned – have someone else to deal with the time-wasting quibbles of tiresome actors. He left her to her own devices and so she learned on the job, she had to. It was a baptism by fire and things only went pear-shaped when Frank retired and was replaced by a schoolboy who decided he would make all the decisions for her, at which point she swiftly resigned.

Frank now lived with his wife in a small terraced house in the outskirts of Epsom, around a half-hour train journey from Charing Cross and within walking distance of one of England's most famous racecourses. Mrs Frank, so-called by her husband, was a cheerful, long-suffering soul who took everything her often curmudgeonly husband did or said with a pinch of salt and a shrug of one shoulder. After Frank's retirement she had agreed to the move from their apartment in Pimlico with alacrity, in the knowledge that it meant Frank was able to spend longer at his beloved Turf and less time getting under her feet at home.

'My point is,' Frank continued eventually, 'in answer to your question, there is only one way to find things out and that is by doing them. If you are going to become a producer then go ahead and produce something.'

He had shown not the least surprise when Violet had written to him, or that she had become a producer, despite his view – which he had made clear over and over in the past – that women were made for housekeeping purposes only; and regardless of the fact that, as Violet saw it, her years spent working as his assistant proved otherwise.

'So what exactly do you want to know?' he asked now.

'That is the whole point,' said Violet. 'I don't know. I don't even know what questions to ask.'

'Hmm.' He tapped his pipe on his knee. 'Well, I'm an old dinosaur now. I've no idea what's going on in the theatre these days and I've no interest in finding out.'

Violet smiled.

'But in essence,' he carried on, 'you need a play, you need money, you need actors, designers, wig makers and all that shenanigans. And you need a theatre.'

'We have the money and the play, that's about it.'

'And when you go looking for actors you need to be careful who to talk to.'

'Oh?'

He then reeled off a long list of names – of agents, Violet surmised. It was not clear whether it was a form of blacklist Frank had created because they were his personal enemies, or for some other reason. The list was very long. Frank had never liked nor understood actors – he had always regarded them as a necessary and annoying evil – so it was more than possible he included actors as well as agents among his *bêtes noirs*.

'They're all fools, to a greater or lesser degree,' he said. 'A woman like you would have no difficulty sorting the sheep from the goats.'

It was in the nature of a backhanded compliment, the nearest a person like Frank ever got to a compliment in the first place.

'Actors, agents, theatre managers, they are by and large *stupid people*,' he said, with emphasis. 'Totally wrapped up in themselves. Here and there is a canny one, and he usually gets out of it at the first opportunity once he's made his fortune. No one with a head on their shoulders would have anything to do with a business that's fundamentally fickle and nonsensical.'

The idea of the magic of theatre, or the sense of wonder that drew so many people into the business would not occur in the mind of someone like Frank Sharp.

'You could say horseracing is equally fickle and nonsensical, if not more so,' Violet ventured.

He nodded in acknowledgment. 'Start with what you know,' he said, 'and proceed from there. Get the script into shape first, you can do that standing on your head. Things will either go right or they won't.'

As advice goes it was not quite what Violet was hoping for, she mused on the train back to Charing Cross. Yet it was all one might expect from the likes of Frank Sharp.

~

The following week she received a letter from Frank containing two separate lists of names. On the first, against each name was an initial which, she eventually worked out, signified Designer (Setting, Lighting, Costumes) or Stage Management (including Stage Crew). The second list comprised two columns headed Yes and No, and beneath them was an even longer list of what she assumed to be agents.

It was typical of Frank to send her advice in the form of a riddle. Yet it was a start, she supposed.

# 5 The script doctor

*SCENE – An elegant drawing room in a house in Bloomsbury. A large sofa centre stage flanked by two occasional tables on either side, two armchairs downstage right and two downstage left, one or two upright chairs set against the walls. Upstage left is a door leading to the hall. A large window right overlooks the street. A sideboard and fireplace take up most of the left wall. It is early evening.*

*As the CURTAIN rises we see a woman, in her late fifties, dressed in a dark-coloured skirt and jacket. This is MRS MORPHETT. She stands motionless in the centre of the room looking about her, lost in thought. After a moment MRS GRACE, the housekeeper, enters, and curtseys.*

MRS GRACE: You rang, madam?

MRS MORPHETT: Thank you Mrs Grace, yes. I have some people coming around this evening, my suffragist friends, there should be around a dozen of them. They will be arriving at nine o'clock, so they will have eaten. But we will need refreshments – tea and coffee and perhaps some cakes. And some of Cook's delicious macaroons.

MRS GRACE: Very well, madam.

MRS M: We are gathering to discuss the question of
     women's right to vote, Mrs Grace. What do you
     think of that?
MRS GRACE: I'm sure it is an excellent idea.
MRS M: It is high time, don't you think? After all,
     women have the right to have our voices heard
     every bit as much as men, don't you agree?
MRS GRACE: Of course, madam.
MRS M: Our aim is to have the issue debated in
     parliament. But that's not easy when parliament is
     peopled entirely by men. It is a kind of vicious
     circle, you see. With the seat of government acting
     like an exclusive men's club why should they even
     consider allowing us women in? It is a long battle.
     It has already been a long battle, and there is more
     to come.
MRS GRACE: Yes, madam.
MRS M: Thank you Grace. I will call you when I need
     you.
MRS GRACE: Thank you madam. (*She curtseys again
     and leaves*)

'Can I stop you there?' said Violet.

'Yes?' said Robbie.

'First of all, a housekeeper would not curtsey.'

'Well, I suppose you should know.'

'Secondly, there is too much exposition. Unnecessary exposition, that's to say.'

'In what sense?'

'It's not the first time Mrs Morphett has hosted a meeting with her suffragist friends, there's absolutely no need for her to explain what it's about to her housekeeper.'

'Then,' Robbie scratched his head, 'how is the audience to understand what's going on?'

'They will grasp it as they go along,' said Violet. 'You need to plunge *in media res*, as the Chief would say.'

'*In media res*. In the midst of things. Interesting.' He smiled sweetly at his script doctor.

'Heaven only knows, they'll soon get the hang of what it's about when the ladies arrive. They do little else but discuss it.'

'Is that another criticism?'

'Robbie, this isn't criticism. This is what I'm here for,' Violet smiled sweetly back.

'Of course.'

They were in Robbie's sitting room, seated now in armchairs, each with a script. Fortunately Violet was not holding a pencil this time.

'In fact, I don't think you need this scene at all,' said Violet. 'You could begin in the middle of the meeting, at the point when Mrs Morphett starts to lose her patience. Or even at the end, with just her and Annie.'

'Whatever you say.' He looked across at Violet. So enchanting, so absorbed.

'Let's move on,' said Violet. She turned over a few pages of script. 'Yes, page 15. Mrs Morphett and Annie.'

> *The ladies have now all departed and we hear the sound of the front door closing offstage. There remain on stage only MRS MORPHETT and her maid ANNIE. MRS M gives a deep sigh and wipes the back of her hand across her forehead. She is exhausted. She feels the movement is not really going anywhere, that these endless meetings with her suffragist friends are not achieving anything. Yet she does not want to give up, she will not give up, not now and not ever. She feels the need to share her feelings with someone, and that someone could only be ANNIE.*

MRS MORPHETT: Well, what an evening!

'Can we halt it there again?' said Violet.

'Now what?'

'Did GBS have a hand in this?'

'GBS? What makes you say that?' Robbie exclaimed, with delight.

'There's no one else who thinks it's a good idea to tell an actress how she should act.'

'Oh.' Robbie's face fell. 'I had thought – well, never mind. Look, a play is more than the words on the page, you know. A play is what is not said, what goes on inside a person's head that they don't . . .'

'I don't dispute that, Algie. But any self-respecting actor, or actress, knows that. Allow them some intelligence. They don't appreciate being told how to do things, or what they're supposed to be thinking.'

'You called me Algie,' said Robbie.

'Did I?' said Violet.

'You haven't called me Algie, since . . .' he paused to think. 'Since we first met.'

'Well,' she smiled, with one half of her face. 'Don't take it personally.'

'Algie is my critic's name,' said Robbie. 'You said you preferred it. You preferred my assumed name. Interesting.'

Violet stared at him for a moment.

'Robbie, Algie, whatever you prefer to be called.' She furrowed her brow momentarily. 'This is – let's get this clear. This is business.'

'Yes dear.'

'We are getting off the subject.'

'You are absolutely right. What was the subject?'

'The subject was telling actresses how to act. They don't like it.'

'Very well, I will remember that.'

She shot him a sharp look.

'Let's carry on.'

MRS M: Do you know Annie, there are times when I
    wonder if it is all worth it?
ANNIE: All what, madam?
MRS M: All this. Such hard work. *(She begins to pace
    the floor, her hands on her hips)* Over all these years,
    so little progress. At times I wonder if we women
    are speaking the same language. None of it seems
    to get through.
ANNIE: Can I tell you what I think, madam?
MRS M: *(she ceases pacing and turns to face ANNIE)* By
    all means.
ANNIE: Well, forgive me for saying this madam, but
    it's all very well what goes on inside a lady's
    drawing room, and it seems to me what's the point
    if none of it is getting outside onto the street?
MRS M: How do you mean?
ANNIE: It seems to me as like it's almost like a secret
    society, what goes on in here. *(She throws a hand to
    her breast in alarm)* Not that I mean it's – nothing
    underhand, you know. What I mean is . . . *(She
    wrings her hands)*
MRS M: *(Gently, encouragingly)* Go on, Annie.
ANNIE is in agony. She is a simple girl and she does
    not know how to articulate her feelings. And there
    is the gap between mistress and servant that she
    doesn't know how to negotiate, despite the fact that
    Mrs Morphett is an exceptionally kind woman.
    Annie does not want to speak out of turn and yet
    she feels she must.
ANNIE: These ladies, your friends, they are clever
    ladies. Very clever. I could see that with my own
    eyes. And they can talk the hind legs off a donkey –
    oh *(she reaches out a hand)* – I don't say that to

offend, madam.

MRS M: (*she smiles*) You are absolutely right, Annie, I would not contradict you for a moment. But what is the point you are trying to make?

ANNIE: What I'm trying to say is – lawksamercy what is it I'm trying to say? They are ladies, if you see what I mean. And most of us, well, there are most of us that aren't.

(*There is a pause while MRS MORPHETT takes this in. She is doing her best to understand what ANNIE, in her charming yet inarticulate way, is trying to say. She thinks she probably has an idea.*)

MRS M: What you're saying Annie – and correct me if I'm wrong – you're saying we ladies are not representative. (*Then, realising ANNIE may not understand the word, she elaborates*) That we are just a small part of society and there is a much larger, and therefore more important, section of the populace who are not included in our campaign.

ANNIE: (*She nods*) Not just not included, they don't have the first idea what you're up to. And they should. (*As Mrs Morphett continues to look at Annie kindly, she grows more courageous*) Just because they're – we're – not ladies, doesn't mean we're stupid. Well some of us maybe. I don't have an education but I know what's what. And I know there are lots of women like me, and they'd like to have a say. They may not have an education but they have minds, and plenty to talk about. (*She stops; she's run out of breath, and courage*)

MRS M: (*She smiles*) Then tell me Annie, how can you help us get our message to these people?

'So!' said Violet. She closed her script.

'Don't tell me,' said Robbie. 'Too many stage directions,

too much telling the actress what's going on in her mind. What else?'

'There is something distinctly patronising about the way you describe what Mrs Morphett is thinking.'

'Give me an example.'

Violet opened the script again and leafed through it briefly. '"*She is doing her best to understand what ANNIE, in her charming yet inarticulate way, is trying to say*".'

'What's wrong with that?'

'You don't find that patronising?'

'It's not what I'm thinking, it's what Mrs Morphett is thinking.'

'What else? Yes, she realises Annie may not understand the word "representative".'

'She probably doesn't.'

'That's not the point.'

'And the audience isn't seeing that, it's just a direction for the . . .' He tailed off. 'An unnecessary one,' he concluded.

'Not just that. It shows a horribly superior attitude on Mrs Morphett's part towards her servant. And I don't think Mrs Morphett is like that.'

'It doesn't really matter though, does it, if the actress understands her? Does it?' He frowned. 'Am I missing something here?'

Violet regarded Robbie steadily.

'Anything else?' he asked.

'"Lawks-a-mercy". Really?'

'Why not? It's a colourful word. Should get a laugh.'

'Is that what it's there for?'

'Nothing wrong with the odd laugh to alleviate a serious moment.'

There was a pause.

'You don't really like my play, do you?' said Robbie finally.

'I love your play Robbie, you know that.' Violet declared, with emphasis. 'I wouldn't have taken it on if I didn't love it.' She softened her expression just a little. 'That's not to say it's perfect. I never thought it was. It's the ideas in it that I love. I just feel it could do with improvement.'

'*I* could do with improvement.'

'I did not say that.'

'I am my play. It's my thoughts you're tearing to shreds.'

'Don't be so touchy.'

'Don't be so imperious.'

'Imperious?' she cried.

And then, to Robbie's relief, she burst into laughter.

# 6 The art of parliamentary filibuster

It was the grand opening of Tree's theatre, attended by His Royal Highness the Prince of Wales. Everyone who was anyone was there. Robbie had been Algernon Lightly that evening, theatre critic for *The Weekly Chronicle*, so he was attending on official business, as he described it. He remembered very little about the play but he remembered every detail about Violet. He'd been introduced to her by Herbert Tree as his 'right-hand woman', as he described her. She was wearing a deep blue satin dress, audaciously scooped at the neck and dangerously accentuating her tiny waist. Her hair – how was her hair? – it was draped gently around the ears and coiled neatly at the back. Her neck was bare. Her arms likewise. Her skin . . .

'Good morning sir.'

'Good morning Jack.'

He greeted the policeman guarding the gate at New Palace Yard outside the House of Commons. He was attending what was scheduled to be a debate on women's suffrage, though his mind was elsewhere. His mind was preoccupied with that moment back in April 1897, when Violet first entered his life.

So where was he?

Yes, they had enjoyed such a charming chat, he and Mrs Graham. She was a widow, or so he was led to believe. She was light-hearted, even frivolous, with a highly infectious laugh. But just as their conversation was getting going she left, without warning. 'I'm so sorry, I have to go,' she said hurriedly, and quite out of the blue, as if the clock had suddenly struck midnight and Cinderella was about to be transformed there and then back into a scullery maid. And off she went. He learned later she'd just spotted her estranged husband across the room.

'This way, sir.'

'Thank you Gordon. How are you today?'

'Very well indeed, thank you sir. Yourself?'

'Thriving.'

He nodded at the security guard and removed his hat as he entered the building itself, that superficially ancient and ridiculously ornate and stuffy edifice where the rules of government were made.

He'd seen her a couple of times after that – was it really only twice? – before she did her disappearing act, yet again. And when she reappeared unexpectedly at the matinée of his play, and he'd found himself asking her if she'd produce that same play in the West End, and she'd accepted, with alacrity, it seemed to him, and . . .

He took the stairs briskly, moving speedily past the stained glass windows of disapproving saints, his feet barely making contact with the carpet.

. . . it may have been his imagination but he had felt a distinct – how can one describe it? – an overwhelming sensation that everything was slotting into place.

'Robbie!'

'Hello Sidney.'

The Reporters' Gallery was far from full. He edged his way between the narrow benches to take a seat beside his colleague from *The Times*.

'It's been a long time. What have you been up to?' asked Sidney.

'I've written a play, as a matter of fact. It's about to be produced in the West End.'

'By Jove. What's it about?'

'Suffragettes, as it happens. You must come.'

'Suffragettes, eh? Did you see them, downstairs in the Strangers' Lobby? Packed full.' Sidney's shoulders heaved with what appeared to be amusement. 'Mrs Pankhurst is there, and her cronies. You should talk to them, tell them you're writing a play about them, they'd be tickled pink. James!' And his colleague turned to greet a new arrival.

Thinking about it now, Robbie had to admit that offer to produce his play to a woman he barely knew had been primarily in order to get her back into his life. And now that she was, in a sense, back in his life, it seemed she was in many ways further away from him than ever. The only thing they had in common was the play, and yet it seemed, paradoxically, it was the play that threatened to push them apart.

Right now, he had offered to cover the upcoming House of Commons debate on women's suffrage, the first for several years apparently, on behalf of *The Weekly Chronicle*, out of interest in the subject of course, and to find possible further material for his play. It was the debate itself that had thrown Robbie's mind back all those years to a conversation he had had one evening around a dinner table with Violet, the actress Lolly Mulligan and their host for the evening, a neighbour of Violet's called Mr Kapps. The evening had been set up, by Lolly, the arch-manipulator, in order for Robbie and Violet to meet for the second time. In the course of it the idea arose that Robbie should write a play, produced by Violet and featuring Lolly in a major role, and under his critic's name of Algernon Lightly Robbie would give it a glowing review. It had been a flippant remark in a light-hearted conversation, but out of it, eventually, had arisen *Mrs*

*Morphett's Macaroons.*

Why Robbie should have chosen to write about women's suffrage he didn't rightly know, though he fancied again it had something to do with Violet, and indeed Lolly, both of whom held strong views on the subject. Whether or not he was aware at the time it was the suffrage movement that had indirectly led to the break-up of Violet's marriage, well, who's to know?

The ladies were now beginning to appear in the Strangers' Gallery, and he spotted Mrs Pankhurst immediately. She carried such an air of authority as she directed members of her entourage to their seats, there was no mistaking her identity. She was no stranger to the Strangers' Gallery it seemed. She sat herself down in the middle of the front row, face stern, staring straight ahead.

First on the agenda that day was a second reading of a Vehicles' Lights Bill, which proposed that all vehicles on the roads, including agricultural carts, should bear lights in front and behind. A simple enough motion, you might think; indeed it was stated by the proposer that 'he did not think that he needed to take up a large amount of the time of the House because he thought there were very few Hon Members who would dispute the advisability of passing this very simple Bill'. However, as Robbie looked on with a mixture of wonder, admiration and increasing disbelief, he witnessed for the first time as a parliamentary reporter the practice known as 'talking out', or filibustering. One by one the Hon Members made objections, objected to other Hon Members' objections, discovered anomalies, disputed the anomalies, repeated themselves, digressed, made jokes, cast aspersions on motor car drivers, cyclists, sheep and farmers who fell asleep in their moving carts, and questioned how a horse or a 'perambulator' was expected to carry lights and in which case where exactly on the body they should be positioned, and so on and so on and so on late into the afternoon.

So it was that, finally, Mr Bamford Slack, Member for Hertfordshire, St. Albans, got to his feet to propose the second reading of the Women's Enfranchisement Bill. He began by declaring he was 'almost appalled' at the House's deliberate attempts to prevent discussion of it, but since it had been deliberated seventeen times previously he did not feel a detailed debate was now necessary. This statement was then challenged by the Hon Member for Middlesex, who had played a significant role in the attempt to prevent the Bill from being discussed in the first place by demonstrating his prowess as chief filibusterer throughout the previous debate, and who now expressed his dismay at the notion that such an important measure could be voted on after a discussion of only two hours. He went on to do what he was so good at, which was digressing, making jokes, false and irrelevant claims and comparisons, and generally filibustering his way through the remainder of the afternoon. So that when Mr Slack called for the question to be put, the Deputy Speaker refused, and the debate was 'adjourned' (Parliament-speak for abandoned).

Robbie had been keeping an eye on Mrs Pankhurst throughout the afternoon. Her expression did not change. She barely seemed to blink. She sat stock still during the whole of the first debate, and only leaned slightly forwards when the Women's Suffrage Bill came onto the agenda. At the close of play she rose immediately and left the Strangers' Gallery, and her lady colleagues followed suit.

Robbie sat motionless for several minutes. It was hardly a noble demonstration of British democracy and it dismayed and astonished him to acknowledge the procedure was entirely legal. He knew something of how long it had taken Mrs Pankhurst and the suffragists to get this far, to finally find an Honourable Member to take up their cause, and to win a place in the ballot. And now this. It beggared belief.

Outside the House the square was teeming with women. One of them was trying to make a speech. The police were attempting to hustle them away from the Commons and so they moved on to the Lords, only to be hustled on again, this time with a good deal of brutality. When Robbie tried to intervene to protect some of the women from police batons he was pushed back, roughly yet politely, with a 'Best to keep out of this, sir'.

Finally the ladies took up position outside Westminster Abbey, where Mrs Pankhurst and others addressed the crowd. 'We waited for eight years,' she told them. 'And now, with the aid and support of the Government, they have talked out our Bill and put us back to where we began. We condemn this Government's action and we have a message for the Prime Minister and all members of parliament: We will not be ignored! This is not the last they've heard of us! We will never give up, not now and not ever!'

Robbie looked on. He was surprised to find tears in his eyes. It was a peaceful demonstration but in the atmosphere of the times it was revolutionary too. And it made an excellent story for tomorrow's newspaper.

# 7 Merry and Gaye

'London is hell if you're poor,' said Merry.

'Anywhere's hell if you're poor,' said Gigi.

'But London most of all. Nobody cares about the poor here. We're invisible. We don't exist.'

Merry picked up her napkin and wiped the condensation from the window of the café in which the two women were sitting and peered out at the street. She was watching a lady in a scarlet dress and matching hat descending from a brougham. It took two footmen to aid her – one to hold the door, the other to take her hand as she came down the steps, followed by a snappily-dressed gentleman – and to pass her to said gentleman like an object, a precious piece of china, so it looked to Meredith.

'So how poor are you, exactly?' Gigi demanded. She was tucking into a large bun covered in pink icing. 'Want some?' she offered, as Merry turned her attention away from the scene outside the window.

Merry shook her head. 'Poor enough,' she said.

'So poor you are sitting inside a café with a hot chocolate,' said Gaye. 'Or am I paying for it?'

Merry shrugged miserably. 'It wasn't how I imagined it.'

'I can't see as why you imagined it any different.'

'You're doing all right, aren't you?' Merry rested her arms on the table. Her eyes were on her friend's iced bun, but her mind was far away.

Gaye reached out a bun-laden fork. 'Go on, it'll do you good.'

Merry backed away. 'I said no.'

'Go on!' Gigi was almost rising out of her seat as she tried to push the fork towards her friend's mouth. 'All right then.' She gave up and swallowed the forkful in one.

'So, what are you doing for a crust?' she asked after a moment.

'Working in a hat shop.' Merry looked up and around at the other customers. The sheer cheerfulness of the place oppressed her.

'A hat shop? Blimey, what a turn-up!  What's it like, working in a hat shop?'

'There are women,' said Merry, 'with all the time in the world, and all the money, and their favourite activity is to spend hours in a hat shop trying on everything they can lay their hands on, and then leaving without buying anything.'

'And you envy them?'

'Who said I envied them?'

'You did, as good as.'

Merry placed her elbow on the table and her chin on her hand. She had to lean at a considerable angle to do this, such was her prodigious height. 'I despise them, I don't envy them.'

'In that case, you should be happy to be poor. Speaking for myself, I don't hate nothing in the world so much as boredom.' Gigi cupped her hands around her steaming cup of cocoa. 'I'd rather sweep the streets than spend all morning shopping and not buying anything.'

Merry nodded in half-hearted agreement. She picked up a teaspoon and toyed with it.

'You're a right bleedin' bundle of misery today,' said her companion. 'You're not thinking of giving up, are you?'

'Giving up the stage?' Merry thought about this for a moment. She looked close to tears. 'What else am I good for?'

'You could go on working in the hat shop. You could open up a shop of your own.'

Merry did not respond to this.

'Anyway, you can always just watch,' Gaye went on. 'Us actresses should always observe people. Who knows, one day you might find yourself playing a rich, bored tart with nothing better to do than waste time in hat shops!' She laughed.

'I didn't think it would be like this,' said Merry. 'I thought once you'd reached the West End stage that was it. There was no looking back.'

'Dunno who told you that. My da used to say the entertainment biz is like a fishbowl, and we're all fish, swimming up and down, and sometimes we're down there on the sea bed and sometimes we're up near the surface and that's the way it is.'

'The only fish at the top of a fishbowl are dead fish,' said Merry.

'Oh yeah, clever clogs. You know what I mean.' Gigi blew on her cocoa, 'It's here today and gone tomorrow in the entertainment biz, always was and always will be. No rhyme nor reason to it.'

'You've done all right,' said Merry.

'That's because I don't care what I do. Haymarket one day, Daly's the next. I'm not a snob like you.' She looked at Merry over the top of her cup, but her friend did not react.

'There's always work at Daly's,' Gigi went on. 'It may not be hoity-toity but it's work, and the pay's not bad. They're always looking for girls for the chorus.'

'The chorus,' said Merry. 'I'd fit well into a chorus,

wouldn't I? I'm about a foot taller than anyone else.'

'True enough.'

'Besides, I can't dance.'

'Anyone with legs and arms can dance,' said Gigi.

They sat in silence for a while, each bent over her cocoa, locked in private contemplation of something or other.

'I'm not a snob,' said Merry eventually. 'I just don't want to take on any old engagement for the sake of taking on an engagement. Once you get known as a Gaiety Girl that's it.'

Gigi laughed merrily. Or perhaps that should be gaily. 'I can't see you as a Gaiety Girl, not in a million years.'

'Well there you are then.'

'I can put in a word for you at Daly's,' she said. 'And who knows, you might get a proposal out of it.'

'A proposal? What sort of proposal?'

'It happens all the time. You'd be surprised at the audiences we get. The best. Or maybe not the best but the flashiest, if you see what I mean. Not the sort you find at His Maj's, or even the Haymarket, but richer, you know. Bigger jewellery, bigger hats, bigger everything. And the only reason them young lads is there for is the girls. I've had the odd proposal myself.' She fluttered her eyelashes coquettishly. 'From an earl, no less.'

'Why would I want to be proposed to?' Merry looked genuinely perplexed.

'Sometimes it's the only way out. If all else fails,' Gigi shrugged, 'a girl can always get hooked.'

'God forbid!'

'Ah well. So long as the hats are keeping the wolf from the door.' Then, a sudden thought: 'Do you remember a woman called Violet Graham?'

'Violet Graham.' Merry shook her head, and then nodded, and then she began to smile, for the first time.

'Mrs Graham! Oh my, did we do one over on her!' She laughed. 'At the Haymarket. You and me, what a double act! She didn't know where to put herself! Violet Graham, yes. She vanished, didn't she, into thin air they said. Whatever happened to Violet Graham?'

'Well, she turned up again, just the other day.' Gigi paused dramatically. 'Casting for a play in the West End.'

There followed a dense silence. Merry studied the tablecloth.

'I didn't see her, not personally,' Gigi added. 'I just heard. On the grapevine.'

'What play?' Merry asked.

'Something to do with suffragettes. Plenty of parts for actresses.' Gigi grinned ruefully. 'You just never know, do you?'

'I don't suppose she remembers us,' said Merry.

'I bet you she does,' said Gaye.

'What's the name of the play?' asked Merry.

'It's got macaroons in it,' said Gaye. 'Mrs – Morpet, Morchitt – something or other.'

'Hmm,' said Merry.

'Anyway. If you want me to put in a word for you at Daly's I will. It's got to be better than hats.' Gigi delved into her bag and produced her purse. 'And I'm getting this.'

'All right. This time.'

'Next time it's on you. And by then if you're not hoofing away at Daly's maybe you'll be taking tea at the Ritz with some handsome young cove who's happy to keep you in feathers and scones for the rest of your life.'

Merry smiled, genuinely. 'Thank you Gigi.'

'Anything to stop you moaning on like a cow with a sore arse,' said her friend.

# 8 The musings of Meredith Martin

Meredith was not born to theatrical parents and her decision to become an actress was both unexpected and unusual. Daughter of a brigadier father and his socialite wife, as a child she was taken by her mother to see Ellen Terry and Henry Irving performing at the Lyceum Theatre in London and was immediately captivated. She was, it turned out, a natural mimic, and so she taught herself to impersonate the two actors: their gestures, their movement and above all, their voices. She dressed up and smeared her face with burnt cork and coloured pencils, and one evening while her parents were entertaining she presented herself before the assembled company and proceeded, without warning or invitation, to perform a scene from *Much Ado About Nothing*, playing both Beatrice and Benedick in the style of Terry and Irving, to the embarrassment of her parents and the unalloyed delight of their guests.

It was the guests who encouraged her, and who regularly invited themselves to the family house to be entertained by her, to the increasing yet futile disapproval of Brigadier and Mrs Stephenson. In time and perhaps inevitably one or two of them suggested Meredith should go on the stage. When she expressed her surprise that an ordinary girl like herself might consider such a thing, and that in any case she had absolutely no idea how to go about it, one lady who appeared to know about such things recommended a school of elocution run by an actor by the name of Willard Featherbridge, who it was said had 'once trod the boards with Irving'.

Meredith had only just turned eighteen when she first stepped across the threshold of Mr Featherbridge's academy. The one-time actor turned out to be a man of substance, in form and in character, with a Falstaffian belly and a voice that could – and, as he was fond of saying, often did – shake the rafters. He spent the best part of his introductory greeting boasting that he had the most sustained vibrato in the West End, which included the Opera House at Covent Garden. He went on to entertain his pupils with his experiences working with Irving, Tree and Terry, and his early days 'at the Lane' with Macready.

Eventually Mr Featherbridge paused his peroration and at last turned his mind to the matter in hand. Elocution, he explained, was a combination of Stance, Gesture, Voice and Expression. He began his classes by teaching his pupils how to stand: one foot slightly in front of the other, at a diagonal; how to make the Gesture Conversational: arm extended, palm upwards, as if to a feature of nature; Energetic: the body inclined forward, arms outstretched, as if to a regiment; and Frightful: shrinking back or recoiling from a ghost or fearsome animal. He described the mechanics of the Larynx and how it related to the Voice. He gave his charges speeches to recite out loud, with precise instructions on how to deliver each phrase according to Pitch (high, middle, low), Force (loud, medium, gentle), Pace (quick, moderate, slow), Emphasis (radical, vanishing, median and compound), and Personation (voice, countenance and gesture).

Meredith learned about the 'Voice Pure', the 'Voice Impure', the 'Speaking Sound' and the 'Musical Sound'.

She learned to intone Shakespeare according to the law of Featherbridge, with Emphasis, Meaning and of course, Full and Resonant Vibrato. None of it bore much resemblance to anything she had ever seen on stage or off it, but Merry threw herself into the whole business with gusto, like any aspiring and gullible young actress in the days before proper training schools. Six months after she first set foot inside Mr Featherbridge's school, and on his advice, Meredith went in search of an agent.

They were an indifferent bunch, she discovered, to the point of downright rudeness. Most of them ignored her completely. Others, more friendly, promised her immediate engagements in the West End in return for a fee ranging from one pound to five. Having parted with a considerable sum of money and on hearing nothing further Miss Stephenson presented herself at the premises of the agents in question, only to find they had disappeared into thin air; the only indication they had ever existed the growing pile of brown envelopes on what had once been their doormat.

Then a chance encounter with a friend of the family led to an introduction to an acquaintance who was in the process of mounting a tour of the provinces. He was, he announced, looking for 'walking ladies'.

The experience proved a baptism of fire, one could say, for the green yet ever-hopeful Meredith. It was a 'fit-up' tour, performing one-night stands in village halls or hastily-erected tents, or other random edifices not designed for theatrical performance. This was followed by further engagements of a similar nature, still as a 'walking lady', on low pay and on occasion, when houses were thin, on no pay at all.

In times things improved. Meredith progressed from tent to actual theatre; she went from 'walking lady' to 'utility' and even on one occasion to 'responsible'.

('Responsible' for what was never explained.) She discovered that if you got a laugh taking a drink from a bottle you could get two laughs from taking two drinks, and so on. She toughened up. She learned to hide her insecurities and modify – or 'cockneyfy', as she herself put it – her accent where needed.

And she remained undaunted. The tougher it got the more determined she became. Having been initially bolstered by a modest allowance from her parents, in the belief that their daughter's apparent madness was no more than a passing phase, after a year not only did they cut off her allowance, they cut off their daughter along with it. And so Meredith Stephenson adopted the stage name of Meredith Martin and never saw her parents again.

The engagement in the West End had come about, like most things in this business, by chance. A chance remark overheard by a fellow actor, a chance meeting with someone connected with the production. Being in the Right Place at the Right Time. And now she was beginning to think it had all been a cruel trick. A false promise of a glowing future.

Such confidence she'd had back then! Stepping out onto the Haymarket stage in front of one of the most sophisticated audiences in the world; working for one of the most esteemed actor-managers London had ever known. Herbert Beerbohm Tree, famous on both sides of the Atlantic, the man with the golden touch. It was not a huge part, but she had made it her own. She did what all actors and actresses have had to do throughout time, she turned what was originally written as a minor role into a distinct character that audiences remembered and remarked upon. She'd received *reviews*. 'What in lesser hands might have been considered a minor role the impressively-built Miss Meredith Martin turned Marjorie Forbes-Wilson into a force to be reckoned with.' She'd received *better* reviews than Gaye Worth. 'Miss Worth, in the minor role of Petunia Russell, rival for the hand of the dashing, spendthrift bounder Jackson Johnson, looks and sounds appealing enough.' *Appealing enough*. Lukewarm, at best.

She might not be as versatile as Miss Gaye Worth but she was a good deal more striking. Her height was with her there, her height and her bearing. She was not a brigadier's daughter for nothing. In a world where actresses were ten-a-penny – and let's face it most of them looked and sounded much the same – she stood out, beyond and above them, literally. And she had a voice to match. Not once did Mr Tree have to yell at her, as he did to virtually everyone else, including Miss Worth, to *Speak up, we cannot hear you in the gallery!* He even remarked on it, during rehearsals. 'At last, an actress who can reach the furthest walls of a theatre, without effort.'

Without effort. How odd, there seemed to be relatively little effort involved. She felt immediately at home in the role, she was happy with her costume, she enjoyed rehearsals, with one notable exception she got on well with her fellow performers, and she was aware of audiences responding to her. She had arrived.

Or so she thought. So she had been led to believe. You do your bit in the provinces, a kind of apprenticeship, you put up with the dreadful conditions because you've been told that it's a necessary preliminary to the big time. And once on your way up you never have to look down again.

That, she was realising fast, was illusion.

It was the hat shop that did it. The very thought of looking for work, of *having* to look for work outside the theatre was anathema to Meredith. Fellow 'resting' actresses found positions working in doubtful dives down the side streets of Soho, or as waitresses in places such as the café on Regent's Street where she had just spent an hour bemoaning her fate to her friend. Or getting married. But she would have none of that. Truth to be told it was not so much *infra dig* as fear – of being mistaken as a prostitute in the first case or getting the order wrong in the second. The third option was simply out of the question. Miss Martin had ambition, and she had talent, and the latter had been encouraged by others to lead to the former. And the former had to be fed, and fed properly.

If life in the theatre is like a goldfish bowl she was scrabbling along on the bottom. She was drowning. Or worse, she was floating on the surface, dead before her time.

She was making her way through Leicester Square to the little hat shop off the Strand. All the best shops were in obscure places, it was a sign of their exclusivity – the more obscure, the more customers had to hunt them down. And Madame Poulesse's hat shop was not the sort of place where a customer would find herself meeting another customer. It was that exclusive, and therefore one of the most expensive milliners in London. If a customer considered it permissible to spend two hours trying on the merchandise without spending anything, the price of the merchandise had to reflect that.

And then, as Merry was about to find out, when the forces of fortune appear to be lined up against you, the wind changes, or a bird sings or a butterfly flaps its wings – and the world shifts on its axis.

# 9 Gaye Worth pulls faces

In the hierarchy of West End theatres Daly's stood somewhere near the middle. Neither low- nor high-brow. Popular yet upper-class. As Gigi herself had said, it attracted the moneyed rather than the discerning. And among the moneyed there was more than a smattering of young, unattached gentlemen, aristocracy and others.

She lied when she said she'd been proposed to by an earl. Propositioned yes, and it was tempting. There were a number of young coves, as she liked to call them, not all of them unmarried, who were looking to set up a girl in a smart apartment in London in return for unlimited access any time of the day or night. The earl in question had made just such a suggestion to Gigi the very first time they met. He'd appeared at the stage door, asked to see her, taken her to dinner at Paganini's and propositioned her, all within the space of one evening. There was only one snag: in return for a life of luxury she was to give up her career in order to pay full attention to himself.

That was all very well as a temporary arrangement, but there was always the chance that a chap might lose interest in a girl, and overnight the apartment and the lifestyle that went with it would be no longer. And then where would she find herself? Throughout her life the theatre had been Gigi's home, her family's home, her family's bread and butter, and now hers. Without it she didn't really exist. Without it she would not know how to fill her day; and not knowing how to fill a day was tantamount to hell for a girl like Gigi Worth.

Unlike her new friend Meredith, Gaye had the arguable luck to have been born into the profession. Her father was what was known in the trade as a 'low comedian' and her mother was a music hall singer. Gaye first appeared on stage at the age of five in a concert alongside her sister and her mother. She liked to claim she was born in a trunk in a theatre dressing room; though the truth – that her mother gave birth between shows on one day and was back on stage the next – was every bit as remarkable. Not for Gaye the bewilderment of the elocution school or the humiliation of the condescending agent. She never had to part with the equivalent of a small fortune to a manager who promised her the earth and then vanished from it. Nor was there, for someone to whom performing was an everyday pastime much like eating or drinking, much sense of romance or glamour about the profession into which she was born and in which, there was never any question, she was expected to spend the rest of her life.

Gaye also did her stint in the provinces but it was by the standards of the day a relatively comfortable experience. She and her sister Nell also worked the one-night stand, but they made sure – or their father did for them – that they were not left to make their own way from fit-up to fit-up. It was their father who arranged most of their engagements, whether they liked it or not. It was he who made sure neither of his daughters was ever forced to work for the sort of manager who made off with the takings before the end of a tour. It was the girls' mother who taught them where to find their own costumes and how to alter and trim them when necessary. It was she who taught them that when a fashionable supporter of the drama left a parcel at the stage door they should make sure to be the first to hear about it and to purloin whatever treasure lay within its wrappings.

As for ambition: if you are born to the profession the word has a very different meaning. While the Meredith Stephensons of this world would have killed for a theatre engagement, the Worth daughters would have been quite happy to quit the business altogether. Gaye's sister Nell did just that. At the age of sixteen she galloped off to marry the local butcher's son and never trod the boards again. Gaye contemplated doing much the same thing but the likes of butchers' sons held no appeal for her. Insofar as she had ambition it was to be freed from the shackles of her family and left to choose her own path and her own way of finding it.

She had no misconceptions about herself. She was passably pretty, she had all the right attributes in more or less the right places, a well-shaped nose in a round, slightly flat face, a neat little mouth above a pert little chin. She had fair hair which she wore untidily, through vanity rather than laziness (it took her some time to achieve the effect each morning). She looked, in brief, like a million other young actresses of a similar build and type and age. She was one of many, unlike Meredith Martin; which meant she was more likely to stay in work regularly, so long as she didn't mind too much where she was or what she played, but unlikely to hit what one might call the big time. Except for one thing: her aptitude for 'stage business'.

It is well known to playwrights and actors in particular that there is a lot more to a play than the words on the page, and that what's known as 'business' can make or break a character. There was a well-known story of an actor called Edward Sothern who was once given the small part of a dim-witted aristocrat named Lord Dundreary in a play called *Our American Cousin*. He agreed to take the part on condition he could do what he liked with it. So he adopted a wig, long side-whiskers, an eyeglass and a general air of bewilderment. He gave milord a lisp and a stutter, and had him tripping over carpets and bumping into furniture. He underwent numerous changes of costume, and inside the pocket of every jacket he wore was a neatly-folded handkerchief which several times throughout the performance, and for reasons unspecified, he took out, unfolded, stared at, then refolded and replaced in his pocket.

None of this had anything much to do with the play that was taking place around him, nor did it cast any particular light on Lord Dundreary himself. But it transformed a minor and forgettably-written character into the star of the show without adding or changing a word of the script. Sothern's side-whiskers alone spawned a fashion known as 'Dundrearies', and as a result of his shenanigans the play was a major hit both in America and in England.

Such was the nature and the power of 'business'.

There were actors who took out copyrights on their business. If a certain performer succeeded in a role thanks to a bit of business that bit of business found its way into the script and was repeated whenever the play was revived. There were other actors who, once the play itself had been approved by the Lord Chamberlain (and Guardian of the Nation's Morals), introduced bits of business into a performance the moment the eye of the censor was no longer upon them.

All this Gaye had been taught early on by her parents. Her father, the low comedian, had a clever trick he liked to play with props. He had learned juggling and tumbling in his youth, and he could not handle an inanimate object on stage without playing with it. If he went to pick up an item from a table it would slip from his fingers as if it had a life of its own, and it would continue to escape his clutches until finally he tripped and ended up flat on his back on the floor, yet still managing to catch the thing before it hit the ground. If handed something by another performer the object in question would appear to fly out of his hands and he would chase it around the room, each time appearing to catch it, only for it to fly away again like a startled starling until he finally succeeded in trapping it. His fellow performers soon got used to him and didn't seem to mind having to stand there looking on like a spare part while he performed his prestidigitations, some of which went on for several minutes until, finally, he won his round of applause.

Gaye could not compete with this, nor did she try. But she did perfect her own manner of business, most of which consisted of face-pulling, at which she was an undisputed mistress. She could hold a squint for minutes on end. She could perform gymnastics with her eyebrows, raising, twisting and wrinkling them both together and independently. She could hold a grotesque expression throughout an entire performance. She had an equally versatile mouth which she could transform into a variety of smiles and snarls, 'moues' or pouts. Miss Martin was not the first, nor would she be the last fellow performer to fall foul of Miss Worth's facial contortions and upstagings.

Needless to say, these carryings-on did not always go down well with the management. What she appeared to get away with at the Haymarket was not, as it turned out, acceptable at Daly's. At Daly's Gigi was just another young woman who could kick a leg and sing more or less in tune. It was not exactly a challenge. So in more ways than one that particular theatre, while a useful stopgap, was not and could never be an ultimate destination for the likes of Gaye Worth.

Besides, the show she was currently appearing in – as

part of the chorus of course – was what fancy people were calling 'the talk of the town' and destined for a long run. Gaye Worth did not like long runs. She got bored all too easily. And when she got bored she was tempted to play up.

# 10 A glimmer of hope

Madame Poulesse was on the whole a benign employer and a keen supporter of the arts. She attended the theatre and opera regularly and from time to time advertised in their programmes. Meredith sometimes wondered if these artistic forays were for appearances only – to show off her latest millinery creation, or to hobnob with future potential clients, or above all, to be *seen*. On the occasion when Merry, out of genuine interest, asked Madame to explain the plot of the play she'd seen the night before Madame became surprisingly vague. She could have recited, with total accuracy, the names of everyone (who was anyone) *in front* of the curtain. What was going on onstage was, Merry surmised, of secondary importance.

This did not stop Madame Poulesse from happily spending the odd hour or two chatting to any of her customers who, like her, were regular attendees about the latest offerings at Drury Lane, or the Lyceum, or even on occasion Daly's. When Merry arrived to be interviewed for the position of assistant Madame was tickled to learn she was an actress and had actually appeared on stage at the Haymarket in the West End. It was this, and the girl's obvious breeding, that encouraged her to employ her. Ladies, of course, like to be served by ladies.

There came into the shop one afternoon a woman with

an ample bosom whom Mme Poulesse greeted as Miss Chester-Bolt. After a cursory glance around, Miss C-B proceeded to settle down with Madame P for what looked like a prolonged chat.

Meredith meanwhile went to stand by the window and look out. There was nothing else for her to do. There wasn't much to look at in a quiet street like theirs. The nearest thing to activity was happening in a pub a few doors down called the Primrose Inn. Meredith had a faint idea it was frequented by actors and actresses, most of them out of work. What a depressing place that must be, she thought. Wild horses wouldn't drag me in there. There could only be one thing worse than being an out-of-work actress and that was to find yourself in the company of other out-of-work actresses.

She was half eavesdropping the conversation that was taking place behind her. (With a voice like Miss Chester-Bolt's it was difficult not to.) The topic was once again the theatre, which Miss CB appeared to frequent even more, well, frequently than her companion. She waxed ecstatic about the latest show at Daly's, the hottest ticket in town apparently, it was only by dint of her connections that Miss CB had managed to see the thing not once, not twice, but . . . (and here she whispered into Madame Poulesse's ear and the two ladies burst into laughter.)

Miss Chester-Bolt prattled on. Madame P sat opposite, head tilted, nodding occasionally, a picture of concentration – though closer scrutiny might have detected a certain glazed look about the eyes. Merry heard enough to establish that Miss C-B was one of those mysterious people actors and actresses rarely get to meet, yet without whom the theatre would probably not exist: she was an investor. She put up the money for plays to be produced. As far as Merry could determine this was all she did. She was not a producer, or a manager. Her involvement in the theatre world was entirely financial.

For a small instant Merry was on full alert. A crazy idea came crashing into her head. *This woman has money. And she invests in theatre. What if . . .*

It was a ridiculous thought.

She took to gazing out of the window again. She observed the passers-by with half-hearted interest. She wondered to herself why it was that actors were so *obvious*. Why a child could pick out an actor from a crowded street. It was not just the clothes, though they played an important part of course. Actors were likely to be far more conscious of appearances than the average Joe. This did not mean they were necessarily smarter. There were actors she knew who were deliberately scruffy – a way of telling the world, she assumed, that they were *artists* and did not give a tinker's hoot what anyone thought of them. (Though the opposite, by definition, was true.) There were yet others who would not dream of being seen in public without . . .

'Mrs Morphett's Macaroons', she heard Miss Chester-Bolt say.

Meredith swung round. Mme Poulesse was shrieking with laughter.

'What a title!' she exclaimed.

'An excellent title,' said Miss C-B, 'for an excellent play.'

'When is it coming on?' asked Mme Poulesse.

'We have no dates yet. We will be looking for our actors soon.'

'And shall you have a name in the lead role?'

'Most probably,' said Miss C-B. 'Negotiations are under way I believe.'

'Excuse me,' said Meredith.

The two ladies turned towards her.

'I couldn't help overhearing. Can I . . . Would you be

able to tell me . . .' How could she put it? 'I am an actress,' she went on, almost bowing to Miss Chester-Bolt. 'I have appeared in the West End. I wondered whether you might give me an address I could write to. When you are casting. And a name. Perhaps. I have had quite a bit of experience. I played Marjorie Forbes-Wilson in *Johnson's Retribution* at the Haymarket a few years ago. With Mr Herbert Tree. That was before he – er – he opened His Majesty's, or Her Majesty's as it was then.' She ground to a halt finally.

Miss Chester-Bolt switched her astonished attention from Miss Martin to Mme Poulesse.

'It is true,' said Madame. 'She is an actress. I believe I may have seen her.'

'Truly?' Miss Chester-Bolt turned back to Miss Martin. 'What is your name?'

'Miss Martin. Miss Meredith Martin.'

Miss Chester-Bolt gazed at her for several moments before speaking. Then she said, 'Write this down.'

There followed a flurry as Mme Poulesse, who appeared every bit as excited as Miss Martin despite the emerging possibility that she might be about to risk losing her assistant, pulled open the drawer of her desk and produced a pad and a pencil.

'Write to this address,' said Miss Chester-Bolt. She mentioned the name of a street which Meredith gleaned, correctly, to be in Battersea. 'Care of Mr Robert Robinson. And the name is Mrs Graham. Mrs Violet Graham.'

# 11 The meeting

'*Earth has not anything to show more fair,*' said Violet.
'You wouldn't think we're perched right on top of a
sewer, would you?' said Robbie.

'You are so romantic Robbie,' said Violet.

They were seated together on a bench on Chelsea
embankment looking out over the grey sludge of the River
Thames. It was a warm summer morning and the trees
were in full leaf.

'How wonderful to live right by the river,' said Violet.

'One day maybe,' said Robbie. 'When we are rich and
grown-up.'

'So,' said Violet, after a comfortable pause, 'give me my
instructions.'

Robbie laughed. 'I will just tell you she is forthright,
and she can be prickly, to the point sometimes of
downright rudeness. But she is not as tough as she seems,
so don't be cowed by her.'

'I will try not to be,' said Violet.

'And if you sense a slight frostiness, don't take it
personally.'

'How else should I take it?' Then before Robbie could
reply Violet added, 'And why should she be frosty to me?
I am pleasant enough. People tend to like me, on the
whole. Don't they?' She glanced at him anxiously.

'I couldn't agree with you more.' He took her hand.

'That is the point.'

There was a long silence as they both turned to stare at the river.

'Robbie,' said Violet eventually, 'sometimes your circumlocution is exasperating.'

'You mean why don't I say what I mean?'

'Exactly.'

'All right. As you know, Miss Chester-Bolt is an essential part of this whole project. We couldn't do it without her.'

'I am aware of that.'

'And with Lolly's cheese magnate on the cusp, shall we say . . .'

'What do you mean, cusp?'

'Her usual. Here today gone tomorrow.'

'I see.'

'We can't afford to antagonise Elizabeth in the slightest way.'

'I have no intention of antagonising her.' Violet released her hand from Robbie's. 'I suspect what you're trying to avoid saying outright is that she has designs on you and she regards me as a rival.'

'I wouldn't presume . . .'

'Well don't be so darned arrogant, Robbie Robinson. If that is the case, say so. I think I can handle myself in most situations, but it helps to know what those situations are.' She took his hand again. 'I won't kiss you on the lips in front of her if that's what you're afraid of. I am still after all a married woman.'

'As I know only too well,' said Robbie glumly. He toyed with her hand. 'We need to do something about that.' He looked at her and she turned away.

They sat in silence for a moment longer.

'Oh,' then said Robbie, 'I nearly forgot.' He fished inside a pocket and pulled out an envelope. 'For you,' he said.

'For me?'

'Sent to my address. Care of.' He winked.

Violet turned the envelope this way and that, as if it might reveal its contents, and its writer, without her having to open it.

'Don't mind me,' said Robbie.

Finally she opened the envelope. She read the contents, read them through again, thought for a moment, refolded the letter and placed it inside her bag. Not until all that was done did she burst out laughing.

'Forgive me,' she said.

'What for?'

'My goodness. It's a long story. It's from someone I used to know, a while back. Well, "know" would be an exaggeration, I think.' She paused, and laughed some more. 'She's heard I am casting for a play called "Mrs Morphett's Macaroons" and she wants a part in it.'

'What's so funny about that?'

'One day I will tell you,' said Violet. She got to her feet. 'So, let's get this over with.'

Elizabeth Chester-Bolt lived in a charming, four-storey ivy-clad house in Cheyne Walk, Chelsea. Until a few years previously it had overlooked the river, but since the building of the sewer, which Robbie had romantically remarked upon, and the embankment that covered it and pushed back the banks of the river by several yards behind a concrete wall, it no longer did, to the dismay of many of the residents of Cheyne Walk and Mrs Chester-Bolt in particular.

The Mother, as Robbie referred to her, appeared to live in a separate part of the same house as her only offspring but was often present whenever Robbie visited; hence his in-depth knowledge of the 'disastrous' changes that had occurred over the past several decades. Miss Chester-Bolt disagreed with her mother on this, and on many things. It was a good-humoured disagreement for the most part. Whenever Mrs C-B launched into her tirade about the terrible 'disruption' which she had had to endure for 'fifty years or more' while they built 'a sewer, of all things, and right here on our doorstep!' – 'Don't exaggerate, mother,' her daughter would interpose, then sigh and flutter her eyelashes at Robbie as if to say, 'Don't listen to the old bat, she has no idea.'

'It is much improved, mama, you have to admit.'

'I admit to nothing,' said the old woman.

Right now, as Robbie and Violet were shown upstairs to the drawing room, the two ladies were already waiting for them. The mother remained seated while Miss Chester-Bolt got to her feet and gave Violet a very obvious once-over.

'Elizabeth, may I present Mrs Violet Graham,' said Robbie. 'Violet, this is my friend and benefactor Miss Chester-Bolt, and there in the shadows is her mother. Good morning Mrs Chester-Bolt!' he shouted. 'She is a little hard of hearing,' he told Violet, unnecessarily.

'You don't have to yell quite so loud,' said her daughter. 'They could hear you next door.'

'Turner used to live next door,' said Mrs Chester-Bolt. 'Indeed?'

'Down the street. Number – what was it Elizabeth?'

'I've no idea, Mama.'

'And Dante Rosetti. He kept a bull in his front garden, until it wrecked it. Now it's all theatrical types. Actors and writers and composers and such.'

'Do you disapprove?'

Mrs Chester-Bolt harrumphed.

Her daughter turned back to her guests with a raised eyebrow. 'You mustn't mind Mama,' she said.

'We used to be able to look out of our windows right

across the river,' grumbled the old lady. 'Right across. There it was, on our doorstep.'

'And inside it, as often as not,' said her daughter.

'And there was no "by your leave", not a word. Just – there they were, one morning, out of the blue, with their paraphernalia, and their machinery, and their noise. Deafening, it was.'

'Mama and Papa lived here for a long time,' Elizabeth explained.

'Deafening. And the dirt! Bits of who knows what, hurtling through the air all over the place! They with their filthy tunnels. I don't know whose idea it was, they just turned up, out of the blue . . .'

'Mama, that's quite enough. Mr Robinson did not come to listen to your ramblings.'

She turned a resigned smile upon Robbie and, while Chester-Bolt senior continued to mutter in the background, and the maid brought them tea in a silver pot on a silver tray, which Miss Chester-Bolt dispensed without looking at or addressing Violet once, she said, to Robbie, 'So, tell me about your day in Parliament.'

Robbie did so. He began by outlining the debate that preceded the debate that never got off the ground. How certain Honourable Members, many but not all of them Scottish, took it upon themselves to regale the House for hours on end on the topic of whether an edict to force all vehicles to carry lights before and aft, as he put it, should be a uniform affair decided by central government or left to the discretion of local authorities and especially including, or excluding, Scotland, whose representatives appeared to consider themselves a Special Case, and therefore responsible for Their Own Rules rather than those foisted upon them by the Honourable Members at Westminster, most if not all of whom had never set foot inside that country. Moreover, they continued, now that

that scourge of humanity called the Motor Car was becoming more and more commonplace, it was unfair to penalise the humble cart driver whose very life was now under peril from men who drove their vehicles at speeds hitherto unknown to mankind or beast, thereby causing great danger to the said humble agriculturalist, who as often as not was asleep at the wheel.

As he spoke Miss Chester-Bolt clapped her hands together and bounced up and down in her chair, giggling with delight, and Violet could not help but notice the more she giggled the more Robbie played as it were to the gallery and the longer and more outrageous the peroration became. By the end of it Robbie was becoming quite hoarse and Miss C-B was crying so hard with laughter she almost fell off her chair.

'Robbie, you are priceless!' she pronounced, dabbing at her eyes.

'But it wasn't funny,' said Robbie. 'That's the point. That is our democracy. These are our representatives. In Parliament.'

Miss Chester-Bolt tried to calm down.

'The outcome was there was no time for the debate on women's suffrage,' Robbie went on. 'And so the women congregated outside the House and Mrs Pankhurst tried to address the crowd but was pushed on by the police. With awful brutality.'

'Oh dear,' said Miss C-B. She wasn't laughing any more.

Robbie frowned. 'Awful brutality,' he repeated. 'My faith in the common decency of the powers that be in this country was shaken to the core.'

There was a long and sober silence. Miss Chester-Bolt looked at her lap. Violet looked at Miss Chester-Bolt. Mrs Chester-Bolt meanwhile continued to mumble away in the background.

'So there you have it,' said Robbie finally. 'Back to square one. But a line has been crossed, I sensed it. I do feel that our timing is right, is perfect.'

'For the play, you mean,' said Miss C-B. 'I understand. I agree, absolutely. So, when do you begin rehearsals?'

'We . . .' he glanced at Violet. 'We haven't commenced casting, not yet. We were hoping for Marie Tempest, for Mrs Morphett. But it's a long shot.'

'She's eager to play a straight part for a change,' said Violet. 'So I believe.'

'Marie Tempest,' said Miss C-B, ignoring Violet totally. 'I saw her at Daly's once. I believe she is a difficult woman.'

Robbie shrugged. 'That's the price you pay when you work in the theatre,' he said, with a wink at Violet.

'So,' it was Violet who rose to her feet first. 'It has been delightful to meet you Miss Chester-Bolt. We don't want to take up any more of your time.'

'There is no need to go quite yet,' said Miss Chester-Bolt, addressing Robbie.

But Robbie was on his feet too. 'A pleasure, as always, Elizabeth. We will keep you informed. Mrs Graham,' he turned to Violet, 'has some changes she wishes to make to the script.'

'What kind of changes?' cried Miss Chester-Bolt.

'She thinks I'm long-winded, which I am, as I demonstrated earlier. And she doesn't like the ending.'

'But the ending is perfect!'

'Thank you.' Robbie gave a little bow. 'But no new play was ever produced without the odd tweak here and there.' Then, raising his voice, he said, 'Farewell, Mrs Chester-Bolt. I trust you will keep well!'

There was no response, other than the faintest sound of a snore.

They left the house and walked in silence along Cheyne

Row in the direction of the river. It was not until they had turned towards Chelsea Bridge that Violet ventured, 'She did not look at me once throughout the whole conversation. I may as well have not been there.'

'I did warn you,' said Robbie.

Violet paused for a moment. She leaned over the balustrade of the Embankment and watched the activity on the river.

'Do you think she will be difficult to work with?' she asked.

'I don't see why,' said Robbie. 'Your paths are not likely to cross that often.'

The river was as busy as ever. Pleasure boats packed with rowdy sightseers steered chaotically between working barges and tugs pulling as many as six lighters stacked high with sacks and crates. Travelling in the opposite direction appeared a rowboat containing three men in blue uniforms and caps, and as it made its way languidly upriver Violet saw the man in the stern gazing down into the water – searching, she assumed, for dead bodies and the odd bloated animal. Below where Robbie and she were standing, on the foreshore and risking being caught by the tide, a couple of young mudlarks foraged for treasure.

'When it comes to money, if it does, you can leave her to me,' Robbie continued.

They resumed walking in the direction of Royal Hospital Road.

'She is besotted, you do realise that.'

'With me?' Robbie snorted. 'Come now, just because she laughs at my jokes.'

'It's blindingly obvious, Robbie, you know perfectly well.'

'We have to treat her . . . . *I* have to treat her with kid gloves, Vi. She's all we have, now we've lost the cheese magnate.' He laughed briefly. 'But she won't interfere. I'll make sure she doesn't.'

'I hope so.'

'She hasn't had an easy life, you know.'

'Oh?'

'Her father was a self-made man. Coal, as far as I remember. He came from humble stock. And like all self-made men he thought if he could make his own fortune from nothing, so could anyone.'

Violet nodded.

'And of course his daughter – his only daughter, mind, his only offspring, come to that – she spent her childhood under his thumb. And by all accounts it was a large and fearsome thumb. So since he died she's done all she can to escape from that thumb only to find she's a bit of a chip off the old block, if you'll forgive the mixed metaphors.'

'Is there a reason you're telling me all this?'

'Is there a reason?' Robbie stopped walking and turned to look at Violet. 'We could not be more different. She and I. The capitalist and . . .'

'The socialist?'

Robbie switched his gaze from Violet to a young lad who was playing dodgems in the road with the traffic.

'I know what you're trying to say, Robbie. We can't always be like the people we have to do business with. We can't always *like* the people we do business with.'

Robbie turned back to Violet with a smile, of relief perhaps. 'So you don't mind?'

'Mind what, precisely?'

'If I allow her to flirt with me. Just a bit? If she laughs a little too loudly at my jokes?'

'You're a vain man, Robbie Robinson,' said Violet. They continued walking, past Chelsea Hospital and the Barracks. 'And if you want my honest opinion, which you're getting whether you like it or not, I am more concerned for her than I am for you.'

'Fair enough,' said Robbie.

They had reached Sloane Square. Robbie looked across at the large brick building on the far side. 'Where would the theatre be without hypocrisy?' he said.

'I beg your pardon?'

'Your words. Way back when. *Mrs Warren's Profession?* Do you remember?'

'I do remember,' said Violet.

'Now there,' Robbie nodded at the brick building. '*There* is true drama.'

Violet followed his look to the sign on the Court Theatre: '*The Voysey Inheritance*'.

'Miss Chester-Bolt would never invest in a play like *that*. She told me as much herself. Anti-capitalist trash.'

'I imagine to a socialist that's a badge of honour,' said Violet, and they both laughed.

# 12 Merry and not so Gaye

'What happened?' exclaimed Merry. 'What did you do?'

'Nothing nobody else don't do,' said Gigi.

'And they sacked you? From Daly's? I thought that was almost impossible.'

Gigi sat with her shoulders hunched. 'I made Lily Elsie laugh.'

'Who's Lily Elsie?'

'I've been understudying that girl since the beginning of the run and she hasn't been off once. Not once. She's gone on with a sore throat when she couldn't sing a note and a sprained ankle when she couldn't dance a step, never mind a Viennese waltz. What sort of behaviour is that?'

'Sounds like professional behaviour to me.'

'I said to her, pleaded, I said "Lil, just one go, a matinée, that's all I want, it's not too much to ask is it?" And she said, "Of course, Gigi".'

'So she's . . .'

'She plays the widow, yes. And then nothing! So I had to think of something else.'

'You deliberately made her laugh. On stage.'

Gigi nodded. 'Right in the middle of her best song. Perfect timing! And of course they called her in and they sacked her, there and then.'

'They sacked the star of the show?'

'For five minutes. Until she shopped me.' Gigi stared gloomily into her cocoa.

Meredith was shocked, and impressed. She was still, despite her years of experience, green around the ears when it came to backstage, or onstage, mischief. She knew it existed, she'd been on the receiving end of it, it was a kind of rite of passage: make the new girl laugh, see her make a fool of herself in front of an audience. She'd just about learned how to cope with that, but you had to be *very* experienced, and *extremely* sophisticated, not to say *exceedingly* bored, to be able to do it to other people.

'What did you do to make her laugh?' She tried to keep the admiration from her voice.

'It's not so much what I said as what I did,' said Gigi. 'And if she'd stuck to her promise I wouldn't have had to do it in the first place. She's only got herself to blame.'

Thus was the logic according to Gaye Worth.

'I couldn't believe my luck, not at first,' she went on. 'I thought at the most they might, you know, suspend her. For a performance or two, as a sort of punishment. That's all I needed. But they didn't, they sacked her there and then. I felt sort of bad about that, to tell the truth. Till she shopped me.'

Meredith offered a piece of almond cake to Gigi, who shook her head.

'Dunno what she said, but they changed their minds just like that,' she clicked her fingers. 'And it was me out on me ear. They didn't even let me tell my side of the story.'

'I don't suppose telling your side of the story would have helped much,' said Meredith.

'It's one thing if you're the star of the show and another if you're just part of the chorus,' Gigi grumbled.

'Don't you think it's disrespectful, to a paying

audience? To make someone laugh on stage?' Meredith took a bite of her cake.

'They don't notice,' said Gigi. 'Audiences don't notice nothing except chorus girls' legs. You can mess up the script, you can dry up – there was an actress once, never knew her lines, kept getting stuck at the same point in the play. So I took her back to the beginning of the scene, I repeated what we'd just said, like giving her another run-up, until she got it. Sometimes we had to do it three times. The audience never noticed a thing.'

'That's different,' said Meredith. 'But to do something *deliberately.*'

'Everyone does it. Tree does it. Mrs Pat does it.'

'That's different too.'

'Have you ever been in a long run? Doing the same old thing night after night? Understudying someone who's never off? Do you know what it's like to be so fed up you could scream?'

Meredith felt uncomfortably prim. She did not recognise the world her friend was describing. When you've been unemployed and forced to eke out a modest living working in a hat shop, to have to listen to someone who had apparently deliberately thrown up an engagement in a theatre like Daly's because of boredom made no sense at all.

'Understudying's a mug's game,' said Gaye. She puffed out her cheeks. 'I was just one *tiny weeny moment*, one *cough*, one *fever*, one *accidental trip on the stairs*, away from being the star.'

'It's terribly unfair, being an understudy.'

'It's a mug's game,' said Gigi, again. 'And being a chorus girl and all.'

'So what are you going to do now?'

'I'm sick of it,' said her friend. She was looking vacantly out of the window at the rain. 'Sick of kowtowing to stupid managers. I want to be my own manager for a change.'

A passing hansom hit a large puddle in the road, spraying water all over an elderly pedestrian. Gigi burst into laughter.

'What?'

She gestured out the window. The elderly man stood stock still on the pavement, soaked from head to toe, shaking his umbrella redundantly after the receding carriage.

'At least something can make you laugh,' said Merry.

'I can always laugh at other people's bad luck,' said Gigi. 'Never me own.'

Merry sniggered. 'You can be quite funny sometimes, Gigi,' she said.

'So they say,' said Gigi. She resumed her glum expression.

'Have you ever thought of being a comedian? On stage?'

'Course I have. I was doing it when I was ten years old.'

'It's such a useful talent. If you can make people laugh you need never be out of work.'

'Are you offering me an engagement?' said Gigi. 'As a low comedian? Or even a high comedian? I'm versatile enough. And desperate enough. Do you know of anyone who is hiring low comedians?' She was leaning rather aggressively across the table and Merry instinctively drew back.

'No, of course I don't. I was just trying to suggest a change from being in the chorus line.'

Gigi sat back. 'That's not the problem.'

'I thought it was. You said it was.'

'The problem is managers. Creeps who think they can rule the roost over everyone. Especially girls. Especially chorus girls. We're just bosoms and fannies to them.'

'Oh!' Merry shrieked, then covered her mouth and glanced around in embarrassment. 'I don't know what the answer is to that,' she said. 'Unless . . .'

There was a pause as each woman became lost in thought. In the same thought, perhaps.

'Unless?' said Gigi.

'We could do something that doesn't require a manager.'

'Such as?'

'Such as hire our own theatre,' said Merry.

Gaye nodded thoughtfully. 'With what?'

'What?'

'As in money.'

'Uh,' said Merry.

'Or,' said Gigi, 'we could do an act, the two of us, and perform it in . . .'

'Where?'

'I don't know. People's drawing rooms. Rich people's drawing rooms.'

'Do you know any rich people?'

'Do you?'

'I used to,' said Merry. 'That's before I got thrown out of the family home.'

'Shame about that. Any chance they'd take you back?'

Merry shook her head. 'Not unless I give up the business altogether.'

'Hmm.'

They resumed their private contemplations. Then: 'We could do recitals,' said Merry.

'What sort of recitals?'

'From Shakespeare.'

'*Shakespeare?*'

'Or something a little lighter perhaps. You could sing something, and dance.'

'And what are you doing meanwhile?'

'I am . . . I am looking on, and maybe making dry comments.'

'Can you do comedy?'

'I don't know, I've never tried.'

'Because,' Gaye was leaning forwards again, this time less aggressively, 'if I was, let's say, the comedian, and you could be a kind of foil. Something for me to bounce off. You can do deadpan, can't you?'

'Deadpan?'

'You do it in real life, after all. So I'm the comedian,' she was thinking as she spoke, 'and I'm making fun of you, say, and you're too stupid to realise.'

'Is that the sort of thing that would appeal to rich people?'

'I'm not thinking of rich people,' said Gigi. 'I'm thinking,' she paused for effect, 'of the man on the street. And the woman.'

'On the *street*?'

'Like street entertainers. You've seen them.'

Merry's mouth was hanging open. 'You're suggesting we become *beggars*?'

'They're not beggars!' Gigi exclaimed. 'They're skilled performers. They're royalty! The thing is, would they accept us?'

'Who?'

'You've got to know what you're doing on the street. They won't put up with rubbish. It's not like Daly's, you can't get away with any old thing. And then, who knows?' Gigi's mind was racing now. 'We might get spotted!'

'Who by?'

'By anyone! By Tree. He might even recognise us. You've seen them outside the theatre, performing to the queues. Tree or Irving or whoever, they must see them too. And who knows where it might lead?'

'I thought you said you didn't want to work with managers again,' said Merry.

The conversation subsided. Both women turned to look out of the window. The rain had stopped and a feeble sun was half-heartedly trying to edge its way through the clouds.

'It was a thought,' said Merry eventually.

Another moment passed.

'I still think it's a good idea,' said Gigi.

'What is?'

'The double act. You could dress as a man. You've got the height. It might be even funnier, what do you think?'

'Maybe.'

'We could work on something first, find somewhere to perform it second.' Gigi thought for a moment. 'After all, there's no point in going onto the street or into some fancy drawing room if we don't have nothing to show them.'

'That is true,' said Merry.

~

It occurred to Meredith as she made her way once again to the little hat shop off the Strand, that she did know one rich person and that was her employer, Mme Poulesse. Madame was well connected, she had to be, it was an essential part of her business. And how delighted she would surely be to have the opportunity to offer her customers something extra by way of an entertainment *in their own drawing rooms*. And that entertainment could be tailored (like her hats) to the customer. So for example a lady married to a lawyer could be given an entertainment *especially written* to a theme based on the law. Or a politician's wife could watch a sketch featuring recognisable members of the Government, done with respect, naturally. Although it would be a stretch to be both funny *and* respectful. And it would demand a lot of work, creating different entertainments on different themes. One could adapt them, naturally, so the lawyer became the politician. Would that make sense? Probably not. Still, it was something to ponder on. She wouldn't broach it with Madame, not quite yet. Not until they had something concrete to offer her.

~

Gaye wandered the streets around Piccadilly, without an aim. She did not want to go home. She had not yet gotten around to explaining to her mother, and more to the point, her father, why she would be home for supper that night, and for nights to come.

She killed time window shopping in Burlington Arcade, then made her way to Green Park. A double-act was all very well but it had to be quite special to attract attention. True, it was unusual to see two women, one dressed as a man, maybe, performing together. But Gigi was not a writer, and nor was Merry, and original material was hard to come by these days. She couldn't very well ask her father, at least not until he had calmed down once he realised why she was no longer at Daly's. Her father had what Gigi considered an old-fashioned and over-developed respect for the people he worked for. To know that his daughter had stepped over the line, deliberately, to the extent that she had been sacked, and from Daly's of all places, was enough to warrant a thrashing, or at the least an extended haranguing. Gigi's father was not an entrepreneur and he did not understand entrepreneurship. Actor-managers made no sense because actors did not understand finance, or business. So let the managers manage and the actors act, and heaven help anyone who tried to mix the two, was his view.

In the end Gigi found herself walking in the direction of the Strand, and down the little side-street to the Primrose Inn. She rather hoped the young actress she'd met before might be there, the one who'd told her about the play her nemesis, Mrs Graham, was producing. Principles are all very well when you're in work and funds. Needs must when you have neither.

So deep in thought was Gigi she walked right past the hat shop – so exclusive you'd barely know it was a hat shop from the outside – without even seeing it.

# 13 Mrs Santenoy

'Mr Robinson, you have a visitor,' announced Mrs Woolly.

It was midway through the evening, just as Robbie was finishing dinner and his housekeeper Mrs Woolly was about to go home.

He got to his feet. 'Oh? And who might that be?'

Lolly Mulligan stood on the front doorstep on tiptoe, grinning like a schoolgirl, beret perched jauntily on the side of her head.

'It's you,' said Robbie. And then with a nod to Mrs Woolly, 'Thank you Mrs Woolly, I can handle this.'

The housekeeper nodded goodnight and walked off into the twilight.

'Good news,' said Lolly. 'Can I come in?'

It was difficult not to be pleased to see Lolly. Robbie stepped aside as she walked straight past him to his front room.

'I've found us a new backer,' she said. She threw off her beret and draped herself on Robbie's chaise longue.

'Oh? Who would that be? Did you reconcile yourself with the cheese magnate?'

'Shipping magnate. Henry was a big cheese in a shipping company Robbie, do pay attention.'

'It was meant as a joke,' said Robbie feebly.

'She's a suffragist.'

'Do suffragists have that kind of money?'

'I don't really know what "that kind of money" is,' said Lolly. 'We never discussed the naked realities. There was one condition though.'

'Which is?'

'She wants a part in the play. And I promised her she could have it.'

'Can she act?'

'I doubt it very much. She gave me her version of a Hamlet soliloquy. *"Oh what a rogue and peasant slave am I!"'* Lolly recited, in a remarkably accurate impersonation. 'I don't even think she's done any amateur stuff. But it obviously means a lot to her. She was almost asphyxiated with ecstasy when I said yes.'

'Well then, what can one say?' said Robbie. He stood hands on hips, looking down at his visitor. 'Well done, Lolly.'

'I gave her your details and I invited her here this evening. What's the time now?' Lolly glanced at the clock on the wall. 'She should be here in around half an hour. Would you happen to have any wine in the place?'

Robbie rubbed his neck. Even he had to struggle at times to keep up with Lolly.

'What is this, Dutch courage?'

Lolly looked at him wide-eyed. 'Why should I need Dutch courage?'

He fetched a bottle of wine from the sideboard.

'Where's Vi?' asked Lolly as Robbie popped the cork from the bottle.

Robbie poured her a glass of wine, and then one for himself, before he said, 'Have you eaten?'

'Not really.'

'I could rustle up something.'

'No, this will do.' Lolly took a large swig. 'Well?'

'Mmm?'

'You heard me.'

'She doesn't live here, you know.'

'I do know.'

'And we are not in one another's pockets.' He sat down and raised his glass in Lolly's direction. 'Cheerio.'

'Cheerio,' repeated Lolly, then: 'I don't think I've ever met anyone so slow off the mark as the two of you. We've booked the church, we've ordered the bridesmaids' dresses, and you haven't even named the day. So, when is it to be?'

Robbie contemplated. 'First, I have not proposed. Second, Vi is still married, technically.' He paused.

'Third?'

Robbie stared into his glass. 'Third – I'm trying to find a polite way of saying it's none of your business. But dear Lolly,' he swirled his wine and smiled across the room at her. 'Everything is your business really, isn't it?'

'I like to think so.' Lolly stood up and then sat down again with her legs tucked under her. 'But I am completely harmless, you know that.'

'I worry about you,' he said.

'Everyone worries about me. I can't imagine why.'

As Violet had herself pointed out, there was either a good deal more or a good deal less than met the eye with Lolly. She led a kind of transitory existence, answerable to nobody but herself, let alone her parents, who alternately locked her out of the house and then opened their arms, and their front door, to her again. They objected to her behaviour, her profession, her clothes, and most of all to the company she kept. They had been known to call her a slut.

But there was nothing sluttish about Lolly. She slept around, as she herself proudly claimed, and was not in the least averse to going several steps further than most actresses in order to 'get herself hired', as she put it. The very mention of her name in the theatrical world produced raised eyebrows and knowing looks. Anyone who was anyone 'knew' Lolly Mulligan.

Moreover it appeared she was, at base, homeless, and rootless, and for a single woman in Edwardian London this implied she was no better than she should be. Yet in her own way Lolly was an honest young woman, even moral. She liked to claim that 'what you see is what you get', which in current society with its façade of fakery and humbug was beyond most people's comprehension.

'So tell me about your suffragist,' said Robbie.

'Her name is Mrs Katherine Savoy. Saveloy. Something beginning with S. Her husband is a lawyer, or maybe a surgeon. Retired, I think. She always wanted to be an actress but her parents wouldn't think of it – well, what parents *would* think of it – and of course she adores me. She saw our play.'

'She did?'

'Don't look so surprised. And she *loved* it. She laughed until she cried, she said. She told me I was the brightest thing on the London stage and I was destined to be another Ellen Terry.' Lolly took a drink of her wine and spluttered.

'What's wrong with that?'

Lolly gave him a look. 'Ellen Terry?' She pulled a face. 'I did feel bad about Henry, as you know. I could have asked him to cough up again, but even I draw the line at times, surprising though that may sound. So anyway, I asked around among the suffragists. I thought they'd all come running, but the only one who did was Mrs Saveloy. Compared with Henry she should be plain sailing. I can even give her the odd acting lesson if need be.'

She smiled sweetly across at Robbie.

'Everyone has their price, don't they?' she said.

'You're a clever woman, Lolly Mulligan,' said Robbie.

'I am, aren't I?' said Lolly. 'I bet you're glad you met me.'

As Robbie was searching for a suitable response to Lolly's remark there came a ring on the doorbell. He sprang to his feet.

'Mr Robinson? My name is Katherine Santenoy.' She stood in the doorway, feet together, hands clasped before her. A slight woman with silver hair and dressed from head to toe in grey. The immediate impression was of a ghost.

'Do come in, Mrs Santenoy, I'm delighted to meet you. How do you do.'

She glided past Robbie into the hallway, where she stood erect, awaiting further instruction.

'I saw your play,' said Mrs Santenoy, as Robbie helped her with her cape and hat.

'So Miss Mulligan told me.'

'And I laughed. How I laughed!'

'I'm so glad.'

'Such an ingenious idea. And fancy, making fun of our venerable members of parliament like that. I never would have thought you could get away with it.'

'Well, you never know until . . .'

'Is she here?'

'Miss Mulligan? She is. Come this way.'

'Oh, my dear!'

Mrs Santenoy greeted Lolly like a long-lost daughter. She advanced across the room with her arms outstretched and enveloped the girl within them. It was, as Lolly said later, a little like being embraced by a phantom.

'This clever little thing, where did you find her?' She was hanging onto Lolly's arm.

'Lolly is the sort of person who finds other people,' said Robbie.

'Clever, clever little thing.' She was shaking Lolly's arm

and Lolly was allowing herself to be jerked back and forth, exaggeratedly, like a rag doll. 'So versatile.' She released Lolly suddenly and the girl collapsed back down onto the chaise longue.

'I always wanted to be an actress when I was young,' continued Mrs Santenoy, breathlessly. 'But my family wouldn't allow it. Or a dancer.' She was closing in on Robbie and he took an imperceptible step backwards. 'But no. Not even amateur. Amateur theatricals were even worse. They were terrific snobs!' She laughed, and her laugh was like bells tinkling, loudly. 'But what a splendid idea. And you wrote it, Mr Robinson, all on your own?'

'All on my . . . Well yes, that's generally how it happens, though other people . . .'

'And the ending! To imagine a world governed entirely by women, what an utterly delightful idea!' She clapped her hands together.

'Can I offer you . . .?'

'And as for the suffragist ladies – I was saying to Miss Mulligan, wasn't I dear? – what *would* those ladies make of it? We do take ourselves awfully seriously you see, Mr Robinson.' She put on a sober face, and then she laughed again. 'Am I talking too much? I generally do when I'm nervous. There. I will be quiet.' She pursed her lips together and, to Robbie's relief, she sat down.

'May I offer you something, Mrs Santenoy? Sherry? Wine? Something hot?'

'Nothing, thank you Mr Robinson. And then . . .' She stopped suddenly.

'You were saying?'

'But I promised to be quiet. Did Miss Mulligan tell you about me, Mr Robinson?'

'As of ten minutes ago, yes.' Robbie sat down and crossed his legs. He was trying very hard not to catch Lolly's eye.

'I am not asking for the lead role, heavens above! Although, of course, should you so decide . . . No, of course not.'

'We were hoping for Miss Marie Tempest. A well-known name does wonders for a play's publicity, you see.'

'Of course. Miss Tempest. I saw her at Daly's, she has a glorious singing voice. Yes, I can see her, perfectly. But of course if you felt able to give me a speaking role, just a few words, it needn't be anything very much. Just enough to, you see, if I were to invite my family and to show them.' She stopped dead again and stared straight ahead of her.

'I can see Mrs Santenoy as Lady Clothgill,' said Lolly.

'Lady Clothgill,' said Robbie. 'Yes, quite possibly.'

Then without warning Mrs Santenoy stood up and walked to the middle of the room. She clasped her hands together and then she began:

> '"Gallop apace, you fiery-footed steeds
> Towards Pheobus' lodging. Such a wagoner
> As Phaethon would whip you to the west
> And bring in cloudy night immediately."

Is that enough? And what comes next, yes . . .

> "Spread thy close curtain, love-performing night,
> That runaways' eyes may wink, and Romeo
> Leap to these arms, untalked of and unseen."

Then, er . . .

> "Come, civil night,
> Thou sober-suited matron, all in black,
> And learn me how to lose a winning match
> Played for a pair of stainless maidenhoods."'

Then, just as suddenly as she had begun, Mrs Santenoy stopped, and sat down again, and looked nervously at the floor.

'All I could think of on the spur of the moment,' she explained apologetically to the carpet. 'I promised myself I wouldn't practise anything in advance, I didn't want to get too worked up. So Juliet, she stays in the mind, doesn't she, once she's lodged herself there.'

'It was . . .'

'Though hardly appropriate, of course. I don't know which of Shakespeare's characters might be more fitting. The nurse, probably.'

'You really did not . . .'

'Or perhaps Queen Margaret. Different play, of course. Except I don't know Queen Margaret. She was batty, wasn't she?'

'Mrs Santenoy.' Robbie leaned forwards and spoke gently. 'You really didn't need to audition for us, you know.'

'Isn't that what actresses do? For an engagement? I thought it was what all actresses did, and actors of course.' She smiled suddenly. 'I rather wanted to, you see. I wanted to see what it was like.'

'And what was it like?'

'Terrifying,' she said, with a broad smile. 'But now it's over I can breathe easily. And I'm not going to ask you what you thought, or whether I've got the part. Miss Mulligan told me all about it, you see.'

'All about what?'

'How actresses "get hired", as she put it.'

To Mrs Santenoy's alarm Robbie burst out laughing.

'Did I say something stupid?' She looked to Lolly for support, but Lolly was glowering at Robbie.

'Forgive me, Mrs Santenoy. Miss Mulligan is absolutely right, that is how actresses get hired. But I think this is a very different case.'

'How much are you looking for?'

Robbie, normally quick on his feet, felt nonetheless wrong-footed by the forthright Mrs Santenoy.

'I need to do some calculations, Mrs Santenoy. Lolly, Miss Mulligan, did rather land you on me, as it were.

Without warning.'

'Oh, well of course.'

'A most delightful landing, I should add.'

'I hope I did not do anything out of turn.'

'On the contrary, you've been very open, and very helpful, and encouraging. And we are delighted to welcome you to our little company.'

'Thank you. Thank you, Mr Robinson. Thank you.' And the gentle lady beamed from ear to ear.

# 14 Lolly stays the night

'You were laughing at her,' said Lolly.

'I did no such thing!' exclaimed Robbie. 'You couldn't even get her name right.'

'She's quite a card, isn't she?'

'I liked her, as a matter of fact.' Robbie was circling the room extinguishing lights.

'Are you trying to tell me something?'

'No. I'm turning down the lights. I thought she was charming. And it was a very brave thing she did this evening.'

He drew apart the curtains and stood by the window for a moment, gazing out.

'I suppose you need a bed for the night.' He spoke without turning around.

'Not necessarily. I am quite comfortable where I am.'

Lolly had kicked off her shoes and was lying flat out on the chaise longue. She closed her eyes. 'Shall you and I have an affair one of these days, Robbie?'

'I'm not married.'

'No, but you soon will be. Should I wait until you are? I'm not sure I mightn't be too old by then.'

He wandered over to her and stood looking down at her. With her eyes closed she looked so young. A child really. But she wasn't a child, not by a long chalk.

'Sit down, Robbie, talk to me.' Without opening her

eyes Lolly shifted her bottom further into the chaise longue to make room for Robbie. She reached out a hand and pulled him down to sit by her.

'So.' She draped an arm languidly over his knee. 'I'm going to give you my opinion on Vi. In my opinion,' she opened her eyes and looked at him, 'it's a meeting of similars, if there is such a thing. And that can be a problem.'

'In what way?'

'You're both' – she made a circling motion in the air with her hand – 'what is the word I'm looking for?'

'Charming?'

'Reticent is what I was looking for. Though that doesn't come close. I was looking for something stronger.' She placed her arm on Robbie's knee again. 'Cautious maybe. Cowardly even.'

'In what sense?'

Lolly turned onto her side and raised herself onto one elbow.

'I've never understood why it is that people who have one bad experience in love assume every experience is going to be the same. It makes no sense to me. No, don't interrupt. I know what you've been through, Robbie, but it seems to me you're little more than a coward when it comes to the human heart.'

'That may well be true. But . . .'

'But nothing. You're getting on for goodness' sake. How old are you?'

Robbie scratched his head as if trying to remember. 'Thirty-five next birthday.'

'You're an old man. A confirmed bachelor. Do you expect to stay that way?'

Robbie took hold of Lolly's hand in his. 'I've no idea, Lolly. But the truth is, if you'll allow me to get a word in edgeways, Violet does not want to get married.'

Lolly stared at him. The light from the street lamp outside was reflecting off his spectacles, which made him look distinctly other-worldly.

'That's no excuse.'

'It is a fact, though. She's still married, and unless and until her husband asks for a divorce – or she asks him, which is hardly likely – that's the way she will stay. And I believe it suits her to stay that way.'

Lolly sat up completely. 'Why?'

'Who knows?'

'You must bed her, immediately,' she said. 'If that's the only way you can get a divorce.'

Robbie was already shaking his head. 'She's not like you, Lolly.'

'Nobody is like me. That doesn't mean you shouldn't bed her. Are you afraid?' Then before he could answer, 'Is she afraid?'

'We haven't exactly broached the subject.'

'"We haven't exactly broached the subject",' she mimicked. 'Heavens above, Robbie. Well then, live with her, why don't you? Or are you afraid of what people might say?'

'Not at all.'

'There you are then.' Lolly bent her knees to her chest and hugged them. 'Ellen Terry had two children out of wedlock and it did her no harm at all.'

'I'm grateful for your concern, Lolly,' said Robbie. 'And now, if you will excuse me.' He stood up and stretched.

Lolly lay back down on the chaise longue. 'Do you think we could include a dance in the play?'

'A what? What kind of dance?'

'Mrs Santenoy is a wonderful dancer. She showed me, the other day. It was a little . . . weird.' She made twisting movements with her arms by way of demonstration. 'Greek, she called it, or maybe Turkish.'

'I'm not sure how that could fit in, but I wouldn't rule it out.' He yawned. 'Are you sure there's nothing I can get you, Lolly?'

She had closed her eyes again. She held out her hand and Robbie kissed it.

'Just a wedding date. That's all I ask,' said Lolly.

Robbie held onto her hand for a moment longer, until he could hear her snoring softly. He left the room quietly and returned a moment later with a blanket, which he laid gently atop the sleeping girl. As he crept away he felt a hand grab the tail of his jacket.

'I have an idea,' said Lolly. 'Come here.' She grabbed hold this time of Robbie's lapel and pulled him down towards her. She whispered into his ear.

Robbie straightened up, and smiled. 'Thank you for the idea Lolly, but I don't suppose it would work.'

'Whyever not?'

'Vi would see right through it.'

'It's worth a try, don't you think? It's what they do in comic opera all the time.'

'In comic opera, yes, exactly. But in real life?'

'Think about it,' said Lolly. With which she turned onto her side dismissively. And Robbie, suitably dismissed, departed the room properly this time.

# 15 The Merry Widow

While Lolly was paying her uninvited visit to Robbie's apartment in Battersea, Violet was attending a performance of the comic opera *The Merry Widow* at Daly's Theatre in Leicester Square.

Comic opera was not Violet's fare of choice, and moreover this particular show had been running for many months and was known as the 'Theatrical Sensation of the Year', which was yet another reason why she had so far avoided it. Her reason for attending on this occasion was her companion, young Olivia, daughter of her recent employers Lord and Lady Armstrong.

During her time working as housekeeper to their Lord- and Ladyships Violet had struck up an unexpected friendship with their daughter. Unexpected, because it was not usual for upstairs and downstairs to form alliances, and certainly not alliances that consisted of intimacies of the kind enjoyed by the then seventeen-year-old Olivia. While it would not be quite accurate to describe the two young women as friends – there was an age disparity of more than ten years, for a start – Violet was the nearest thing Olivia had to a confidante. And even though Violet was no longer working for the Armstrongs they considered her to be a distinctly positive influence on their daughter, and so they asked her if she wouldn't mind, on occasion, accompanying Olivia to the theatre to a show of their daughter's choice —and of course at their expense.

So that is how Violet found herself sitting with her ward in the centre of the stalls of Daly's Theatre, alongside the best, or at least the gaudiest, of London society. She herself would have preferred the pit or the gallery where the 'real people' sat. And she would have preferred almost anything to the bit of fluffy nonsense she was about to sit through. On the other hand, as a fledgling producer it was necessary, she acknowledged, to know what else was going on in town, not least to witness the show that had taken over London society and spawned a number of crazes. In particular there was the *Merry Widow* hat, a ridiculously broad-brimmed affair, worn by the widow herself, which was adorned with feathers and chiffon and flowers and everything it seemed but the garden furniture. There were *Merry Widow* tea sets, *Merry Widow* jewellery, *Merry Widow* cigars and even, rumour had it, *Merry Widow* corsets. And of course *everyone* was dancing the Viennese Waltz.

So it was with a cold and sceptical heart that Violet sat and watched as the lights dimmed and the curtain rose on Madame Glawari, the eponymous widow who, left a fortune by her late husband, returns to the country of her birth, ostensibly to find a replacement. She meets up again with Count Danilo, an old flame, the man she was meant to marry until class, snobbery and an uncle got in the way. And now their romance is rekindled and then re-snuffed, as Danilo, having been once forbidden (by the aforementioned uncle) from marrying a woman because she had no money, now declares he cannot marry the same woman because she has too much of it. There is music, and singing, and the stage fills with beautiful women in flowing skirts dancing the Viennese Waltz. There is a sub-plot involving a fan and an affair between the Ambassador's wife and a Frenchman. And more dancing. At last, thanks to a verbal trick on the part of the widow, the lovers are reconciled and the company rejoices and waltzes into the sunset.

It was a show to penetrate the hardest of carapaces and despite her deep-rooted resistance, Violet was completely won over. It was both cleverer and wittier than she had expected. The settings were predictably sumptuous, the costumes glorious, the singing and the performances largely sublime. She might have taken issue with the tendency of almost everyone on stage to over-emphasise everything they said, and in particular with the Ambassador, who accompanied every *double-entendre* with a grimace; and the Ambassador's wife, who was relentlessly *arch*. Yet as the show wore on, so Violet warmed to the old buffoon and his cheeky wife and even found herself laughing out loud more than once. Young Lily Elsie as the widow, barely twenty-one years old, was a revelation. And when the thirty-piece orchestra struck up the famous *Merry Widow* waltz and the dancers began to swirl and twirl around the stage it was all Violet, along with Olivia and no doubt the rest of the audience, could do not to leap onto the stage and join them.

All told it was an unexpectedly moving experience for a practical, unsentimental person such as Violet. As the curtain finally fell after endless curtain calls, she was not the only member of the audience caught dabbing at her eyes. It was romance on a grand scale. It was theatre on a grand scale, with its power to transport the most cynical person away from their humdrum existence to a world of music and dancing and make-believe and lovely frocks. The story of love that blossoms and then fades and then blossoms again struck a very personal chord, and she wondered for a moment, had Robbie been there with her whether or not she would have . . .

Now she was just being sentimental.

As they turned to leave Violet caught sight of the familiar outline of Elizabeth Chester-Bolt. She waved, but not for the first time the lady appeared to look right through her.

Outside the theatre Violet deposited young Olivia into the safe hands of family friends with whom she was staying the night. She was contemplating which route to take home when she heard her name called from what appeared to be the inside of a brougham, the door of which stood open.

'Mrs Graham!' It was more of a command than a greeting. 'May I offer you a lift?'

Now that was unexpected. Violet approached the carriage cautiously.

'That is very kind of you, Miss Chester-Bolt, but I live in quite the opposite direction to you.'

'No matter, get in.'

She hesitated. She wanted to refuse but she couldn't immediately think of a reason to do so. And besides, it was late, and it was chilly, and there was a heavy demand for cabs. She climbed in.

'Where to?'

She gave Miss Chester-Bolt her address, which the lady relayed to the driver before turning to Violet and saying, 'What did you think of the show tonight? Extravagant, isn't it? I've seen it five times. It has caused quite a stir here, and in Vienna, and quite right too. For once extreme wealth is not regarded as evil. The notion of a woman who is the centre of attention solely because of her money is a novel one, and I like it very much. And the idea that a man refuses to marry a woman *because* she is wealthy is clever and ingenious, don't you agree? I can identify with that myself. You may wonder why I am not yet married, many people do, and it is for the very same reason, not because I have not received offers – because I assure you I have, plenty of them – but because I do not believe they are given honestly.'

She paused, and Violet realised she was expected to respond.

'It's a shame,' she said, 'you have so little trust.'

'Whereas you do not have any such excuse. You are lucky. The question is, why would a woman such as yourself remain unmarried? I understand you are estranged from your husband.'

'That is true, yes.'

'Not yet divorced. That is an awkward situation to be in, I grant you. Such is the way of things for us women, divorce is not easy to obtain without adultery. Which must be proven. It not only has to take place, it has to be seen to take place.'

It was not the direction Violet expected any conversation between herself and Miss Chester-Bolt to take, one-sided as it was. She was intrigued, and not a little apprehensive, as to where this particular one was going.

'I see there is a certain attraction between Mr Robinson and yourself, am I right?'

Again that was unexpected. She suspected a trap.

'We are good friends, yes, and working partners.'

'That is not the impression I get. I have known Robbie for some time and I recognise an attraction when I see one.'

Violet shifted uncomfortably. 'Then you know more than me,' she said.

'Come now,' said Miss Chester-Bolt, 'don't be coy, you know as well as I do.'

'We are working together to put a show on, there is nothing more to it than that.' Violet was trying her best not to sound defensive, or insulted, though she felt both.

'You must take me for a complete fool,' said Miss C-B. 'Or perhaps you think you might be offending me in some way. Perhaps you think I have my own designs on Robbie.'

There was no appropriate response to that.

'And you did not want to upset me because you need my money.' Miss Chester-Bolt sighed, a touch melodramatically. 'Because in the end it always comes down to money. And nobody can be completely honest with me so long as there is money involved.'

She had been looking out of the window while she spoke, her eyes on the road. Now she turned to face Violet directly. In the dim light of the carriage interior Violet was aware of a pair of eyes boring into her very soul.

'I see you are struggling to find an answer, and I understand why. You don't know whether to agree with me at the risk of offending me, or to continue to disagree with me at the risk of offending me. It is a cleft stick.'

'I think you've rather lost me, Miss Chester-Bolt.'

'Elizabeth, please.'

'What exactly do you want me to say?'

Miss Chester-Bolt turned her face away from Violet and Vi thought she saw a hint of tears in her eyes.

'I know I frighten people. I do not have the social skills of some, yourself included, I've no doubt. I have a habit of snubbing people, not because . . . ' She hesitated. 'Not intentionally.'

She stopped. Violet waited.

'I do not know who my true friends are. I do not know if I have any true friends. It has made me suspicious, of everyone. Of the most innocent of people, like yourself.'

She stopped speaking again, and it occurred to Violet, with some surprise, that the lady was perhaps attempting to apologise for her abrupt behaviour.

'So all I wish to say, when it comes to the play, and to

Robbie, you do what you like. Take no notice of me. It is your venture, I am just an old . . .' she sighed. 'I know nothing. I do have views, but they should not stand in the way of your play.'

'We will consult with you, obviously.'

The carriage was drawing up outside Violet's house.

'Is this where you live?' Elizabeth peered through the window at the tall house. 'Gracious me, where on earth are we?'

'Shoreditch,' said Violet.

'*Shoreditch?* What makes you want to live here?' she cried. 'Is it salubrious?'

'Far from it. But it's all I can afford. And it suits me. I don't need much.'

'You could lodge me with me if you'd like to.'

'Oh. That's extraordinarily kind of you, but I would not presume.'

'You would not be presuming. You could act as a buffer between my mama and myself.'

Violet laughed, and then checked herself. Miss Chester-Bolt was not making a joke.

They sat for a moment in silence. Elizabeth was staring straight ahead.

'Very well,' she said. And then leaning across Violet she opened the door and said, 'Goodnight.'

'Goodnight,' said Violet, as she clambered out of the carriage and stood watching as the vehicle, with its extraordinary occupant, sped away down the road.

## 16 What Lolly did next

It was one of the more bizarre offers that Violet had ever received, and a little bit of her, a *tiny* bit of her, was tempted. To see the world from the viewpoint of a four-storey house in Cheyne Walk overlooking the river? Imagine it.

Besides, she rather fancied the idea of being able to work on Miss Chester-Bolt. Of getting her to soften up a bit, to harness her aggressiveness and mistrust of the people she mixed with. Encourage her to make a joke or two. What an achievement that would be.

Not to mention her clothes. Wealth did not always go hand in hand with style, especially in Elizabeth's case. Her appearance would be greatly enhanced by, say, gentler tones of colour. Last night she had been adorned from head to foot in violent purple. The previous occasion she'd been encased in something resembling custard. All of it suggested a woman who enjoyed being looked at, but with admiration, not with what Violet had already perceived as badly-suppressed mirth.

Then there was the mother, grumbling away in the shadows. Violet would make an excellent 'buffer'. She had spent years keeping the peace between volatile people. It had been her virtual stock-in-trade.

The problem was, if one did agree to go to live with Miss Chester-Bolt how would one ever escape?

These were the thoughts that preoccupied Violet as she made her way to Battersea the following morning. She looked forward to sharing her experiences with Robbie. Not all of them, of course; she respected Miss Chester-Bolt's confidentiality. He did not need to know of the offer to go and live with her. He perhaps did not need to know how hard the lady found it to apologise for her behaviour, or even if her ramblings were intended as an apology in the first place. He did not need to know quite how unhappy and mistrustful his benefactor was.

Or perhaps he already knew. All the same, it made for an interesting story.

As she stood on his doorstep about to ring his bell it occurred to Violet that he was living almost within sight of Cheyne Walk. If you looked across the river you could just about make out the ivy-clad four-storey houses on the far side of the Thames. This made her chuckle, and she was still chuckling when Robbie opened his door.

'Good joke?' he enquired, as he stepped aside for Violet to enter.

'I was just thinking,' she said, as she entered and took off her hat, 'you are almost within eyesight of Cheyne Walk. Miss Chester-Bolt might just be spying on you from her top floor window.'

'She wouldn't find much to spy on.' He removed Violet's cape from her shoulders and ushered her into the front room.

'It so happens,' she said, 'I saw her last night. At Daly's. She gave me a lift home.'

'Did she indeed?'

'We had a very – odd talk. She told me quite a lot about herself.'

'She is inclined to do that.'

'But I barely know her. And on the only occasion I met her she ignored me completely.' Violet perched herself on

Robbie's chaise longue, pushing aside a blanket as she did so. 'As she appeared to do likewise at the theatre. She is a strange soul.'

'Not a particularly happy one, I don't think.' Robbie stood looking down at Violet, his hands in his pockets as usual. 'Can I get you anything? A glass of water? Tea? Turkish coffee?'

'Turkish coffee, what is that?'

'It is my latest fad. It's very strong. It wakes you up and keeps you going like nothing else on earth.'

'I've only just had breakfast, thank you Robbie. I don't need anything.'

'Right you are.' He tugged at his trouser legs and sat down opposite Violet. 'And what did you make of *The Merry Widow*? Did you know Elizabeth has seen it fifteen times?'

'Fifteen? She confessed to five.'

'Ah well, then maybe she did not truly confide in you. She is ashamed, you see. She would hate to think anyone regarded her as a romantic.' He looked at Violet over his spectacles. 'I imagine you hated it, for the same reason.'

'As a matter of fact, I did not hate it at all.'

Robbie raised an eyebrow.

'I was all set to hate it, you're right, but it was difficult not to be swept along.' Violet squirmed slightly in what looked like embarrassment. 'So there you are.' She glanced at Robbie out of the corner of her eye. 'Why are you looking at me like that?' she demanded.

'No reason in particular,' said Robbie. 'You are a strange and unpredictable mixture, that's all I . . .'

'Good morning!' came a familiar voice.

Lolly was standing in the doorway wearing nothing but a towel draped vaguely around her skinny body. She strolled across to Violet, leaned over the back of the chaise longue and gave her a peck on the cheek, and when she straightened up not all of the towel went with her.

'Oops!' She made a clumsy attempt to cover herself. 'Lovely to see you, Vi.'

'You too, Lolly,' said Violet. 'What are you doing here?'

It was pretty obvious to Violet what Lolly was, or had been, doing there.

'She spent the night,' said Robbie.

'Ah.'

'On the chaise longue.'

'Oh.'

She wasn't sure but she thought she saw Lolly throw Robbie a cross look.

'Is it all right if I dress in your room, Robbie?'

'Of course. You know where it is.'

'See you shortly, Vi.'

'Yes, Lolly.'

There was a silence.

'So, where were we?' he asked.

If Lolly had really spent the night on the chaise longue, why were her clothes not there? Presumably they were in Robbie's bedroom, in which case, how did they get there?

'Vi?'

'Sorry?'

She always had wondered about Lolly. Lolly usually only went for married men, but even she made exceptions. Presumably. In this case anyway.

'Are you all right?'

It did seem a bit of a betrayal. She couldn't honestly see why; she had no hold over Robbie, they were not even engaged.

'Just a bit taken aback, that's all,' said Violet.

'Don't mind Lolly. You know what she's like.'

'I'm not sure I do,' said Violet.

Or of course it could all be a set-up – she wouldn't put it past him. Past the both of them. She sat for the moment gazing vacantly out of the window. She felt surprisingly cross.

'She also introduced me to a new backer, a suffragist by the name of Mrs Santenoy. To replace the unlamented Henry Poll-Perkins.'

'Oh, excellent.'

'So you see Lolly does have her uses.'

Sometimes he infuriated Violet more than she cared to admit. It was the lopsided smile, the knowing manner, the ridiculously casual way he sat there with one leg hooked over the other, showing his socks.

'I have been . . .' Violet began.

'Don't mind me,' said Lolly. She had padded back into the room, fully dressed and barefoot. She slid onto an armchair and sat sideways, her legs draped over one arm of the chair.

'I have been in touch with a couple of casting agents,' said Violet.

'I've also let it be known,' said Lolly, 'here and there. You will probably be receiving a few letters, if you haven't already. I could make suggestions.'

She looked back and forth to Robbie and Violet, enquiringly.

'That won't be necessary Lolly, thank you,' said Violet.

'That's very kind Lolly, thank you,' said Robbie, more or less at the same time.

'All right, I won't say a word.' Lolly placed a finger on her lips.

It was absolutely impossible. Violet stood up suddenly.

'Are you going somewhere?' Robbie uncrossed his legs and sat up.

'Yes, I think I've suddenly remembered an appointment,' said Violet.

'Oh, not on my account!' Lolly sprang to her feet and scrabbled under a chair for her shoes. 'I'm going. Right now. Before you can say "good riddance, Lolly"!'

She made for the door. 'Off I go!' she said merrily, and gave a little skip. 'Goodbye Vi, see you again soon.'

'Goodbye Lolly.'

There was a hiatus as Robbie saw Lolly to the door. Violet sat down again. She was trying not to eavesdrop on their whispered conversation. She heard the front door go.

To her surprise and horror she found she wanted to cry.

Robbie reappeared. He stood in the doorway and looked across the room at her. 'Are you all right, Vi?' he asked gently.

'What was all that about?' she sniffed, and fumbled in her bag for a handkerchief.

'That was Lolly being mischievous. As only Lolly can.'

He went to her and reached out a hand, and after a moment Violet took it and allowed him to pull her to her feet and to draw her close.

He placed his arms around her and they stood there together for a moment, quite still, in the middle of the room. Then Robbie began to hum, and to move his feet in a waltz movement, slowly to begin with, and as Violet began to move with him so he quickened the pace, and she found herself taking hold of her skirt just as she'd seen them do on stage the night before; and with Robbie's firm hand on her back weaving them deftly through the furniture they twirled and swirled about the room to the waltz from *The Merry Widow*.

# 17 What now?

Gaye was not particularly afraid of her father. She had managed to sneak far more serious lies past him over the years. There was the abortion, when she was almost too young to know what such a thing was, and she took to her bed in agony for two days claiming she'd eaten a bad oyster. The worst part of that was trying to stop him calling the doctor. There was the dog she brought home one day claiming she'd found him abandoned in the local park. She did feel bad about that. Dog stealing was pretty poor behaviour by anyone's standards, even though he had followed her for so far she had almost managed to convince herself he'd wanted to be stolen.

Being sacked from a job was nothing by comparison. Just another hiccup in the life of a young actress. It happened all the time. Late for rehearsals. Drunk during rehearsals. Stealing costumes. She'd never been guilty of any of that. Playing up on stage was part and parcel of being a chorus girl. So when she swung the wheel around and told him it was she who giggled on stage, who was made to giggle on stage by Lily Elsie herself, and that it was only because Lily was the star and she, Gaye, the chorus girl that it was Gaye who was sacked and not Lily, while her father was not fooled for a moment – she was too much of an old hand to fall victim to a bit of on-stage horseplay – he believed it enough to let her get away with a clip around the ear and a few insults, and that was about it.

'So now what?' he demanded. He was standing in the kitchen, his fingers playing on the back of a chair. Her father had been an ace on the squeezebox when such a thing was fashionable, and he continued playing it even when he no longer owned one.

'What do you mean?'

'How are you going to pay the rent?' His feet were twitching too. He was, Gigi realised now if not before, an inveterate twitcher.

'I'll think of something.'

'You'd better,' said her father. 'Or you'll be back in the halls before you know what's what.'

It was a strange kind of a threat, but an effective one. Once she'd done her stint in music hall and left it the last thing an aspiring performer wanted to do was take a step backwards. Up to four shows a day, rowdy drunken audiences, freezing dressing rooms, men who thought it perfectly acceptable to invite themselves backstage to watch the ladies dressing, and undressing. Seasoned performers found a way to cope with it, but Gigi had had enough of it.

'I'm working on a double-act as it happens,' she said.

'Oh yeah? You and who else?'

She described Merry, briefly – her tall, elegant and shriekingly funny (exaggerations essential) friend, who could do anything and everything.

'And what are you using for material?'

'We're writing it ourselves.'

Her father's fingers paused in their drumming for a moment and then resumed.

'Since when have you ever written anything?'

'There's always a first time.'

'Huh.' Her father continued to stare at her.

'Thanks for your encouragement,' said Gigi.

~

Try as she might there were very few times when Merry managed to arrive home without alerting her landlady, Mrs Vlatsky. However quiet she was, at the final click of the front door the woman was there, in the hallway, her topknot bobbing, smiling, anxious.

'Mairie, my dear, how are you, how was your day?'

She spoke with a heavy East European accent, possibly Polish. She fluttered, and fussed, and she invariably asked after Mme Pou – she could never quite remember her name – but she knew the shop. She knew *of* the shop, of course she'd never been inside, it was not – how does one say it? – within her reach.

Merry sensed Mrs Vlatsky – 'Call me Pani, my dear' – was not quite what she seemed. No doubt the accent was genuine, it seemed consistent enough, but she suspected the lady's background was invented. As was her ability to read cards and see into the future. Moreover there was no sign of a Mr or a Herr or a Pan Vlatsky, and every time Merry tried to mention the subject Mrs V became exceedingly coy. But when a person is your landlady and is, on the whole, friendly enough; and you are regularly behind on the rent, and she doesn't badger you about it, well, what business is it of yours?

Mrs Vlatsky, Pani, claimed she had once been a clairvoyant. She had read crystals, or whatever you do with crystals, and she had toured the Continent with a travelling circus. *"See your future with Madame Vlatsky!"* That was until a distant relative unexpectedly left her enough money to buy a house in Lambeth, since when she had let rooms out to a series of 'waifs and strays'. Before she began working in the hat shop Merry had been out of work for some time and struggling to pay the rent. And now that she was earning, albeit a pittance, there was still no way she felt able to catch up. 'One day, Mrs Pani, I promise,' she would say, repeatedly, at which Mrs V would wag a finger, and her head, topknot included, and insist, 'No no no. We shall consult the cards.' And she'd grab hold of Merry by the arm, pull her into her sitting room and sit her down, fetch her a cup of tea and 'Read her future'.

She was a small woman, permanently in a hurry and hunched over, as if she had no time to straighten up. She had long, thick black hair which she twisted carelessly into a rough knot on the top of her head. The topknot itself had a life of its own, always one step behind its owner. When Mrs V hurried to greet someone at the front door the topknot hurried with her and continued quivering long after the rest of her had ground to a halt. Sometimes as the evening wore on the topknot grew weary, and began to droop sideways, and eventually to start to unravel. This was generally a hint that it was time for Mrs Vlatsky to pack up her cards and go to bed.

Merry was puzzled by the cards. They were ordinary playing cards, and Mrs V would lay them out with great care, muttering all the while: 'Good . . . Yes . . . Oh! . . . Well . . . There!' Merry could not make head nor tail of her method, if indeed she had one. She could not identify bad news cards from good news cards. But whenever there was a decision to be made – such as when Merry would eventually hit 'the big time' and be able to pay Pani her back rent – out they would come. She laughed at them to begin with. But it was not a laughing matter to Mrs Vlatsky. Cards were serious business. Without the cards she could not get up in the morning. Merry was tempted to ask her if she set out her cards on her eiderdown before she got up, but that was no doubt a frivolous remark too far. So she got used to it, and she didn't laugh any more.

On this occasion she told Pani she was thinking of

teaming up with a fellow actress to create a double act, and what did she think?

'A dooble act?' the lady exclaimed. Her topknot wobbled.

'We were thinking of touring the night spots. Or maybe even . . .' she hesitated, 'performing on the street.'

'We shall see what do the cards say,' said Mrs V. She frowned with concentration as she went through the motion of laying them out, muttering, smiling occasionally and then frowning again.

'Well?' Merry asked.

Mrs Vlatsky stared at the cards for a long moment. 'They seem to be saying, I can't make it out exactly, two things.'

'Which are?'

'On the one hand this is promising.' She pointed at a five of hearts. 'There are good things. On the other,' she indicated a two of spades, 'this is not so good. I think it is saying, be careful.'

'Be careful of what?'

'That I cannot tell you.' Mrs Vlatsky bent over the cards, as if seeking further enlightenment. 'I cannot make it out.'

'Oh.' It was all very well laughing at the cards, but when it came to it it was difficult not to be disconcerted. 'So are they telling me yes, or no?' Merry wanted to know.

'They are saying yes. Oh yes. But . . .'

Pani leaned back. Her topknot was beginning to lurch sideways and she instinctively pushed it upright again. She looked at Merry with a concerned expression. 'They are telling me different things. They are saying, on the one hand, this will be a mistake. But on the other . . .' she peered at the cards again and fingered one or two of them thoughtfully. 'In the end,' she said, 'you will triumph. This is what the cards are telling me. In a new way.

Unexpected.'

'What do you mean, unexpected?' Merry asked.

'Let us say, I have not seen this before.' She gestured at the cards. 'This way. I think it means,' her hand went to her chin to stroke an imaginary beard. 'Good things! In the end. At last,' she added for good measure.

With which Mrs Vlatsky leaned back in her chair and beamed at her companion, and her companion gave her a watery smile in return.

# 18 It's not as easy as you think

The greatest innovations often stem from the oddest beginnings.

What stimulates a person to be truly creative? To be truly creative is to make something out of nothing: to splash paint onto a blank canvas, produce notes from a piano without music, fill a blank sheet of paper with words. And not just any words, or notes, or splashes of paint.

To perform is not to create. A performer is an interpreter, not a creator. He, or in this case she, has to have material to perform. Material that by and large has been written by someone else: Shakespeare, or Wilde, or Sheridan, or even, in the case of music hall, Arthur Lloyd. Even the humblest music hall performer has to have something written by someone to perform in a venue owned by somebody to an audience someone else has managed to persuade to buy tickets yet someone else has printed.

Yes, of course, a comedian can write his own material. Or better still, steal it. Most material is either stolen or 'plagiarised' – is there a difference? – or at best, adapted from something created elsewhere. Not every performer needs a theatre or a music hall to perform in. Gaye's own father had, in lean times, performed in the back rooms of pubs. As a small child she'd passed the hat around for him on these occasions. He had even written the odd joke himself, 'adapted' of course from elsewhere, and in time he'd learned to ad lib. But the very notion of creating an act, single, double, or multiple, from scratch, using material that did not exist, to be performed who knows where, was to a man like Gaye's father not unlike flying to the moon.

The spur for this particular double act on the part of Merry and Gaye was a mix of desperation and boredom, and that is a heady mix. If you are fed up with corrupt managers, or managers in general, or being told what to do, or worse, not being allowed to do what you know you can do, as was the case with Gigi Worth, then there is only one thing for you: create your own future using whatever resources you can summon.

If on the other hand, like Merry you are sick to death of being treated like a nobody by women with too much money in a world that is at best superficial and at worst exploitative and, yes, even corrupt (those hats were made by women whose yearly wages would barely cover the cost of the trimmings), then there is only one thing you can do: create your own future using whatever resources you can summon.

Thus it was that Meredith and Gaye were sitting in Merry's room on the second floor of the house in Lambeth one weekday evening. Gaye was lounging on the bed, Merry was stretched out on her tiny sofa, her head protruding from one end, her legs the other. There was silence, as each of them delved into their innermost beings in search of a nugget of gold in the shape of an Idea.

The usually talkative couple were compelled into silence by their mutual promise that neither of them would say a word that did not constitute the beginnings of an Idea. They would not gossip. They would not get distracted. It was very, very hard. They were both straining. Somewhere in the room with them was the kernel of a thought that could set the wheels of a fledgling theme in motion. And once in motion the train of brilliance would set off down the track of innovation to arrive, eventually, at the destination of success that would place Merry and Gaye firmly on the theatrical map.

There may have been similar thoughts buzzing through each of their brains: We need a jumping-off point, something to get us started. A topic, however irrelevant, that we can toss from one to the other, and as we do so so the topic itself will develop, and mutate, until it in no way resembles the topic we started out with. Or, another thought may be running: We need someone else to get us started. Someone who is used to this sort of thing. A writer, in other words.

The women who hated the whole idea of having to kowtow to a manager or a shop owner were now desperately looking for someone to tell them what to do.

The silence went on for some time. Merry shifted her body so her head was now resting on the arm of the sofa and her legs were dangling off the end of it. Gaye, fighting sleep, sat up in the bed, gave the pillow a good pummel and lay back down again.

Time passed.

'You're not falling asleep, are you?' said Merry eventually, breaking the rule.

'Fat chance. Your bed is far too uncomfortable. There's something moving inside your mattress,' said Gigi. 'Honest to God.'

'What are you saying, that I have bed bugs?'

'More like bed rats.'

Merry sat up straight. 'That's disgusting.'

'Sure is. I don't know how you put up with it.'

'Nobody's forcing you to lie there. I have to lie there every night.'

'More fool you, having to sleep with rats.'

'There are no rats!'

'Then what's the problem?'

'There isn't one. You're the one with the problem.'

'Who, me? I don't have to sleep here every night, thank God.'

'Lucky you.'

'So you *do* have rats.'

'I never said anything about rats. You're the one with the fixation on rats!'

There was a pause, and the two women did a strange thing: they burst out laughing.

It wasn't much perhaps. But it was, or could be, the nugget of something that might just develop into the beginnings of what could be termed an Idea.

~

So that is how it was. It can happen to any of us. The moment the brain stops straining and the mind allows itself to roam and to drift in any direction it chooses, or better still no direction at all, miracles can occur.

It was not a miracle exactly, but it was enough to wake the two ladies up and spur them into action.

Insults. They would base their act on mutual insults. As in life, so in art. The characters would develop from that. The aim of each sketch, the punchline, would be the ultimate put-down, the last word, the final, all-conquering comeuppance.

It was the early hours of the morning before Merry told Gaye it was time she went home.

'Do you have the money for a cab?' she asked.

'What do you take me for, someone with savings? I never saved anything in my life. I never had to.'

'So what do you intend to do?'

'Stay here.' Gaye began to climb into Merry's bed.

'You're going to sleep in my bed,' said Merry.

'Where else?'

'With the rats.'

'Hah! So you admit there are rats.' Gaye drew the sheets up to her chin and snuggled into the pillows.

'It's my bed,' said Merry.

Gaye yawned widely and loudly.

'Did you hear me? You spent the evening insulting my bed, and now you're sleeping in it.'

'I'm not sleeping. You're not letting me.'

'And where am I supposed to sleep?'

'It's your room. You decide.' Gaye closed her eyes and began to snore.

'You are impossible. I've got half a mind,' Merry staggered to her feet, 'to throw you out, of my bed and my room!' She strode over to the bed and stood towering over it, and so its occupant shrank further into the sheets until she fancied she was invisible.

'Did you hear me?' Merry demanded.

'I heard you,' came the muffled voice of Gaye. 'But I ain't working no more.'

'This isn't work, this is real life!'

'What's the difference?'

'*Quid dicis tu cursus ego maior quam vobis*!' exclaimed Meredith. She did not have the benefit of an expensive education for nothing.

'What?' Gaye's head emerged from the bedclothes.

'I said, "Watch what you say, I am bigger than you".'

'Was that Latin? That was really comical!' Gaye propped herself on one elbow. 'We could use that, in the act.'

'I thought you said you weren't working any more.'

'No, really. You could be, what, you could be a teacher, a school teacher. And I'm a kid. I can play kids, easy. And . . .'

'And?' Meredith sat down on the bed next to Gaye.

Mrs Vlatsky's words were nibbling away at something in the deep recesses of her brain: "You will triumph!" 'Go on,' she said.

In the end, even the wildest imagination could not come up with an idea that doesn't have its roots in what is fancifully called real life.

# 19 Talking to the sky

A young gentleman, taking a short cut along St Martin's Street towards Trafalgar Square one morning, was curious to see two people – one female, one purportedly male – performing what appeared to be a sketch in an obscure corner close to the steps of the National Gallery. They had no audience. Indeed, so detached were they from the throng filling the piazza it was only by sheer chance that the eye, and ear, of the young man were caught sufficiently for him to pause for a moment and watch.

It was difficult to hear much of what was being said amid the hubbub of traffic and other ambient interruptions. But as far he could gather the turn consisted of a teacher, played by the tall woman, and her pupil, played by the smaller woman dressed as a boy. They appeared to be exchanging insults, and the boy being somewhat brighter than the teacher seemed to be gaining the upper hand until the teacher began to resort to Latin. At this point the boy pouted, made loud fart noises and tried to drown the other's voice by singing loud and obscene songs very out of tune.

The young man smiled, winked at the ladies and dropped a coin into their hat before continuing on his way.

'Well,' said Merry. 'It has to get better than this.' She

sank down onto the steps.

'Of course it'll get better,' said Gaye, as she joined her.

The out-of-the-way corner of the square was a choice made out of necessity. The two ladies had arrived earlier in the morning to find all the prime spots in the busy piazza taken up by jugglers, gipsy bands, contortionists, fire eaters, performing dogs and child acrobats, all of whom were surrounded by onlookers, cheering and laughing and applauding and, so one might suppose, filling the hats that were passed around. When Merry and Gaye tried to set themselves up at the foot of Nelson's Column they were hustled on by a burly gentleman in clown make-up who informed them, rather rudely, thought Merry, that they were 'in his spot'. The idea that there were such things as 'spots' came as news to both of them. So they moved around the square to the northern end opposite the National Gallery, where the same thing happened. This time it was a child ballerina, with legs like twigs and eyes like rapiers and who despite her size and her fragility was infinitely more frightening than the burly gentleman.

So this was how they ended up in what could have been described as the quietest corner of the square, where there were very few passers-by, only one or two of whom even glanced in their direction, and nobody other than the young gentleman actually thought to stop and listen to what they were saying.

'Just as well,' said Merry.

'What do you mean?' said Gaye.

'We're no good, are we?'

'It's a start,' said Gaye.

'And nobody can hear us. Even when we yell. We need to do something more . . .'

'Physical?'

'Loud. We need an instrument. A drum, or something.'

The legitimacy or otherwise of what they, and indeed all the other street performers, were doing was not something either of them had looked into very closely. They had both seen performers outside theatres and other places of entertainment being moved on by the police. Suffice to say, the less you know the less you worry.

The world of street entertainers, they were in the process of learning, was one only properly understood by the entertainers themselves. Gaye had once referred to them as 'royalty', and while this was not the most obvious word one might think of to describe the raggle-taggle bunch of chancers, like royalty theirs was a closed world, with its own hierarchy and its own rules, none of which were immediately clear to an outsider. They were members of a club, it seemed, and they did not welcome new members.

'I told you it was a bad idea,' said Merry.

'You got a better one?'

Merry shrugged.

'You could play the penny whistle,' Gigi suggested.

'The *penny whistle*? Who's going to hear that? Besides, I don't know how to play a penny whistle.'

'We could black up.'

'Don't be vulgar.'

'Or, how about this? We could park ourselves outside a posh house in Park Lane say, till they pay us to shove off. Or a hospital.'

'Why a hospital?' asked Merry.

''Cos it has sick people in it.'

'Now you're truly scraping the barrel.'

Gigi started picking at a thread in her skirt.

'*Nil desperandum*,' said Merry. She got to her feet.

'What?'

'Never give up. We're here now, we might as well carry on for a while.'

Nobody ever cracked it first time. As the day wore on so the two ladies grew in confidence, and volume. It takes guts, after all, to stand on a street corner and talk to the sky, as that it how it feels when one has no audience. By mid afternoon they were beginning to attract the attention of the odd pedestrian and his dog. And her child. It was the children who did it. Tugging at the hands of their minders they stood there gawping, and when they saw that one of these funny ladies was playing a naughty schoolboy they began to shriek with laughter. When the schoolboy started making fart noises they were in paroxysms. The words of the rude song went right over the heads of the little ones but shocked their minders, so Gigi substituted the worst of them with more fart noises, and soon the grown-ups were laughing as loudly as the toddlers. There were never more than a dozen of them in the audience at any one time, and Merry and Gaye had yet to learn the technique of passing the hat around before the onlookers dispersed. Because it is surprising how quickly a bunch of people can dissolve into thin air at the first sight of such a thing.

It was a long day, and an exhausting one. And their takings barely covered the bottom of the hat.

'It's a start,' said Gaye, again.

'You mean we're going to carry on?' said Merry.

'Now we know what works.'

Merry stared glumly into the hat. 'Sixpence, at most.'

'We need to pass the hat around sooner.'

'How do we do that?'

'In character.'

'Which character?'

'I'm the one they were laughing at most.'

'Just because you made fart noises.'

'Who cares, they were laughing.'

'They laughed at my Latin. Some of them.'

'Told you so. What was it you were saying?'

'"*Et fac quod dicis perfide et dabo vos umquam habuit in vita maximus longe.*"

'Which means?'

'Do as I say you horrible little worm or I'll give you the biggest spanking you ever had in your life.'

'Sounds better in Latin,' said Gaye.

'Most things do,' said Merry.

'Did you see them little ones, doubled over. I swear I thought some of 'em were going to be sick with laughing.'

'It's easy to make a child laugh.'

'Don't matter. It's . . .'

' . . . a start, I know. All the same, is that all we're here for, to make children laugh?'

'We'll get the hang of it. We'll get better.'

'It couldn't get a lot worse. I blame Mrs Vlatsky,' said Merry.

'Mrs Vlatsky? What's she got to do with it?'

Merry did not respond.

It had not, as days go, been much to write home about. Later perhaps, once the disappointment of their earlier failure and the day's takings had subsided, they could congratulate themselves on their courage and their enterprise. And their persistence. For as everyone knows, nothing worthwhile can be achieved without persistence.

'Do you really want to keep doing this?' asked Merry wearily.

'Dunno,' said Gaye. 'Do you?'

# 20 A question of divorce

One morning Violet received an unexpected visitor.

She had not seen her old friend Veronica Ann since Violet had separated from her husband, which was getting on for ten years ago. It was Veronica and her hubby who'd introduced Vi to the man she went on to marry in a rush of eagerness to escape the stifling tedium of her family home. The two girls had been school friends and were happily known as 'the two Vees' or, as Violet's husband-to-be remarked on the first occasion they'd met, 'The W.' (How Violet had laughed at that.)

However when Violet left the marital home, friends, as they tend to do, took sides, and Vee and her husband Cecil unsurprisingly dumped her in favour of the man she had 'deserted'. On the face of it Violet was very much the villain of the piece: she'd married a handsome, well-to-do gentleman with a steady position in the civil service, and enjoyed his large Bloomsbury house with servants and everything a young woman could possibly wish for for five whole years without producing any children. And then one day she'd upped and left just like that.

That was the story put about by Vi's husband Anthony. But it was only part of the picture of course. Violet had walked out of the marriage mostly because she had made the mistake of walking into it in the first place. Or rather rushing, too quickly and out of desperation, without doing the usual things a young woman should do, such as consider carefully whether her escape route from the family home wasn't leading her from one prison to another. She had married a man she knew very little about. She married Anthony because he made her laugh, but it became clear very quickly that they were far from compatible. He disapproved of Violet's association with the suffragists and he could not understand why she had failed to provide him with children – which was obviously her fault. He did not see why she should feel the need for anything that he, his house and all its trappings could not provide. He could not recognise her longing for something, anything, in the form of mental stimulation.

So here were the two women in their thirties, standing on the threshold of Violet's room in a rundown house in Shoreditch, staring at one another with a mixture of surprise, horror and embarrassment. How on earth, Violet was thinking, had Anthony managed to track her down yet again, after all this time?

'Vee,' she said, uncertainly.

'Vi,' said Vee, tentatively. Then, 'May I come in?'

'Of course.'

They exchanged the usual conventional commonplaces of two people who have not seen one another for some time, while managing to avoid any mention of the rift that had pushed them apart in the first place. It was some time before Violet finally broke the atmosphere abruptly to enquire of her estranged friend the purpose of her visit.

'Oh,' said Vee, almost with surprise. 'Do you mind if I sit down?'

Violet indicated a chair, upon which the other woman sat, awkwardly and heavily. Violet noticed, with some satisfaction, that her friend had become even plumper and clumsier in the years since she'd seen her. She detected signs of the aching joints that excess weight brings with it.

Moreover Vee was looking years older than the thirty-something she was, perhaps due in part to the however-many children she had produced and about whom she could, given half a chance, talk *ad infinitum*.

'So,' said Violet. 'What's this about?'

'I've been wondering about you,' said Vee. 'How you've been getting along.'

Violet glared at Vee with as much hostility as her naturally unhostile nature could muster. 'You took your time.'

She was not going to make it easy. Vee reminded Violet too much of her estranged husband and the life that had gone with it. The woman she thought had been her friend, possibly her only friend, had not just betrayed her but done so without explanation.

'You have to understand . . .'

What an expression that is, thought Violet. Does it not always preface an excuse for something unpardonable? No. I do not have to understand anything.

'I'm sorry, I wasn't listening to what you were saying,' she said baldly.

'You have to understand how it was, back then. Cecil and Anthony are cousins after all. We had no choice.'

'If you say so.'

'It hurt me of course, I can't tell you how much.'

'I am sorry to hear it.'

'There is no need to be sarcastic,' said Vee.

Violet would have liked to have said it was water under the bridge, but she didn't want to give the woman the satisfaction.

'Please get to the point,' she said instead. 'Although I can imagine what it is.'

'Yes. Anthony wants a divorce.'

Violet nodded.

'He wants to get married again, but you know, the

divorce laws . . .'

Violet knew the divorce laws as well as she knew her own name, but she was curious to hear Veronica Ann's definition of them.

'It has to be adultery, either way.'

Violet waited.

'He does not want any unpleasantness, he holds no grudges against you. In fact,' Vee laughed briefly, 'he says he has you to thank for not staying with him. It seems he's met someone far more suitable.' She looked momentarily alarmed. 'His words, not mine.'

'I'm delighted for him. He is welcome to his divorce.'

'But that's the problem, you see. It isn't quite as straightforward as that.'

'One of us has to prove the other's adultery.'

Vee nodded uncomfortably. 'Might I ask if there is anyone else?'

'Is it you asking or is it Anthony?'

Vee gave a strange, straight-lipped smile. 'It's me,' she said. 'On behalf of Anthony.'

'If you've been in touch with Anthony you will know the answer to that.'

'Ah.' Vee's brow wrinkled. This was not in her script.

'So what is your suggestion? Yours and Anthony's? I presume you have one.'

'Well, the general rule is,' Vee cleared her throat, 'if both parties are in agreement, even if, er, adultery is not taking place, it can be arranged.'

Violet suddenly wanted to laugh. How ridiculous this all is, she thought. Here I am, taking out all my anger on my innocent and well-meaning friend, the woman I almost grew up with, who I have fond memories of living in a large and chaotic house where she was always tripping over something, first the furniture and later her children, who seemed to be everywhere. Who has been given the unwelcome task of trying to organise a divorce between her erstwhile best friend and her husband's cousin. Who did what any woman would have done ten years ago and followed her husband's lead and cut her friend out of her life altogether.

So Violet did something unexpected: she smiled, genuinely.

'Very well,' she said, and she sat back in her chair. 'Tell me your plan.'

Vee took a deep breath. 'Anthony wants to marry again, and between you and me he's been living with her anyway for some time, but the point is, now he wants children.' She paused for a moment to collect herself. 'So, you could get a legal separation but that would not allow either of you to remarry. And he could continue to live as he is, with . . . but then the children would be born out of wedlock.' She looked up to see Violet almost laughing. 'So,' she pushed a wandering strand of hair away from her eyes, 'it has to be divorce. And you could divorce him for adultery, if you wish, but he doesn't want that. He believes he is the innocent party, you see.'

If there was ever such a ludicrous law, created by men, it was the law that decreed that in a divorce there had to be an innocent party and a guilty one.

'So where does that leave us?' Violet folded her hands on her lap.

'Well,' Vee coughed into her hand, 'if you were to commit adultery it would mean the naming of the third party, and all court costs to be paid by the third party.'

'The co-respondent.'

'Correct. However,' Vee held up a hand to forestall the objection that was not forthcoming, 'Anthony has agreed to pay all costs. If you are in agreement.'

'And if I'm not?' I am not a nice person, thought Violet.

Vee looked slightly stumped for a moment. 'I think he

is expecting, he is hoping that after everything, after you . . just left him, it is the least you can do.'

Vee had not looked Violet in the eye throughout the conversation, but she did so now, and she was surprised to see the smile on her old friend's face.

'What if the third party does not want to commit adultery?'

'Then – we thought of that – we would have to fake it. You would have to fake it. There are ways and means.'

She was puzzled now, poor woman, by Violet's smile, which she took, understandably, to be sarcastic.

'Oh Vee,' said Violet. 'Dearest Vee, how did we get to be here?'

Vee frowned.

'Years ago, all those years ago, we'd have laughed at this. After all, it is laughable, isn't it?

Vee smiled cautiously.

'There are a lot of things that are laughable, if you're not caught up in them.' Violet chuckled briefly.

She sat gazing at the wall for a long moment, while her companion, perched as she was on the edge of her chair, tried not to look at her. Finally she said, 'I am happy to do whatever you want me to do. If the third party is happy to be named, then so be it.'

'And you will need a witness,' Vee added anxiously.

'That,' said Violet, 'might be difficult. But I will do my best, how's that?'

'Thank you Vi,' said Vee.

Violet stood up suddenly and held out her arms.

'And now, please stand up so I can give you a hug.'

Vee hesitated. She was clutching onto the arms of her chair. She got to her feet, slowly, and allowed her friend to embrace her. And once she was assured it was not all part of some wicked game, she returned the embrace with relief and gusto.

## 21 How to leave a marriage

The law is an ass, Violet muttered to herself.

She understood the so-called sanctity of marriage and the importance of marriage vows. She had once taken both of them very seriously. In truth she had thought a lot longer and harder about leaving her husband than she had about marrying him. What she had not done was given any thought to the aftermath of her so-called desertion. She had been too busy finding somewhere to live and a way to support herself. She had walked out of the marriage with nothing, she had asked for nothing and been offered nothing, and that was only fair. It was no less than she felt she deserved. And so she had drawn what she hoped was a line under the whole sorry business.

But that is not how the law of the country viewed things. A person could not just walk out of a marriage and pretend it had never happened. What if, after some years a couple proved to be mutually incompatible and wished to annul the arrangement? That was when lawyers had to become involved, at great expense, and there had to be a guilty party and an innocent party even when there was neither, and there had to be a third party even when such a person did not exist. In the end, in order presumably to uphold public morality, a couple who simply no longer wished to live together had to cheat and lie their way to some kind of separation, at great expense and distress to themselves and to everyone around them.

That is how it looked to Violet.

A year or so ago Anthony had hired a private detective to hunt Violet down at her old lodgings in Crighton Street near Camden Town. It had terrified her at the time, so much so that she left London almost overnight to take up a position as a housekeeper in the country. And she had changed her name, yet again.

She had changed her name before, after she left Anthony. It had been a way of putting her mistakes, as she saw them, behind her and giving herself a new start. Besides, a surname like Turnip was not one a woman might want to hang onto. By the time she was thirty Violet had acquired four surnames: the name she was born with, the name she married into, the name she assumed when she left her husband and went to work in the theatre, and the name she took on when she left London to become a housekeeper. Each name signified a new life and a new start. Perhaps unconsciously, she thought, she was trying them all out for size, the names and the identities, until she found one that fitted.

For now she had reverted to Mrs Graham, as that was the name by which she was known by Robbie and Lolly and all the friends she'd made during her working life in the theatre. When she had left her position as housekeeper in order to produce Robbie's play Violet had as it were returned to an older name and an older life, albeit in a different guise and with different expectations.

Yet one way or another Anthony always managed to track her down. This time it was through her parents, so Vee told her.

Violet was both angry and amused. Angry to think that whatever a woman does when she's barely nineteen years old can come back to haunt her older self. That what might be deemed a minor misdemeanour, the sort of stupid behaviour all young things get up to before they are old enough to know better, can be held against them long after it took place, like a criminal record. It had been an experiment, and it hadn't worked. And if a young woman isn't allowed to experiment, how is she to know how to live her life?

However, according to the law incompatibility was not a good enough reason for a man and a woman to want to separate. There had to be adultery involved, and a third party implicated. This, for Violet, was the sticking point.

Before Vee had departed, the pair of them once again the best of friends, Violet had managed to reassure her she would 'fix everything'. If divorcing Anthony was the only way to get rid of him for good and all, so be it, she had no objection. Even if she had no idea how to go about arranging it.

She imagined the conversation: 'Dear Robbie, my husband wants to divorce me. So please will you sleep with me tonight, in full view of a private detective?'

What sort of a law was that?

~

Shoreditch, while home to Shakespeare and to the very first playhouses that appeared in the city in the sixteenth century, was in the early part of the twentieth better known for lower forms of entertainment. At one point it boasted more music halls and 'penny gaffs' – rooms often attached to public houses, where for one penny a person could drink the night away and enjoy all manner of entertainment from a motley group of singers, dancers and acrobats – than anywhere else in London. It was colourful, it was rowdy, it was rough, it was cheerful, and Violet loved it. Unlike in the sunny uplands of Bloomsbury, or even to some extent Camden Town, it was a place where a stranger would talk to you in the street – while as often as not picking your pocket. Nobody questioned who you were and where you came from. In so many ways it suited Violet perfectly.

The penny gaffs had more or less gone now but the musical entertainments continued to proliferate. It was not the West End, geographically or culturally, although it liked to think it could outdo that ritzier part of London in spectacle and popularity. Shakespeare still lurked on the edges of his old neighbourhood now and again, as did opera.

Violet had never set foot inside a music hall, much as she wanted to. It was not the sort of place a single woman frequented unless she was looking for trade. Besides, there had never been the time. If she was not working on Robbie's play she was tutoring. She had rent to pay, after all.

Violet had had no visitors in her new place other than Vee. There had been no one to invite, and when it came to business, since Robbie's apartment in Battersea was the nearest thing they had to a production office it became their natural meeting place. What he might make of her simple set of rooms was anyone's guess. Notwithstanding, Violet took out her pen and wrote him a letter.

*'Dear Robbie. I would like to invite you to call on me tomorrow, if possible, at a time to suit you. I have something to discuss with you. It has nothing to do with the play, and I'd feel happier if I were on my own home ground.'*

Then she tore the letter up. It sounded far too formal and calculated. She'd bring it up in conversation one of these days. Soon.

She tried to think back to the conversation they'd had – it wasn't so long ago – when she agreed to produce Robbie's play. There had been some mention of marriage – not a proposal as such, more of an understanding. And she had put it out of her mind. Tried to put it out of her mind, because . . . And since the day they'd first begun working together the subject of marriage had not arisen. The closest they had come to romance was dancing around Robbie's drawing room while he hummed the tune to *The Merry Widow Waltz*. That had been a charming moment. But she'd nipped it in the bud after a couple of minutes to get back to work.

Why? If challenged she'd have mumbled something to do with not wanting to mix business with pleasure. Or, perhaps more appositely, that she was perfectly happy as a single working woman living an independent life doing exactly what she wanted precisely as she chose to do it. That her boat was steady and did not need rocking.

Yet so long as her estranged husband was around, Violet could not slip into complacency. Robbie would not wait forever. Moreover the Robbies of this world, men who not only did not object to a wife who worked but who positively encouraged it, did not grow on trees.

She began to panic. Had she lost him already? If so, she had nobody to blame but herself. Oh Robbie, dear Robbie, I haven't been that good to you, have I? she thought.

Veronica Ann's visit had been more timely than Violet realised. She was galvanised, and not a moment too soon.

She had an idea: she would invite Robbie to a night out together at a music hall, preferably somewhere nearby. Then afterwards she would ask him back for an after-show drink and pop the question, so to speak. That way she could kill two birds with one stone. If all went well she could kill the whole flock.

## 22 The modern lady milliner

In the drawing room of an elegant Victorian terraced house in a quiet street off Knightsbridge a recital was about to take place.

Meredith Martin took up her position in the middle of the room, upright and composed. She was dressed simply yet stylishly, if a touch primly, in a dark green silk dress that followed the contours of her lengthy body from head to toe in the fashionable 'S-shape' – bust thrust forwards, bottom thrust back – the only adornment a simple enamel brooch pinned to her waistline. The whole effect was carefully designed to set off her hat, or rather her series of hats. She placed one hand on the pianoforte for support (and because she'd seen it done elsewhere).

Standing beside her was Gaye Worth. She was also dressed simply, if less strikingly, in a light blue dress with ruched sleeves and a sailor-style collar. She wore a straw hat decorated with flowers, the sort of thing a child might wear, as that indeed was the intended effect.

Seated before them in a half circle were a dozen or so of Mme Poulesse's friends, ready to be entertained. At the piano sat Monsieur Poulesse. When the assembled company were ready and settled, and with a nod to M Poulesse, Merry began to sing, in her own fashion and to a tune that would have been familiar to all those present.

MERRY:

  I am the very model of a modern lady milliner,
  I own a little hat shop near the Strand (you may have
      been in there),
  My clients are exclusively the cream of our society,
  I'm known for my discretion and my taste and my
      propriety.

  *(She adjusts her hat minutely and continues)*

  I know the latest fashion and I'd say that I'm ahead of it,
  You'll never find a hat that's out of style, I just get rid of
      it,
  I've simple hats and fancy hats with trimmings and with
      featherers,
  I've hats for all occasions and for every kind of
      weatherers.

GAYE: *(accompanying the words of the chorus with a strange
little bobbing motion)*

  She's hats for all occasions and for every kind of
      weatherers,
  She's hats for all occasions and for every kind of
      weatherers,
  She's hats for all occasions and for every kind of
      weather-weather-ers.'

  *(During the following verses Gaye hands Merry a series of
  hats, each one more outlandish than the last. As the hats
  exchange hands so they became jumbled, muddled and
  dropped, intentionally or otherwise.)*

MERRY:

  Each model is unique, you will find there's only one of
      it,

Fads and mass production, I'll have absolutely none of
    it,
No Merry Widow nonsense and no passing whims or
    silliness,
For I'm the very model of a modern lady millin'ress.

GAYE: (*chorus*)
    No Merry Widow nonsense and no passing whims or
        silliness,
    For she's the very model of a modern lady millin'ress.

MERRY:
    I've curly brims and floppy brims and hats completely
        brimless,
    Panamas with ribbons on, irregular or rimless,
    I've Buckets, I have Cartwheels, I have Gainsboroughs
        with flowers on,
    Tricorns, tam o'shanters, and a cloche with Eiffel Towers
        on.

    Wedding hats and party hats, Derby hats and toques,
    I've hats from off the shelf, made to measure and
        bespoke,
    I've bretons and I've turbans, on the straight or
        asymmetrical,
    Berets plain or stripy or with patterns diametrical.

GAYE: (*chorus*)
    Berets plain or stripy or with patterns diametrical,
    Berets plain or stripy or with patterns diametrical,
    Berets plain or stripy or with patterns diametri-metrical.

    (*The tempo of the music slows*)

MERRY:
  Each bonnet is a statement, every beret tells a story,
  A hat is so much more than just a mere accesso*sory*,
  I've sober hats and jaunty hats, for fun'rals or festivities,
  Hats for servants, mistresses, and maids of all
    proclivities.

  There are hats to make a maiden swoon, hats to dance a
    reel in,
  Picture hats to hide beneath or cloches all-revealing,
  Boaters that will guide you in your speech and your
    behaviour,
  Yes, a hat can be your dearest friend, a hat can be your
    saviour.

GAYE: *(chorus)*
  A hat can be your dearest friend, a hat can be your
    saviour.
  A hat can be your dearest friend, a hat can be your
    saviour.
  A hat can be your dearest friend, a hat can be your
    saviour-saviour-er.

MERRY:
  From the promenades of Paris to the salons of Sofia,
  You'll find my darlings perched on every noble head
    you see-a,
  In halls of fame throughout the world my name is all-
    familiar,
  I am the very model of a modern lady milliner.

GAYE: *(chorus)*
  In halls of fame throughout the world her name is all-
    familiar,
  She is the very model of a modern lady milliner.

When it was over the audience erupted into loud applause and choruses of 'Hoorahs!' and 'Encores!' Some of the gentlemen, and one or two of the ladies, got to their feet. Merry and Gaye, with a smilingly reticent Monsieur Poulesse, curtseyed and beamed and mouthed 'Thank you' and 'Merci' for what seemed like a good five minutes.

Afterwards, once her guests had departed, Mme Poulesse took hold of Merry's shoulders and gave her a French hug. (As in held at a distance, with no other parts of the body touching.)

'*Magnifique!*' she exclaimed. 'Not forgetting you, dear child.' This she addressed to Gaye, who curtseyed sardonically, before Madame turned her attention back to the star of the show. 'But my dear, what a triumph!'

A little bell in the guise of Mrs Vlatsky's voice tinkled in the back of Merry's brain.

She smiled modestly. 'I can't really sing, you know,' she said.

Gaye muttered something.

'I beg your pardon?' said Mme Poulesse.

'Nothing,' said Gaye.

'But I did think it wouldn't matter too much,' Merry went on. 'It's the words that count, after all.'

'It is the words that count,' agreed Mme Poulesse, beaming. 'And how you "put it across" – is that how you say it? That is what matters.'

~

'Well?' said Merry.

'Well what?' said Gaye.

'How did I do?'

They were walking down Sloane Street together away from Mme Poulesse's.

'Not bad.' Gaye shrugged. 'Shame you can't sing.'

'But it didn't matter. When the words go so fast there

isn't much opportunity for singing.'

There came no reply.

'Are you sulking?'

'Why would I sulk?'

'Because I was getting all the attention. It was meant to be the other way around, wasn't it? You were meant to be the featured one, and I was your – what did you call it? Your foil.' Merry laughed, elegantly. She caught sight of her reflection in a shop window and smiled to herself. She was feeling stylishly superior in her simple-yet-modish green dress with matching cape.

'I got laughs too, don't forget.'

'Of course. I couldn't have done it without you.'

The patronising tone of that remark was not lost on either of them.

'Next time,' said Gaye, 'I do the singing and you the chorus. It's only fair.'

'But they're my lyrics.'

'So?'

'And I honestly think – I know you're a far better singer than me, but I honestly feel it's better this way around.'

'Why do you say that?'

'Because I'm,' Merry gestured at herself, 'taller. And more naturally authoritative. And because of the way I deliver it, deadpan. Isn't that what you said I was good at once?'

Gaye did not reply.

'That way, it comes across as much funnier. Whereas if you were to do it, your natural cheekiness wouldn't work at all. Not at all. It isn't a cheeky song.'

'I can do more than cheeky.'

'You could build up your part,' suggested Merry, rather pompously. 'You're good at the business, after all. So long,' she added quickly, 'as you don't distract from the words.'

'How can I do business without distracting from the words?'

'The business with the hats gets laughs anyway.'

'And by the way, did you get permission from Mr Gilbert to use his words?'

Merry did not reply to this.

'Didn't think so. What if he found out?'

'He won't.'

'He might.'

'He'd be flattered,' said Merry.

Gaye made a rather vulgar noise.

They had arrived at Sloane Square, in the shadow of the Court Theatre, where they were to part company.

Merry puffed out her chest, like a pigeon. 'I think we may be made, Gigi,' she said. 'Or at least for a while, for as long as Mme Poulesse has enough friends.'

'It's a one-shot turn.'

'What's wrong with that?'

'You can't make a career out of a one-shot turn.'

'Well, it's good enough to be going along with. And I tell you what,' she turned her imperious gaze upon her little friend. 'Next time, you do it. We'll see how it goes. How is that?'

In return, Gaye bestowed upon her colleague a sickly smile, which was unfortunately largely unseen in the shadow of the streetlights. Then she blew her a kiss and wandered off in the direction of Pimlico.

Merry watched her go, anxiously, like a mother observing her child walking to school for the first time. Then she headed off into the underground station.

~

Gaye Worth never did get to play her version of the 'Modern Lady Milliner'. When Merry brought up the subject of her *pièce de résistance* with Mme Poulesse subsequently the lady smiled, and agreed that yes, it had been a *triomphe*, and then changed the subject.

A week after the event as Meredith was arriving home Mrs Vlatsky burst from her room, her topknot quivering with excitement. 'Miss Mairie!' she cried.

'I'm sorry Mrs Vlatsky, I have to – '

'There is a gentleman to see you!'

'A gentleman?'

From behind Mrs Vlatsky appeared the small, rotund figure of Monsieur Poulesse. He was mangling his hat in his hands.

'Mam'selle Martin.' He held out his hand, which Merry took with some trepidation. 'Forgive me, I needed to call on you to explain.'

'Oh? Explain what?'

They were standing all three together in the hallway. Mrs Vlatsky was the only one who was smiling, and she was showing no signs of departing.

'Mrs Vlatsky, would you mind?' Merry gave her a weak smile.

Mrs V bowed, said something inaudible, and backed away into her front room, still smiling.

'So?' Merry drew herself up to her full height and turned her haughty gaze upon the diminutive M Poulesse. There must have been nearly a foot's difference between them and she was making the most of it. 'What can I do for you?' She placed one hand on a hip and the other on the hallway table.

'Do you think we could . . .?' M Poulesse made a vague gesture. 'Is there somewhere a little more private?'

Merry hesitated for a moment, and then without speaking she led the way up to her room on the second floor. As she stepped this way and that, turning on lights and divesting herself of her outerwear, M Poulesse danced from one foot to the other, trying to keep out of her way.

'Do sit down,' said Merry.

But he seemed disinclined to do so. He stood before her, his hat still in his hands, and began to speak rapidly.

'You may be wondering, I expect you are. It is most unfortunate, very unfortunate, but there was simply nothing, you understand, please, nothing I could do.'

'What are you talking about?'

M Poulesse ran a hand over his bald head and took a deep breath. 'Your song. As you know, Madame Poulesse loved it very much, as did her friends. Only her friends told her . . . told her . . .'

'Yes?'

'What a shame it was you were not such a good singer, and Madame Poulesse agreed.' He paused, and cleared his throat. 'I tried to tell to her, how does it matter, she presents the song so perfectly, never mind her voice is not . . . However, Madame made an arrangement for a friend, for a friend to – who is an opera singer, a professional singer. She arranged . . .'

'She arranged for what?'

She guessed the answer, she just wanted to make it as difficult as possible for poor M Poulesse.

'For the lady, for her friend, to perform the song.'

'She stole my song.'

'*Alors*, it is not truly your song, is it?'

'My words.'

Mr Poulesse bowed his head in acknowledgement. 'Believe me, I told her no, it was not right, I tried to stop her. But she insisted. Insisted.' He adopted a solemn face. 'She was most adamant, and when Madame is adamant, she . . .' He shook his head. 'So I, she forced me, to give her the music. With the words.' He was addressing the floor. 'And there it is.'

There was a very long moment while Merry stared at Monsieur Poulesse with no expression whatsoever, and

Monsieur Poulesse continued to gaze in agony at the floor.

'I apologise. I apologise from my heart, please believe me.' He clutched onto his chest by way of illustration. 'I hope you will accept.'

'Thank you Monsieur Poulesse,' said Merry. She turned away from him dismissively and appeared to focus her gaze on the far wall. The agonising silence continued for a few more seconds and then, as Merry's attention seemed to be no longer upon him, Monsieur Poulesse turned and made his escape as quickly and quietly as he could.

Her attention *was* upon him. Or rather it was upon Mme Poulesse, the woman who had had the effrontery to hire a real (as in professional opera) singer to perform Merry's (purloined, without permission) lyrics based on the (purloined without permission) words of Mr Gilbert to the (ditto) music of (the late, which meant it didn't count) Mr Sullivan from their popular operetta *The Pirates of Penzance*.

'How dare she!' Merry exclaimed out loud. She stood up, grabbed the cushion off her chair and flung it across the room. 'I shall report her! I shall report her to Mr Gilbert!' And she sat down again.

She began to laugh. Even Merry had to see the funny side. Even she had to admit she did not have the proverbial *jambe pour se tenir debout*.

It was back to square one.

## 23 Violet and Robbie visit the music hall

'Music hall?' Robbie raised an eyebrow. 'Are you sure? They're low places, hardly suitable for someone like yourself.'

'Don't be so pompous, Robbie,' said Violet.

'I'm only trying to protect you,' said Robbie. 'So, let me think.'

He was familiar with them all, he claimed. He boasted he'd misspent his youth in them. So now he had to consider which of them might provide Violet with an authentic music hall experience – for her 'virgin visit' he called it – without compromising her artistic sensibilities or placing her in mortal danger.

'I am not the fragrant flower you take me for,' she remarked. 'But I do draw the line at grotesques.'

'"Grotesques"?'

'No giants or midgets or ladies with beards,' she explained. 'And no performing animals.'

'No animals? Not even the speaking dog?'

'Especially not the speaking dog.'

'Well, that narrows the field. Let's see . . .' He ran through a few and dismissed them – 'too large, too raucous, too coarse, too infested' – before he finally plumped for The Cuckoo. It was large enough to be authentic, he said, and small enough to make a quick exit from if their lives were endangered. It was situated in a side street off Commercial Road and it offered what Robbie described as 'a mixed bag': Shakespeare one week, opera the next, vaudeville the week after. Music hall, he told Violet, was not genuine music hall unless it included a good deal of rowdiness and a serious risk of death, by fire from onstage pyrotechnics or asphyxiation from offstage smokers.

'If you are trying to frighten me you are not succeeding,' said Violet.

She was nervous before the event however, not because of the event itself but because of the purpose behind the event, which was, to put it baldly, her seduction of Robbie. She was afraid she might lose her nerve and mishandle it. The whole thing seemed too contrived. She realised now she would have done better to have confronted him directly rather than working towards it in this ludicrously roundabout kind of a way.

She spent an inordinate amount of time deciding what to wear: not too respectable yet not showy; modest yet suggestive. In the end she chose a deep aquamarine dress with just a hint of a plunge in the neckline, plain-sleeved to the wrist and, on instruction from Robbie, devoid of jewellery - 'They'd have that off you before you had time to sit down'. On her head she wore a simple turban designed not to obscure the view of anyone who happened to be seated behind her. Robbie pronounced her 'a picture', and squeezed her hand as he helped her into the cab.

As music halls go The Cuckoo was on the small side. It held maybe a thousand people, no more, and it was crammed to the rafters. Violet did feel slightly self-conscious as she took her seat, but unlike in the smarter environs of the West End nobody appeared to take the slightest notice of anyone else unless they knew them; in which case they thought nothing of conducting a conversation at shout level from one row to another.

The evening was hosted by a Master of Ceremonies in top hat and tails. He set the tone for the evening with barbed remarks directed for the most part at the upper classes: 'Ladies and gents,' he began, 'though we don't get many of them here, I don't think,' he added with a chuckle.

The whole auditorium was like the gallery of a West End theatre. The audience expressed their opinion of each act with uninhibited abandon. There were boos for Jerome the Exotic Juggler (the 'Exotic' was neither obvious nor explained, which maybe accounted for it), but cheers and yells of approval for most of the comedy acts. These included a surreal sketch featuring a bewildered policeman and a much smarter criminal who was trying unsuccessfully to turn himself in, and an act so veiled in innuendo Violet could not understand a word of it. There were frequent references to railways which, judging by the audience's response, was code for something else entirely. One seemingly innocent song, delivered with rather more gusto than the face-value words merited, featured a piano tuner:

> 'At first he'd tune it gently, then he'd tune it strong,
> Then he'd touch a short note, then he'd run along,
> Then he'd go with a vengeance, enough to break the key,
> At last he tuned whene'er he got an opportunity.'

There were a number of musical items delivered by women dressed as young girls singing naughty songs with feigned innocence. Charlie the Conjuror, who managed to keep up a deadpan patter about the behind-the-scenes goings-on of well-known politicians – never mentioned by name but easily identifiable – while producing rabbits from his pocket and strings of scarves from the leg of a table, brought the house down. One lady acrobat who performed what Violet considered to be a first-rate display of agility and grace induced boos and slow handclaps. Another young lady who executed a mediocre dance in a distinctly bored manner won wolf-whistles and encores; perhaps because she was, as one audience member pointed out, loudly, 'Putting it out all over, Marlene'. There were obvious favourites, and a newcomer had to work extra hard to win the audience's attention. One young woman delivered what Violet took at first to be a song completely in mime until she realised the poor girl was simply unable to make herself heard above the hubbub.

It was raucous, it was raw and it was rowdy, but it was never obscene and never downright crude. It was both disarmingly childish and surprisingly sophisticated. The Censor being the Father of the Innuendo, as Robbie had said to Violet at one point, virtually every act contained a subtext. On the face of it the lady was singing a harmless song about a journey in a railway carriage and the gentleman an innocent ditty about a piano tuner. If the authorities claimed to find the songs vulgar they only had their own grubby minds to blame, was the prevailing get-out.

It was Violet's choice to walk home, and in order to forestall the ultimate topic of the evening she chattered non-stop all the way. She gave Robbie a detailed description of every act – 'I was there too, remember,' he mildly if pointlessly reminded her – which of them she particularly enjoyed and which of them she did not. When that was exhausted she turned her attention to the audience, and how their reaction told her when she was completely missing the point 'because of some code' such as railways, and when she was not, such as in the piano tuner. She felt quite proud of herself about that. She told him about her delight at her discovery of the subtext and how it reminded her of the Enlightenment . . .

'The Enlightenment?'

. . . When the French *philosophes* used irony and classical references in order to condemn the status quo and the established Church without arousing the ire of either.

'Ah, as in a secret language. I see, I think.'

. . . And wasn't it marvellous how art and hypocrisy go hand in hand, not just in the West End but all over. Why, if there weren't such a thing as a Censor, whether it was the Lord Chamberlain or the London County Council, writers would have nothing to write about and performers nothing to perform.

'Is that not a little far-fetched?'

'Well yes, maybe,' she rushed on, 'but you know what I mean. Ultimately all art is a celebration of the appalling and glorious complexity of mankind.'

Even Violet realised she was going off the rails a bit, to coin another railway metaphor. But by then they had reached her front door and she had to say, 'Will you come in?'

'It's late,' said Robbie.

'Not so late. And there is something I have to say to you.'

'In that case . . .' Robbie stood there while she fumbled for her keys and opened her front door – it took some doing, her hand was inexplicably shaking – and they stepped inside.

'Follow me.'

She led him up the stairs to her room on the first floor. When they reached her landing she stopped, and blinked once or twice.

'Are you intending to seduce me?' he asked.

'What makes you say that?' She spoke more sharply than she intended.

'I can't imagine,' said Robbie. He was still smiling as Violet opened the door to her sitting room and ushered him inside.

She removed her hat, took a deep breath and sank into an armchair. Then she threw her head back as if transfixed by something on the ceiling, and Robbie had to resist an overwhelming urge to kiss her neck.

'I've never been here before,' he remarked. 'Might I perhaps turn on a light or two?'

When Violet did not reply he searched for the light switches and took in the room. In the dimness it looked rather gloomy, yet cosy enough. He took a turn around, it did not take long, and the next time he glanced in Violet's direction she was sitting upright in her chair staring at him.

'So?' said Robbie. He sat down. 'What is it you wanted to say to me?'

Violet was still staring at him as if he wasn't exactly there.

'I was wondering,' she began, 'if we should . . .' She cleared her throat. 'What we should be doing about hiring a theatre.'

'It's funny you should ask that. Because I was going to suggest, after this evening, if we shouldn't have a word with Sam.'

'Who's Sam?' she asked feebly.

'He owns The Cuckoo, and other halls besides.' Forget the West End, Robbie went on, it was an unnecessary stretch financially. Costs were ridiculous, they would have to fill the theatre every night to get their money back. Not to mention the hypocritical audiences (he added for good measure, with a chuckle). Far better to try the play out in a genuine theatre with a genuine audience, like tonight's, with minimum costs and a ready-made crowd that's not afraid to tell you exactly what they think. The only sticking point might be Elizabeth. She wouldn't be seen dead in a music hall, but he felt sure he could talk her round. He'd have a word with Sam the next day. The Cuckoo might not be the ideal place but there were plenty of others. And then it would be full steam ahead.

He stopped, finally, and asked Violet what she thought. She was still staring at him as if she were seeing through him. He had the distinct impression she had not been listening to a word he'd said.

'You're tired,' he said. He got to his feet.

'Are you going?' She tried unsuccessfully to keep the anxiety from her voice.

'Unless you have other ideas?'

She opened her mouth to say something and then closed it again.

'You're tired,' Robbie repeated. He went to her and kissed her on the top of her head. 'Goodnight,' he said.

He picked up his coat and hat and left.

# 24 Mrs Santenoy goes to gaol

The subject of finding a theatre, which had dropped out of Violet's mouth by sheer chance and as a diversionary tactic, was nonetheless pertinent.

For a producer, she was in the process of learning, the finding of the right theatre is one of the most important aspects of putting on a play, and one of the trickiest to get right. In the West End in particular, theatres that were not already occupied by a regular company under the auspices of an actor-manager such as Herbert Tree or the Bancrofts were much sought-after, and their owners or managers could demand ridiculous hire fees. Moreover plays did not always run to form: the predicted sure-fire favourite might fail to attract an audience and have to close at short notice, at a huge loss to everyone involved, while an outsider might prove surprisingly popular, and no theatre manager wanted to curtail the run of a play that was pulling in audiences. All of which meant that things could happen very suddenly and the alert producer needed to be ready to jump in the moment a suitable theatre became vacant. Otherwise months could go by and nothing become available, at which point other problems would inevitably arise.

Just as Robbie and Violet thought that they were ready to set their production machine properly in motion – they had a finished script, and thanks to Robbie's friend Sam the choice of no fewer than three theatres in the East End, which meant they could begin the process of casting – two vital cogs in the machinery went missing. One was Lolly, the other Mrs Santenoy.

After a good deal of detective work the truants were eventually located: in the South of France and in prison respectively.

Tired of hanging around, Lolly had decided to take herself, or allow herself to be taken, on a sojourn to Cap Ferrat. This produced the following series of telegrams between her and Robbie.

> ROBBIE: *Where the hell are you stop come home immediately stop*
> LOLLY: *Tell me first if you are actually ready to produce the play darling otherwise I see no reason to come home it's so beautiful here stop I was beginning to think it was never going to happen stop*
> ROBBIE: *You should have told me stop we begin rehearsing immediately stop*
> LOLLY: *Very well I'll be on the next train home don't begin without me stop*

Mrs Santenoy was a very different matter.

The suffragettes, as Robbie had witnessed, were beginning to step up their strategy of civil disobedience. Under the guidance of Mrs Pankhurst and her daughter Christabel they were becoming more and more militant. Having failed to have the issue of women's suffrage debated in Parliament, and having been fobbed off yet again with more false promises of 'Of course women will be given the vote but *not just yet*', they were now a near-regular presence outside the House, in large numbers. On one occasion they marched *en masse* from their 'headquarters' at Caxton Hall to Parliament Square and were charged by policemen on horseback. A number of them were taken into custody and accused of 'obstructing police', and sentenced to two weeks in prison. Which was how Mrs Santenoy and some of her fellow suffragettes found themselves in Holloway.

The notion that a gentle and mature soul like Mrs Santenoy should be thrown into a hellhole such as Holloway Prison struck terror into Violet's heart. It also threatened to upset the whole delicate process of *Mrs Morphett's Macaroons*. Robbie took the news in his stride. In fact he admitted – perhaps unwisely – that it could provide excellent publicity for his play, featuring as it would a Real Life Suffragette and Gaolbird.

'How can you say such a thing, Robbie?' Violet exclaimed.

'Do not worry, my dear,' he replied. 'I will pay her a visit, if I'm allowed, and we'll see what's what.'

'I think I should do that,' said Violet.

~

The very sight of the medieval fortress that was Holloway Prison was so intimidating that Violet had to fight the urge to bolt. After a few deep breaths and a bit of searching however she found her way to reception, where she informed the uniformed woman behind the desk that she had come to visit Mrs Santenoy.

'Who?'

'Santenoy. S-A-N-T . . .'

'Never mind.' The woman ran a bony finger down a list of names on a ledger until she found what she was looking for.

'No visitors,' she said.

'I beg your pardon?'

'No visitors.'

'Oh.'

Violet stood there stupefied. She had not, naively, anticipated such a complete and immediate brush-off.

'Then may I leave her a message?'

'No messages.'

'What, not even a note?'

'Not even a note.'

'In that case . . .' Violet frowned, and looked around the room as if seeking inspiration from an invisible ally. 'Then what can I do?' she asked rather pathetically.

'There's nothing you can do,' said the woman wearily, and Violet wondered how many times she'd had this conversation before. 'Unless you want to pay her fine.'

'Fine?'

The woman consulted the ledger again. 'Twenty shillings,' she said. 'If you happen to have that on you.'

'And if I did, which I don't, would she be released right away?'

'That depends on her,' said the woman. 'We'd be happy to let her go.' She gave Violet a lopsided smile.

Violet made to leave but turned back. 'How is she?' she asked.

The woman shrugged. 'I don't know anything except what's in here.' She tapped the ledger. 'There've been no complaints that I'm aware of.'

'She's not a young woman.' Violet began.

'There's plenty of them in here.' The woman relented slightly. 'She's only here for two weeks.'

'What sort of conditions does she have to put up with?'

'She's second division, which means she's in a cell on her own. She has a bed. And a stool. She has a lovely green frock to wear with fetching little arrows on it, an apron, also with arrows, and a dainty little white cap. She's given three meals a day, one bath a week and an hour's exercise per day in the prison yard.' She rattled it off by rote.

'Is she allowed to mix with other prisoners?'

'No, except in the exercise yard. And then she's not permitted to communicate with anyone.'

'What if she's ill?'

'We have a hospital.' The woman was in the circumstances being friendly enough and Violet did not want to test her patience too far. But the idea of an elderly woman, who by the way she had never met, having to eke out day after day alone in a cell with no communication with anyone, wearing grubby prison garb that was quite possibly infested, was almost more than Violet could bear. She felt if she left now she would be failing both herself and Mrs Santenoy.

'Did Mrs Santenoy have the opportunity to pay the fine herself?' she enquired.

'When she was sentenced? Probably, yes. Most of them do and most of them refuse.'

'Most of "them"?'

'These women. Suffragette women. Don't ask me why. Pride maybe, or maybe they can't wait to spend a week or two at His Majesty's pleasure.' She laughed, and showed a set of yellow teeth. Then the smile vanished and she leaned over the desk to Violet. 'Look duckie, don't waste your time here. She'll be out soon enough, there's nothing you can do meanwhile. She'll be all right, most of them get out of here pretty much unscathed.'

'Would you,' Violet said tentatively, 'just tell her I was here? Mrs Graham, Violet Graham. We haven't met you see.' But the woman was already shaking her head.

'No,' she said. 'And again no. Whatever the question is, the answer is no. It's tough but there it is. Good day to you, Mrs Graham.'

# 25 The cat among the pigeons

'A music hall?' cried Miss Chester-Bolt. Robbie suppressed a splutter. He couldn't help thinking what a perfect Lady Bracknell Elizabeth would make.

'What makes you think I'd be seen dead inside a music hall?'

'I wouldn't like to see you dead anywhere, Elizabeth.'

'A woman in a place like that is likely to be arrested. . .'

'No, no, you're quite wrong.'

'. . . especially if she's on her own. I can't imagine what you were thinking of.'

'I'm not talking about one of those cheap gin palace.'

'And in *Shoreditch* of all places!'

'It's a perfectly legitimate theatre, they do straight plays there, often. Shakespeare even.'

'I don't believe I've ever been to Shoreditch and I don't believe I ever shall.' She had clearly wiped her mind completely of her recent trip to drop off Violet.

'You're out of date, Elizabeth. We're in the twentieth century now.'

'Are we indeed? And what difference does that make?'

They were in Elizabeth's drawing room overlooking the Thames in Cheyne Walk. The lady herself was pacing up and down the room, swishing the skirt of her dress dramatically. Of her mother there was no sign.

'Do you think I would even *contemplate* a place that was frequented by . . .' Robbie ran out of words. He stood with his hands in his pockets, rocking back and forth on his heels.

'What's wrong with the West End?' Elizabeth stopped pacing for a moment.

'There's nothing wrong with the West End. Except for the cost. And the availability.'

'Cost? What cost?'

'I have the figures somewhere, if you want to see them.' Robbie made for his briefcase, which was leaning up against the chair he had not yet managed to sit in.

'I don't need to see the *figures*. I'm asking you why the cost is such a problem?'

'Because it is. It costs around twice as much to produce a play in the West End as it does in the East.' He gave up on the briefcase.

'It was never on the cards,' Elizabeth pronounced. 'Why, if it had been I would never have been involved in the first place, you should know that, Robbie.'

Robbie sighed, despite himself. 'And we have another problem.'

'Which is?'

'Our other backer, the lady suffragette, is in gaol.'

'In *gaol*? Oh!' To his surprise Elizabeth let out a guffaw. 'Of course! She's a suffragette! I had heard they were sending some of them to prison. So, what is the problem? Bad publicity? You don't want the word to get out that someone connected to your play is in prison? I would have thought quite the opposite. I can see the poster now.' She splayed her hands as if she were imagining it. '"*Mrs Morphett's Macaroons*, starring a genuine suffragette and inmate of Holloway Prison".'

'Don't be crass, Elizabeth,' said Robbie. He seemed to have forgotten he'd had the self-same thought himself.

Elizabeth turned to him as if he were a truanting child. 'Crass? Robbie. Never before have you accused me of being crass.'

'That's because you've never said anything crass before,' said Robbie, with a strained smile. 'Think what Mrs Santenoy would have to say. Besides, she is hardly the star of the show.'

'That's as may be.' Elizabeth patted him on the arm. 'Come now. Let's sit down and have a cup of tea and catch our breath.'

They did so. Elizabeth rang for tea and while they waited they chatted about inconsequentials.

'I have already set the wheels in motion,' Robbie told her, as he drank his tea. 'On the basis of the Shoreditch theatre.'

'Well, that was presumptuous of you.'

'I knew you wouldn't like it, which is why I presented it to you as a *fait accompli*.'

'And not only presumptuous,' said Elizabeth, reaching for the plate of cakes, 'but highly risky. You know I could withdraw my cooperation at any moment.' She offered him a cake, which he refused.

'I am horribly aware of that, naturally,' said Robbie. 'The point is, Mrs Santenoy had agreed to invest in our little piece, in return for being given a small part in it.'

'Who's Mrs Santenoy?'

Robbie suppressed another sigh. 'She's the lady . . .'

'Gaolbird. I see.' Elizabeth snorted. 'Well, you are playing a dangerous game,' she said. 'So that means you are out of pocket, is that what you're saying?'

'Partly, yes.'

'And you need me to stump up more.'

'That's not what I'm asking.'

'Then what are you asking?'

'I am asking to keep costs down so I don't have to ask

you to stump up more, as you delicately put it.'

'There's nothing delicate about money,' said Elizabeth. She picked up a cake from the plate she was still holding and held it in the air for a moment. 'So, where are we exactly? Do you have your actors yet?' She placed the cake in her mouth.

'We are holding auditions shortly,' said Robbie. 'Mrs Graham is looking after that.'

Elizabeth chewed briefly and swallowed. 'And Marie Tempest?'

'Even if we could afford Marie Tempest . . .'

'I wish you'd stop talking about what you can and can't afford, Robbie. That's the trouble with you artistic types, you think of nothing else but money.'

Robbie sat back in his chair. He felt suddenly tired. 'That's very true, I don't deny it. But as I was saying, even if we could afford Marie Tempest I don't believe she is right for the part. We have a much better contender in Mrs Leonora Heyday.'

'Mrs Leonora Heyday, never heard of her.'

Elizabeth was still holding the plate of cakes. She was gazing at it in puzzlement, as if not quite knowing what to do with it.

'Go on,' said Robbie. 'Have another one.'

'I wish Lucille wouldn't bring cakes every time I ask for tea,' she said. 'They will make me fat.'

'Have you tried telling her not to?'

Elizabeth did not reply and popped another cake into her mouth.

'So as you see,' Robbie made the most of it while Elizabeth's mouth was otherwise engaged, 'we have a timetable to work towards now, we can't put the brakes on just like that.'

'Well,' Elizabeth brushed some cake crumbs from her bosom, 'that is your problem, Robbie. You got yourself into this predicament, it's up to you to get yourself out of it. You and Mrs Graham, of course.' She gave him a sickly smile. Then with some effort, the plate of cakes still in her hand, she leant across to Robbie. 'Take this from me, before I finish them off.'

He did so and placed it down on a table.

'Remember, when I first agreed to invest in your play it was partly for the prestige.' She spoke, as only Elizabeth could do, with no irony whatsoever. 'People invest in artistic enterprises for all sorts of reasons. Some of them do it for the allure, the bright lights and the big names. Some of them do it for fun, like betting on a horse. Very few people do it for the art, as you know. As for me,' she automatically reached across for a cake and checked herself, 'I do it for entirely philanthropic reasons. Investing in new and untried talent. Introducing exciting young – and not so young – artists to the world, giving people like yourself a leg-up. And in the case of *Mrs Morphett*, because it concerns a cause in which I believe very strongly.'

She stopped abruptly. Robbie waited.

'But I have a reputation, and that reputation means a lot to me, and to others, I believe,' she went on. 'I'm sure there are people who are happy to put their money into the music hall but I am not one of them.'

'What you mean is,' said Robbie, 'and try not to take this the wrong way Elizabeth, that you are a snob.'

'With my money I can afford to be,' said the lady. Then, 'How is Mrs Graham?' she asked.

Robbie hesitated a split second before replying. 'She is very well, thank you for asking.'

'When are you getting married?'

'What makes you think we are getting married?'

'I am not an idiot, Robbie. How else did you manage to coax Mrs Graham into this enterprise in the first place? It's not as if her experience counts for much.'

'What do you mean?'

'Tell me one useful thing she has done so far with *Mrs Morphett.*'

'She's improved on the script.'

'The one thing that did not need doing. What else?'

There was a long silence. Robbie took a deep breath. 'What is this, Elizabeth? Why the interrogation? Violet is doing everything one could expect, and with great competence.'

'Then why do we not yet have an opening date?'

'Because these things take time, and coordination.'

'Because you've been too busy sleeping with her, I wouldn't wonder.'

'I'm not going to answer that.'

'Because it is none of my business.'

'Partly, yes. And because I am not here to talk about Violet.' He took a drink of his tea and tried to outstare her.

'Well as far as I can see you've been doing all the work so far. You'd be better off without her, in my view. You've become transfixed by that woman, I can't imagine why. You're normally such a sensible person, Robbie.'

Robbie replaced his teacup upon the tray with the utmost care and got to his feet.

'And now I've offended you.'

He did not respond to that.

'You managed perfectly well without Mrs Graham before, there were no hold-ups then.'

'Producing a play as a single matinée is very different to producing it as a regular run,' said Robbie. 'And no, don't interrupt me please, Elizabeth. If you cannot trust me, trust *us*, to do whatever is best for the production then we will have to part ways.'

'Oh, Robbie, don't be so sensitive!'

But he was already on his way out of the door.

'Please excuse me, Elizabeth,' he said with a wan smile.

'I have things to do. I will let you know about theatres as soon as we have news.'

His last impression of the lady as he departed the room was of a mouth gaping open in a very red face. It was not until Robbie had left the house completely and was halfway across Battersea Bridge that he allowed himself to unclench his fists and breathe normally.

# 26 Lady Caroline Daly

Lady Caroline Daly gazed at her reflection in the mirror of her dressing table. It was her favourite occupation – and why not, when you were as beautiful as Lady Caroline? She picked up a silver hairbrush, embossed with her initials (a gift from her husband), and languidly drew it through her long, lustrous golden hair.

Robbie watched her from the bed. He loved to observe this ritual. He loved to see the way her body moved inside her all-but transparent wrap. Everything Caroline did was graceful. Even when she sneezed, or on occasion burped, she did so with elegance, and a total lack of effort.

After some minutes she ceased brushing, and with one last longing glance at herself she rose, and pulled at the tie around her waist, allowing her wrap to slip from her like a second skin. And there she stood, in the full glory of her nakedness. Her unblemished, slender body, almost white in the dim light of the bedside lamp.

She slipped into the bed beside him and lay flat on her back gazing at the ceiling. What a disappointment that must be, after her own reflection, thought Robbie a touch wickedly. He turned onto his stomach and began to stroke her, first her breasts and then her stomach and beyond. He shifted closer so his lips could follow his hand, and he started to kiss her, her cheek, her neck, her breasts, and on and on down her body, lingering to play awhile with the erogenous bits. She moved beneath him and lifted her arms above her head and spread her legs (the hussy!). Then when she was ready for him he lingered a little longer, until she was beginning to squirm and almost to cry out for him. Not till then did he enter her.

Her body continued to move beneath his, her arms still stretched above her head, her pelvis thrusting, feeling him deep inside her. Even in the midst of lovemaking Lady Caroline was still glorious, more so as she forgot herself, forgot she was the most beautiful woman in the universe, and that it didn't matter if her mouth opened so wide you could see her tonsils, and her face contorted with sheer, uninhibited lust was still breathtakingly beautiful. More so, if such a thing were possible.

The lovemaking lasted as long as possible. Robbie was the conductor here, holding back on the pace, controlling his own and her movements so things didn't go too fast. When the tempo threatened to run away with them he withdrew, and he would find other ways to please her in other positions. Then when it was time he would enter her again, and as they approached the final crescendo, so he allowed the pace to quicken and events to happen as they were bound to happen until they at last arrived, hopefully simultaneously, at the final clash of cymbals. At which point he arched his body over hers and looked down into her face and saw Violet.

Then he woke up.

Dreams are strange things. Not exactly fiction, not quite fact, but something in between. Memories and hopes, but more often fears. Unfinished business. Lost people. There was never much obvious rhyme or reason for them, and just as you thought you'd packed a particular aspect of your past away for good out it would pop from some hidden corner. Lady Caroline Daly. Fancy that.

Robbie turned and lit his bedside lamp. He lay there for some time, his hands behind his head, thinking.

Lady Caroline Daly. He never had quite worked out what that particular interlude was all about. He had stepped into it so easily, with very little thought, very little idea where it was all going to go. It was a daytime romance, if you could call it a romance in the first place. She was a married woman. And she was married in every sense, not like Violet.

It was a little daylight bubble, in the Daly house in Eaton Square. Blinds drawn. Servants and husband miraculously absent. Afternoons when he should have been doing other things. It existed outside the real world and it brought a great deal of pleasure to two people, without – Robbie liked to imagine – harming anyone else. The possible risks, of discovery or even of pregnancy, were never discussed.

Discussion in general was not a part of their relationship. Caroline, bless her cherished heart, did not have too much to talk about. It was why she was so beautiful, was Robbie's contention. Hers was a face untouched by trouble or doubt, or the darker uncertainties of deep thinking. A child's face in a way. There was a kind of calm blankness about her, like a banal watercolour, appealing in its simplicity and its inoffensiveness. He felt completely comfortable with her.

And when it ended, which it had to do, he was devastated. He had no idea why, they had so very little in common except for their lovemaking. And while he could remember the hurt, oddly enough he could not remember the cause of the break-up. Presumably Lord Daly found out about it, there was no way of knowing. The invitations to visit suddenly ceased, and when he called on her she was permanently 'out'. And of course the moment she was gone he yearned and longed for her so badly he thought he was going mad.

For a fundamentally sensible man like Robbie it was terrifying. He felt his life had ended, that there was no point to anything any more. In all the time of their affair he had neglected everything else. His friends, his family, a good deal of his work even, everything and everyone that had once meant so much to him, none of it mattered while he focused his attention all-consumingly on the dazzling, delicious, ultimately destructive Lady Caroline Daly.

But what are dreams for? They must have a purpose, even if you had to hunt to find it. Was it a warning? It felt like it. And if so, about what? Did he still unconsciously yearn for Lady Caroline? He didn't think so; he barely gave her a thought these days, which was faintly troubling in itself perhaps.

And then there was Violet. How did she fit in? And why was her face on his pillow so disturbing? She was everything Caroline was not: she was clever, and funny, and unpredictable, and she was beautiful, if not in the classic way Caroline was beautiful. Violet was more like an oil painting that changed according to the light, or her mood. There was depth in that face, and the beginnings of the lines of experience that add so much more interest to a woman.

He had fallen so easily into bed with Caroline Daly, so what was stopping him from doing the same with Violet Graham? Or Violet Turnip – he must not forget her married name.

It wasn't good enough to say love is foolish. In some cases maybe it was not foolish enough.

Robbie turned off his bedside light and lay for the rest of the night gazing sleeplessly at the ceiling.

# 27 Troubled waters

'He was talking about putting it on at a *music hall*!' cried Elizabeth Chester-Bolt. 'Sometimes I do wonder about that man, Mrs Graham. I wonder about his judgment.'

'Yes, I agree it was a long shot. I think Robbie sometimes has an overdeveloped idea of his powers of persuasion.' Violet gave a slightly twisted smile and carried on before she could be interrupted. 'That said, he was not talking about a music hall. He was talking about a legitimate theatre in the East End. They do have them, you know.'

'Do they? Well, I would know nothing about that.' Miss Chester-Bolt wrinkled her nose. 'So I told him that was out of the question and he needs to find somewhere else.'

'If I may say so, Elizabeth, you have a slightly distorted idea of East End audiences. They are surprisingly sophisticated.'

'Sophisticated? In the East End?' Elizabeth snorted.

'Very quick off the mark. And not afraid to express their opinion. I do believe *Mrs Morphett* would find a very comfortable home in an East End theatre.'

Elizabeth snorted again, louder this time. 'What would an East End audience know about the suffragettes?'

'Exactly! That's partly the point.'

'Hrrmph.'

Violet had arrived uninvited at Cheyne Walk, half expecting, more than half expecting, to be turned away at the doorstep. But Elizabeth had admitted her, with alacrity or so it seemed. It almost looked as if she was as anxious to talk to Violet as Violet was to her.

It was Robbie who had unwittingly summoned her there. It appeared there had been some kind of a row, and Robbie was in a bad way. Violet had never seen him like it before. He was barely dressed as she arrived at his apartment earlier that morning. Mrs Woolly had greeted her at the front door with a grimace, as if to say 'Don't ask me'. The man who prided himself on his appearance was looking positively scruffy. Why, he was still in his slippers!

'Goodness me, what happened to you?' said Violet.

And his hair was unbrushed. He was running a hand through it when she appeared in his sitting room and he barely looked at her.

'I didn't sleep,' he said abruptly.

'I am so sorry.' Violet stepped further into the room. She had not removed her cape or her hat, nor had she been invited to. 'Were you worried about the play?'

'Yes. No. That wasn't it.'

That Elizabeth Chester-Bolt had dismissed the idea of a theatre in the East End came as no surprise at all to Violet. Nor did the fact that Robbie had failed to talk her round.

'Wretched woman! If I had the choice I would . . .'

'Wring her neck?'

He didn't laugh. That was concerning.

'Robbie.' Violet took both his hands in hers. He did not pull back but he still refused to look at her. 'Robbie, what is the matter?'

'She is impossible. Simply and utterly.'

'Would you like me to have a word with her?'

'No!' He said, almost as a shout. He looked at Violet

briefly and then away again. 'It's best if you keep out of this. Besides, when Elizabeth is set on something nothing will change her mind.'

'Robbie,' said Violet again. She was still holding onto his hands. 'It's only a theatre.'

'Yes, I know.'

'Look at me, please.'

He did. His expression was so crestfallen she wanted to take him by the shoulders and give him a hug. Instead she said, 'I'll have a word with her. Right now. The worst she can do is slam the door in my face.'

And that is how Violet ended up in Miss Chester-Bolt's drawing room, with little or no ideas or intentions other than to do what she could to bridge the rift that had developed between the two most crucial members of the whole enterprise.

The lady of the house was sitting in an armchair near the window, so she could gaze out of it without straining. With the light behind her she was little more than a silhouette, if a substantial one. She did not get up when Violet stepped into the room.

'I understand your objections,' Violet resumed. 'And I appreciate the aim of our play is not just to educate the unenlightened.'

'Or enlighten the uneducated,' said the other woman, with what sounded like a snigger. Violet nodded in acknowledgement of Miss Chester-Bolt's rare attempt at a joke.

'Robbie likes to think of himself as a man of the people,' said Violet. 'A bit of him has an aversion to what he considers the pomposity and hypocrisy of the West End theatre.'

'He shouldn't be working in this business then,' said Elizabeth.

'And he thought, we both thought, we were doing the

right thing.'

'Well, you were both wrong.'

'At the same time we have reached what you might call the point of no return, Elizabeth. If we delay things any longer we may lose our actors.'

'You've cast it already?'

'Not altogether, no. We have our leads, they are the important ones. The rest are . . .'

'Do you have the faintest idea what you are doing?' cried Miss Chester-Bolt.

She had swivelled in her seat to confront Violet directly. There followed a moment's silence, while Violet absorbed the shock.

'I thought you said you were not going to interfere,' she said, as evenly as she could.

There was a full minute's silence while Elizabeth composed herself. Then she began, in a voice so quiet you could barely hear her.

'You know Mrs Graham, Violet, when I decided to take on Robbie's little venture it was for love. No, not that kind of love. I like to think of myself as a philanthropist, it's why I support the theatre in the first place. I believed in his play despite it being an unknown entity, as was he. And then along you come, another unknown entity. So here I am, taking a giant leap of faith.' She paused, and gazed out of the window for so long Violet thought she had lost her thread. 'That is why,' she said, returning her attention to her uninvited guest, 'I feel the need to intervene.'

Violet waited.

'When Robbie first spoke of you he told me you were the ideal person to produce his play,' she went on. 'He said you knew all about actors, and scripts, and whatnot. When I asked him about your experience he didn't seem concerned that you had never produced a play before.

Now I see why he hired you, and it certainly wasn't for your experience as a producer.'

'Go on,' said Violet, against her instincts.

'If you are asking me to spell it out for you I may be tempted to be vulgar.'

Violet suppressed a laugh. 'You think he only hired me because . . .?'

'He wanted you in his bed, precisely.'

Violet blinked.

'A passably pretty girl has a lot to contend with,' continued the lady magisterially, 'I imagine, not being one myself. It must be tempting to use her feminine wiles to get what she wants without having to work at it.'

Violet thought for a long moment before she replied.

'Elizabeth.' She spoke softly, and calmly, as if to a small child. 'For nearly five years I worked for the busiest, and the most successful actor-manager the West End has ever known. If you are looking for someone to vouch for me, at this late stage, I am sure Mr Tree would be happy to oblige.'

'I expect he had you in his bed too,' said the lady.

Normally one could have laughed off such a conversation as banter. But Elizabeth Chester-Bolt was not one for such things. Bantering requires a degree of humour, which she did not have. Violet was confused about what lay behind the conversation. Not jealousy, of her and Robbie, surely not. She was being tested, yet again, she got that. But she'd had enough of finding herself on the defensive.

She got to her feet.

'Where are you going?' demanded her hostess.

'To find a theatre,' she said. 'I will have one within the week, within calling distance of the Strand, and I will let you know when I have.'

'You don't have to be so abrupt, Violet.'

Violet paused in the doorway. She took a few steps towards Miss C-B and smiled down at her. 'Since you are obviously in a state of high anxiety I would hate to have to prolong it, Elizabeth,' she said. 'Time is of the essence.'

As she went to leave Miss Chester-Bolt said, 'Do you know anything at all about Robbie's past?'

Violet stopped. 'I beg your pardon?'

The lady of the house was once again gazing out of the window. There was a pause during which Violet wondered if she'd heard right, or whether the other woman's remark was even intended for her. She waited just long enough, and then she turned and went.

As she made her way down the richly-carpeted staircase to the front door it occurred to Violet, with a good deal of annoyance, that in a world so dominated by men the biggest obstacles to progress and happiness were all too frequently women.

# 28 Felix Overbrand

From Cheyne Walk Violet made her way home via the West End.

Between the snobbery of Elizabeth Chester-Bolt on the one hand and the would-be radical socialism of Robbie Robinson on the other there was bound to be tension. It was a wonder they had managed to work together so successfully thus far. There had to be more to the apparent rift than a simple row about theatres, Violet realised. But she'd learned enough about arguments between people to know it was best to keep out of them as much as possible. And if Miss Chester-Bolt doubted her abilities then the best thing Violet could do right now was prove her wrong.

There was more than one kind of snobbery, it occurred to Violet as she passed the self-important façade of Daly's in Leicester Square, and that was the snobbery that turned its nose up at something simply because it was popular. It was the same sort of snobbery that considered the Court Theatre to be superior to, for example, His Majesty's, because it offered the kind of fare that challenged its audiences to think, and on occasion to question the status quo, through the works of Harley Granville-Barker and of course, GBS. Robbie would have killed to have his play produced there, and he would have needed to.

In the West End of 1905 every other building appeared to be a theatre or a music hall, most if not all of them offering the kind of fluff that Violet scorned and Elizabeth secretly cherished. She struggled to see *Mrs Morphett's Macaroons* in any of them.

Violet threaded her way through the busy streets to Charing Cross Road, past a brand new and vast edifice which grandly called itself the 'Coliseum', boasting a 'triple electric revolving stage' and two different variety shows four times daily. On she went towards the Strand, the heart of London's theatre and home to musical comedy: at the Vaudeville, the Savoy, the Gaiety and the famous Tivoli Theatre of Varieties, to name just a few. Travelling eastwards, past Rimmel's, 'The Scenter of the Strand', she peered up a side street by the Adelphi Theatre (currently showing *Hamlet*, featuring Henry Irving's son H B; at last a bit of class, thought Violet, secretly) and spotted the Touchstone Theatre.

She'd been there, she was sure she had, at least once, though she could not for the life of her remember what she'd seen. It was out of the way yet in the heart of theatreland, an unpretentious, strictly functional building created, she recalled, as a true labour of love by its owner, whose name had escaped her. It appeared, unusually, to be dark. This intrigued Violet.

She retraced her steps and approached the gentleman inside the box office of the Adelphi. 'Excuse me, but do you happen to know,' she enquired, 'what's going on at the Touchstone?'

'Not much,' replied the box office clerk.

'It's not due for demolition, is it?'

'Not as far as I know. He's choosy about what he puts on, he can afford to be, not like most people.' The gentleman in the box office rested his ivory-skinned, clean-shaven chin upon his hand and regarded Violet coolly.

'By "he" you mean . . .?'

'Mr Felix Overbrand is his name.'

'And have you any idea where I might find this Mr Overbrand?'

'You could try his club,' said the man.

'Which would be?'

'The Garrick. It's just round the corner, you can't miss it.'

'Yes, I know where the Garrick Club is, thank you.'

Dammit, she thought. The Garrick.

Violet knew as much about the Garrick Club as it is possible for any woman to know, for women, famously, were not allowed within its portals. It was a club for theatricals, and intellectuals, male only, membership by personal recommendation. There was always a long waiting list. Still, nothing ventured.

Violet made her way back down the Strand and along Bedford Street to the Garrick. The more she thought about it, the more perfect she thought the Touchstone would be. Not too big, centrally situated, run by a man of independent mind, and apparently means, and most important of all, she could think of nothing about it that either Elizabeth or Robbie could possibly object to. She was trying hard to remember the play she'd seen there. It had been out of the ordinary, that's about all she could recall.

'Good morning,' she said politely to the silver-haired gentleman behind the reception desk of the Garrick Club. He regarded her warily. 'I wondered if by chance Mr Overbrand happens to be on the premises at the moment?'

The wary look did not go away.

'I am sorry, madam, we are unable to disclose which of our members is currently in attendance at any particular moment. However if you would care to leave a message I will attempt to pass it on to Mr Overbrand at some point. Are you acquainted with the gentleman, may I ask?'

She rather thought that was none of his business, and that if he felt unable to disclose a harmless piece of information to her she had the right to do likewise.

'In a professional sense, yes,' she replied, obliquely yet firmly.

The gentleman produced a pad and pencil. 'If you would care to inscribe your details here, madam, along with any message you would like to impart, I will do my best to make sure the gentleman in question receives it, in due course.'

'Thank you,' said Violet. She scribbled on the notepad. It all felt vaguely ridiculous and probably a waste of time, but not least in defiance of the receptionist's supercilious attitude she took her time as she wrote a rather long message, explaining who she was and that she had a play that was looking for a theatre, with some urgency, and if Mr Overbrand felt inclined and interested she would be most obliged if he could arrange a time for them to meet and discuss terms.

'There,' she said eventually. And with a smile and a nod she turned and left.

On arriving home in Shoreditch she immediately sat down to write to Frank Sharp. Did he know of any theatres that might suit their play, in the West End or its approximations? And by the way, what did he know, if anything, about Felix Overbrand?

She had barely sealed the envelope when there came a ring on the doorbell.

'Special delivery,' said the young lad on the doorstep.

'For me? Oh.' Then, as the boy remained standing there, 'Does it expect a reply?'

The boy nodded. 'Right away.'

She tore open the envelope.

*'Mrs Graham, kindly tell the boy when you are able to visit me to discuss your proposal, the sooner the better, regards Felix*

*Overbrand.'*

'Well I never,' said Violet.

~

To say that Felix Overbrand was an oddity in the Edwardian theatre scene would be a gross understatement. He had made his money, a lot of it, through the manufacture of munitions and he spent it on what some people snootily described as his 'hobby', which was the theatre. He had none of the effete, cultured attitude of the Herbert Trees of this world nor the grasping, commercially-motivated greed of the music hall owner. He was interested neither in making money nor in making a name for himself, or for anyone else, on the West End stage. He had no inclinations to act or to write or to design. He was first and foremost a businessman, and a supremely successful one. He had built his own theatre out of his own money.

Overbrand's taste was also idiosyncratic. You could say he took on plays that found it difficult to find homes elsewhere, which is not to say they did not have potential, commercial or artistic. He liked to take a gamble and he didn't care a fig if the piece was written by a total newcomer and featured a cast of dozens of similar unknowns. The motivation behind his 'hobby' was a topic of some speculation among fellow members of the Garrick Club, as was the origin of his membership. No one owned up to having recommended him in the first place. He was not married and he appeared to have no immediate family or direct dependants. Some thought his theatre was simply a diversion and his way of atoning for the millions he earned making machines that killed people. Others simply wrote him off as a maverick. The kind of plays his theatre had presented in its relatively short life to date threw little light on what made the man tick. There was the odd comedy, one or two melodramas, two musicals, small-scale, one revival of Shakespeare (*Pericles*) and an obscure Wilde (*The Duchess of Padua*).

Some of this information was contained in the letter that Frank subsequently wrote to Violet in response to her questions. But by the time his letter dropped onto her doormat it was already too late.

~

Felix Overbrand was small and chubby and partly bald. It was difficult to put an age on him – the baldness didn't help – but Violet surmised he was somewhere between forty and fifty-five. He looked like a man who lived well and cared not a jot what people thought of him. His 'interview' with Violet was businesslike, and brief, and to the point. He stared at her throughout, without expression and certainly without a hint of flirtation. It took place in what he called his 'office' above the theatre itself. It didn't look as if much, if any, work had ever gone on in there. Despite the warmth of the early autumn day the room was cold, and there were cobwebs on the closed window. There was a desk and two chairs, a slice of carpet on bare floorboards and a couple of empty shelves and that was it. Violet was to learn subsequently that Mr Overbrand conducted most of his meetings in the Garrick Club itself, since those meetings without exception were between men.

Despite his expressionless stare he seemed nervous, and she wondered if this had to do with her sex. He did not seem like a man who was comfortable in the company of women. He fidgeted, with his cuffs, the odd item – a blotter, a pen, a pad – on his desk, even his watch, which he took out several times during the course of the interview and replaced without looking at it; at which point when Violet asked, Did he have to be elsewhere? Or Was she taking up too much of his time? He shook his head with some vigour, and Violet put that down to yet another nervous tic.

'Tell me about your play,' he said. And so she did, broadly and then in some detail. She told him about the try-out performance the previous year, which had been attended by many of the leading lights of the West End theatre – she could name them for him if he wished (he didn't) – and had garnered such *excellent* notices. As for who Robbie Robinson was, well he was initially a reporter but he had written *many* plays and he was *extremely* talented, and well-informed.

Overbrand didn't go for the puffery. The more Violet puffed the more he fidgeted. 'Yes yes yes,' he interrupted, after a while, as if he'd heard it all before, which he no doubt had, albeit from lips other than Violet's. When she mentioned Marie Tempest, which she did in passing – 'She was interested but in the end she was otherwise engaged,' she lied – he began muttering under his breath. Likewise when Violet began burbling about the worthiness and the topicality of the subject-matter. The less he responded the more she burbled, the more he fidgeted. In the end she just shut up, sat back and waited.

'Well,' said Mr Overbrand finally. He opened a drawer of his desk and peered inside, closed the drawer again and opened another until finally he pulled out a large ledger, which he opened, hunted for a page, smoothed the spine with a chubby finger and said: 'When do you want it?'

# 29 The audition

There was already a gaggle of people hanging around the stage door of the Criterion Theatre as Violet arrived at 10.30 one October morning, to the disgruntlement of the stage doorkeeper, whose name appeared to be Lewis. 'They were not called until 11,' she explained apologetically. 'Perhaps there is somewhere where they could congregate? Inside?'

He nodded grumpily and led them all down the narrow corridor to a dark and slightly grim room at the end of it. Why green rooms – where actors gather backstage to chat, or to eat and drink between shows – were so-called Violet had never managed to establish. Once settled, the silent and surly Lewis took Violet on and through the wings onto the stage, where he left her.

Theatres in the daytime are strange places, Violet mused as she stood on stage looking out over the empty auditorium. By comparison with most West End theatres this was one of the smallest. But she could still feel its throb and its mystery and the invisible eyes gazing at her from the empty seats.

She was both nervous and excited. It had taken months, much longer than Violet – or indeed Robbie, not to say Elizabeth Chester-Bolt – had ever imagined. In the end the business of finding a theatre had been the easiest part of it. And that had happened pretty much by chance.

When Mr Overbrand produced his ledger and asked Violet about dates, and she'd given him one off the top of her head only a few weeks away, and he'd nodded and made notes, it all seemed to happen in such a rush she barely remembered what she'd said. She was so overwhelmed at having managed so swiftly and simply to do what she had rashly promised to do only the day before: find a theatre within shouting distance of the Strand, not too big, terms to be discussed. It had been worth it, the whole humiliation, the trials and tribulations, just to see the look on Elizabeth Chester-Bolt's face when she delivered the news later that same day.

As Frank had said, the theatre business followed no rules. It was what made it all the more exciting, to Violet if not to the likes of Frank Smart.

She was still standing on stage when Robbie arrived, clutching a large cardboard box.

'There's the most spectacular row going on in the green room,' he said. He placed the box down on the floor as he divested himself of his hat and coat. 'It's like a double-act. Two women having a right old go at one another. If they're anything like as hilarious onstage as they are off we should definitely include them in the show.'

'Good morning, Robbie,' said Violet.

'Good morning, darling girl.' He leant over to Violet and kissed her on the cheek. An onlooker might almost have taken them for a married couple. Or maybe simply old friends.

Robbie jumped down into the auditorium and gazed up at the stage. 'We'll put ourselves a little way back I think, so we're not as it were on top of them. I used to hate auditions when I was a thesp.'

He picked up the cardboard box from the stage and threaded his way through the rows of seats to Row H.

'Since when were you a thesp?'

'Only amateur stuff, when I was a stripling. All the same, it's a tough process. You get half a minute to prove yourself and that's it. We need to get some lights up. I wonder if there's a stage manager about.'

As if on cue the mournful Lewis appeared from the wings.

'Oh, hello. Are you not the stage doorkeeper?'

Lewis shrugged. 'Stage doorkeeper, electrician, you name it.'

'Well, that's grand. Do you think we could have some lights on the stage?'

Lewis disappeared, and a couple of minutes later the stage was flooded with light.

Violet jumped down from the stage and went to join Robbie.

'What's the plan?'

'We'll work in groups of five,' he said. 'I have five scripts, and we'll hand them round and give them each a speech or two to read, at random, and swap about as necessary. When I think we've found our woman, or our man, I'll give you a nod, and of course if any of them catch your eye make a note of them. I'll need you to make sure we have the right names.'

He was in a very merry mood. No doubt he too was glad to be doing something practical at long last. 'How many people do we have?'

'I'm expecting twenty,' said Violet.

'Excellent. Then if we're ready I'll go and fetch them.'

He was back in no time with the string of actresses – they were mostly actresses – and a few actors. He sat them all down in the stalls a few rows in front of Row H.

She spotted Merry first. Merry was the sort of person one did spot, since she was a good head and shoulders taller than her fellow actresses. Automatically Violet looked around for Gaye and – hey presto, there she was!

They were not together, in fact they rather looked as if they were avoiding one another as they took their seats at either end of Row F. Like two people who have just had a massive row and had determined never to speak to one another again, thought Violet.

She had to laugh, to herself. When she had received Meredith's letter offering her services for *Mrs Morphett* she was so taken aback by her cheek she did not know how to respond. She had wrestled with her conscience – she did not like to think she was one to hold a grudge for so long – and in the meantime somehow forgot to reply. And now here she was, Meredith Martin and her friend and rival Gaye Worth. Both of them. How they had managed to gate-crash the audition heaven only knew.

Robbie was addressing the assembled company from the stage.

'Ladies and gentlemen, thank you all for coming. Please make yourselves as comfortable as you possibly can.' He was rubbing his hands together. Violet had never seen him so keyed up.

'My name is Robbie Robinson and I am the writer of this little bit of nonsense. My producer is Mrs Graham.' He gestured to Violet, and as one the assembled company, with two notable exceptions, turned to look at her.

'This play,' Robbie went on, 'is about suffragists and suffragettes, of how the one became the other. It is a comic piece about a serious subject, and I hope it comes off as such.

He then explained his audition process, the swapping of roles, at random, how they should all relax and enjoy themselves, haha, nobody has read the script before so nobody is expecting anything approaching a performance.

'So don't worry about a thing and try to enjoy it, however far-fetched that may sound.'

He looked, Violet thought, not without pride, in total

control. You'd think he'd been doing this sort of thing all his life. It helped that he was a young(ish) and handsome(ish) man talking to a group of mostly women. But you could also see them hanging on his every word.

It was a long morning. Robbie did exactly as promised, handing out the scripts in random groups and swapping roles until he felt he had found a suitable contender, at which point he nodded to Violet and she made a note of the name. When one of the actresses asked him why he was reading in the part of Annie Addeley he explained sweetly that that part had been cast and the actress concerned was currently in the South of France and expected back any time. And that Lady Clothgill was currently being held in Holloway Gaol but would with a bit of luck be out in time for rehearsals.

At lunchtime he finally called a halt. He thanked everyone and told them what a pleasant morning it had been and he hoped they had enjoyed it, and he would be in touch with their agents, or themselves personally, very soon.

'But perhaps,' he said, as the attendees prepared to leave, 'I might ask two of the ladies to stay behind for a moment.'

To Violet's dismay he indicated first Merry and then Gaye. 'Kindly remind me of your names,' he said to them.

They glanced briefly at one another.

'Meredith Martin.'

'Gaye Worth.'

'Miss Martin and Miss Worth. On stage please, if you wouldn't mind.'

Now what? thought Violet.

As the rest departed the two ladies in question climbed uncertainly onto the stage. Gigi had put her jacket back on and was looking uncharacteristically sheepish.

'When I arrived this morning,' Robbie said to them

genially, 'I interrupted an argument between the two of you. I wondered what it was about.'

The two women glared first at one another and then at Robbie and said nothing.

'I'm asking out of curiosity, nothing else,' he said. 'I'm not about to chide you, it's got nothing to do with me. I was intrigued. You looked like two people who have worked together before and I wondered if that was the case.'

Merry broke the silence first.

'I was surprised to see her here,' she said, with a jerk of the head towards Gigi.

'Me too,' said Gaye.

'And why was that?' asked Robbie politely.

The two women looked at one another again and then back at Robbie.

'We were supposed to be working together,' said Merry.

'On an act, a double-act,' said Gigi.

'Ah,' said Robbie. 'I wondered. Go on.'

'I was the comic, she was the foil. We had it worked out,' said Gigi.

'In a side street off Trafalgar Square,' said Merry. 'We had six people in the audience.'

'And all of them kids.'

'We made sixpence,' said Merry.

Again they looked at one another in perfect synchronicity.

Merry thrust out a hip. 'And I wrote a song,' she said. 'I wrote new words to the tune of "A Modern Major General".'

'I know the song,' said Robbie.

'About millinery,' said Gigi.

'We performed it to a private audience, it went down a storm,' said Merry.

'Excellent.' Robbie nodded. He stood in the stalls with his hands in his pockets, smiling up at the two women on stage. 'Perhaps you'd like to perform one of your sketches to us now.'

Yet again Merry and Gaye looked at one another, only this time it was not so much in hostility as in a kind of unspoken agreement.

'We'll do the song,' they said together.

And so they did. With no accompaniment, and no props, they performed Merry's "Modern Lady Milliner" as they had done at its one and only performance in Mme Poulesse's drawing room. Gigi, lacking props to play with, replaced the hats with other complicated bits of cleverly improvised business that threatened to distract from Merry's patter; at which point Merry glared at her without breaking her stride, all of which added to the hilarity. At the end of it Robbie applauded enthusiastically, as did, with a flicker of restraint, Violet.

'Splendid!' he said. 'Absolutely splendid. Well done. Does Mr Gilbert know about this?'

'No,' replied the two women simultaneously.

'And where did you perform the song before?'

'At Madame Poulesse's residence. In Knightsbridge,' said Merry. 'To an invited audience.'

'She makes hats,' said Gaye.

'I see,' said Robbie. 'Thank you, Miss Martin and Miss Worth. We will be in touch very soon.'

As they were about to exit through the wings Gaye stopped suddenly and turned back.

'Yes?' said Robbie.

'Er, you may not have our address. Our addresses,' she said.

Violet had never seen Gaye look so uncomfortable before.

'I am sure we have,' said Robbie. 'You will be on the

list, Mrs Graham has all your details.'

'Well, maybe not.'

Robbie looked enquiringly at Violet.

'That is the case,' said she. 'They are not on the list.'

'Oh?' Robbie looked from one to the other in confusion.

'But never mind. If we need to get hold of you we will.' She gave the two ladies her best patronising smile and turned her back on them. It was a petty gesture but it was satisfying too. Gaye hesitated a moment longer and then she departed properly.

'Pure gold!' exclaimed Robbie, the moment the ladies had gone. 'I never saw such synchronicity. We have to have them in the show. And what hostility to one another, that was quite genuine. Why are you looking at me like that?'

'It's a long story,' said Violet. 'So what did you have in mind for them?'

Robbie paced up and down in the space between the stage and the front row. 'We'll write them in. Somehow. As they are.'

Violet leaned on the back of the seat in front of her. 'You know what they did to me once?'

Robbie ceased pacing. 'Tell me.'

And so Violet told Robbie the story of her humiliation, by ritual, at the hands of Misses Martin and Worth, and not long after she had begun working in Herbert Tree's company when by her own admission she 'knew nothing'. Of how she tried to remonstrate first with Miss Martin and then Miss Worth and then with both of them together, at which point the two women whom she had assumed to be deadly rivals appeared to join forces specifically in order to make her, Violet, feel an utter fool.

'It felt as if they'd rehearsed beforehand,' she said. 'Like a double act. I was impressed, despite everything.'

'So that's why they weren't on your list. How did they

get to hear about the auditions?'

'I have no idea,' said Violet. 'They wrote to me. At least one of them did, I think it was Meredith.'

'And?'

'I never responded.' Violet grimaced. 'As to how they found their way here this morning – they are resourceful, I'll give them that.'

'So you don't want them in the show,' said Robbie.

'I'm not saying that.'

'Then what are you saying?'

These wretched women, Violet was thinking, it's as if they're following me around deliberately to make my life a misery. To reward them by offering them parts in Robbie's play, in *her* play, went completely against the grain. As did their uninvited presence that very morning. Everything these ladies did, from their appalling behaviour towards Violet all those years ago to the sheer cheek of gate-crashing her audition, irritated – and impressed her – beyond all imagining.

Robbie was still waiting for her response. And she realised, with some alarm, that he was genuinely hanging on her word. That if she refused to give the ladies parts in the play he would not argue with her but he just might never forgive her.

'First they humiliate me, then they turn up for a casting session uninvited. What do you think I should do?'

Robbie nodded in reluctant acquiescence.

'I have no objection to having them in the show, if you believe there are parts for them,' she said stiffly.

Robbie gazed at Violet long and hard. 'Thank you, my darling girl,' he said.

# 30 Lolly Mulligan hatches a plot

When Robbie's telegram had arrived Lolly had to think for a moment before replying. She felt very comfortable in Cap Ferrat and she was becoming horribly used to sipping champagne on the terrace of the villa belonging to the Hon William Sackworthy (not his real name of course) overlooking the Med. It seemed a shame to interrupt something that had never happened before in her life and was not likely ever to happen again. From where she was sitting London, with its fog and its traffic and its bustle and its anxieties, looked less and less appealing.

She'd really only found herself lounging by the Med on a whim, because the offer was there, and there was not much else going on in her life, least of all the play. The play. That interminable business. It had not been like that first time around at the Comedy. There was Robbie, and Winnie from costumes, and Hans Kapps (whatever happened to Mr Kapps?) and the woman with the bosom who put up the money for it all; and not forgetting Henry of course, dear Henry, the big cheese in shipping, who adored her so much he agreed to pay not just for the hire of the theatre but a handsome wage for her, which included rehearsals. It had all seemed so easy then. So what was the hold-up now?

She couldn't really, although she was tempted to,

blame Violet. Dearest Violet, whom she loved deeply, but who had never produced a play before and had only been brought on board by Robbie because he wanted to sleep with her. He could deny it all he liked but she could tell, could Lolly, she knew them both well enough. She knew them possibly better than they knew themselves. She had every faith in Violet, had Lolly. But there comes a time when any self-respecting actress can no longer afford to hang around, and that's where the South of France came in.

Her part in *Mrs Morphett's Macaroons* had been especially written for her by Robbie Robinson. There were not many actresses who had plays written for them, even by a writer who had never had a play produced before. This one was created specifically to show off Lolly's extraordinary versatility and skill with accents. The role of a parlour maid who becomes a leading light in the suffrage movement and ends up as the first female member of parliament was a character who, in a different world with the odd element of it tweaked here and there, Lolly felt she could almost have been in real life.

But instead she was becoming the sort of person who agrees to spend a week on the French Riviera with a rich and amusing married man.

There was one problem however: after day upon day of sunshine, over-indulgence and pretty good sex, Lolly was beginning to feel something she recognised as boredom.

So it was that she bade a tearful goodbye to the Hon William and caught the overnight express train to London. The journey gave her time to ponder, and to plot. And so it was that on the very day that Robbie and Violet were reviewing their actors on stage at the Criterion Theatre Lolly decided to visit Robbie's apartment in Battersea.

The door was answered by his housekeeper, Mrs Woolly. Upon opening it she discovered a slim young redheaded woman dressed from head to foot in orange and brown, who stood upon the threshold on one foot and said, 'Hello Mrs Woolly, is Mr Robinson in?'

'I'm afraid not, Miss – er – Mulligan,' replied the good woman.

'I hoped as much,' said Lolly. 'May I come in?'

Without waiting for an answer she stepped past Mrs Woolly into the hallway and through to Robbie's drawing room, removing her shawl as she did so.

'It's you I want to speak to, Mrs Woolly,' she said.

'Me, miss?'

'Yes, as it happens. On a matter of the utmost secrecy. Sit down, do.'

She had never been ordered to sit down in her master's drawing room by anyone, let alone Mr Robinson. Nonetheless Mrs Woolly sat, and looked at her visitor, and waited.

Lolly perched herself daintily on the edge of the chaise longue. The last time they had met Lolly had spent the night on it, Mrs Woolly recalled.

'I am going to ask you to do something for me,' said Lolly. 'It is not strictly legal but it is not illegal, do you understand?'

No, she did not, but Mrs Woolly nodded anyway.

'It won't get you into trouble, I promise you.' Lolly smiled her most winsome smile, then: 'How long have you worked for Mr Robinson, Mrs Woolly?'

'I'd say getting on for five years, Miss Mulligan.'

'And you know him terribly well, don't you? I always think a housekeeper knows her master better than anyone, especially if he is a bachelor.' Lolly winked, and gave a merry little laugh. 'I bet you would do anything for him, wouldn't you Mrs Woolly?'

She cocked her head to one side. She could be a right tease when she wanted, thought Mrs Woolly.

'Within reason,' she replied warily.

'Of course. That goes without saying. The point is,' Lolly looked away for a moment, as if to collect her thoughts. 'What I'm about to ask you to do will transform his life in the best way imaginable. What do you say?' She turned back to Mrs Woolly, still smiling.

'I don't say anything until I know what it is,' said Mrs Woolly.

'Then I will tell you. It's just a bit of fun really,' said Lolly.

# 31 Merry & Gaye fire their guns

Meanwhile, in Piccadilly:

'Take that, Mme Poulesse!' roared Merry. She was striding down the street as fast as her long legs could carry her, so fast indeed that grown men in bowler hats were forced to leap out of her way. 'He loved us!'

'Don't be so sure,' said Gigi. She was having to run to keep up. 'And you didn't answer my question.'

'What question?'

'What were you doing there?'

Merry stopped dead. 'What were *you* doing there?'

'And don't think just because he said he liked us it means nothing. They do that all the time, they tell you you're the best thing since silk bloomers and you never hear from them again.'

Merry glared at Gigi. 'We'll see.'

'Besides, she recognised us.'

'Who did?' The two women continued walking in the direction of Green Park, not quite so fast this time.

'Mrs Graham, of course. Who else?'

'I didn't give her a thought.'

'Well, I did. She knew exactly who we were, and that we weren't on her list.'

'So what?' said Merry.

'You never told me you were looking for another engagement.'

'Why should I? You are not my manager.'

'But we're a team. We work as a team. We agreed.'

'I don't remember any agreement,' said Merry. 'And I don't recall you telling me you were looking for another engagement either.'

'If we hadn't both been there together, and done the song thing together, he would never have noticed us in the first place.'

'He wouldn't have noticed us in the first place if it wasn't for that God-awful row.'

'You started it.'

'I did not! And what if I did, I was simply taken aback to see you.'

'And what do you think I was feeling?'

'Anyway, how did you get to hear about the audition?' demanded Merry.

Gaye hesitated. 'A little birdie told me,' she said.

'And so you turned up, just like that.'

'Just like that! Just like you.'

'I wrote to her,' said Merry.

'What?'

'So she has my address. They can contact me.'

'But she said you weren't on the list.'

'She never replied.'

'So we're quits,' said Gigi.

They stopped again. They had reached Green Park.

'Look,' said Gigi, 'we stand a much better chance working together, whether you like it or not.'

Merry did not respond. She was looking around her.

'Did you hear what I said? So how's about we try to get on together?'

Merry switched her gaze to her companion. It was a cold gaze. 'Who said we did not get on together?'

'Every time we meet, we have a spat. Who gets to do what. What someone didn't tell the other one. It's barmy.'

Merry smiled, for the first time. 'But isn't that what we do? Our "stock-in-trade"? Isn't that what our act is all about?'

'Our act maybe. But in real life.'

'What's the difference?'

Gigi gave an exaggerated sigh. She looked across the road and spotted a teashop on the far side. 'There's a teashop, right there,' she said.

'So?'

'Are you arguing for the sake of arguing?'

Merry shrugged. 'Very well,' she said.

They threaded their way through the traffic to the teashop. Once they were ensconced at a table near the window – Gigi would not tolerate a table anywhere else – with cups of tea and hot chocolate and walnut cake for Merry and an iced bun for Gaye, Gigi said: 'We could always try the music halls.'

'I am not going near a music hall.'

'We'd go down well there. There's no one else doing what we do. They'd love us.'

'It is not what I was put on earth to do,' said Merry pompously, and she gulped her hot chocolate.

'You don't know, you haven't tried. And who knows, we might be spotted.'

'It'd be like going backwards. From the West End theatre to the music halls? It's an admission of defeat.'

'Can you think of a what else?'

'I am a serious actress,' said Merry, seriously.

Gigi laughed. 'Oh, yep-de-doodle, I'd forgotten.' She looked out of the window for a moment. It was a bleak day, the sky a blanket of cloud, matching her mood.

'In any case, didn't you once say you'd be glad never to see the inside of a music hall again?' Merry remarked.

Gaye shrugged. 'But this is different.' She turned her attention back to her companion. 'So, you got any better ideas?'

'We're going to be performing in Mrs Morphett's Macaroons, I can feel it.'

'You think so.'

'And I am going to invite Mme Poulesse and her apology of a husband and I'm going to tell the world what they did to me.'

'I'm sure the world is dying to know.'

They ate and drank in silence for a moment.

'How d'you suppose they're going to fit us into their play?' said Gigi. 'I couldn't see any parts for us.'

'They are going to write parts for us,' Merry pronounced.

It was surprising, it surprised even Meredith, how one's confidence, absent for so long, could return so suddenly and so completely, simply on the strength of someone's approval. 'Or parts around us. That is what writers do, when they see something that inspires them. Or someone.' She said it all quite without irony and even Gigi had to be a little impressed. 'Or they could ask us to write our own material. In the context of the play, of course.'

Gigi shook her head. She did not share her companion's optimism. She felt things were running away from her somewhat.

She may have been more versatile than Merry, but the truth facing Gigi was plain: on her own, she was no more than another fluffy performer who could sing and dance. An ideal chorus member and little more. With Merry she could be something else, whatever that something else might turn out to be. Which meant she needed Merry more than Merry needed her. This was not a good situation for anyone to find herself in, especially since the two of them found it almost impossible to agree on anything. Worse, Gigi did not trust her companion, as she felt equally sure her companion did not trust her.

On the other hand, maybe a mutual distrust was not the worst base to build a working relationship on, she concluded.

# 32 Acts of defiance

When Mrs Santenoy arrived at Holloway Prison she was in a state of high excitement. For a woman from what society termed 'a privileged background', married for nearly forty years, the experience of going to prison was without question the most extraordinary event in the sixty-eight years of her life. Even as she was lined up against a wall with her fellow protestors and given a rudimentary medical examination, Mrs Santenoy still felt the strangest thrill of adventure. She saw herself as an actress in a play, going through the rudiments of being sent to prison without any idea of what lay ahead of her.

On instruction from the prison wardress she was made to undress – 'Completely?' – 'Completely' – and given some old, stained underclothing, brown woollen stockings and a green serge dress that really was stamped all over with broad arrows. She hunted for but did not find a matching pair of shoes to wear from a huge basket, after which, laden with sheets, a towel, a mug of water and a thick slice of rough bread she was shown to her cell. Even then it all felt quite unreal and startlingly melodramatic. She sank exhausted onto the hard wooden bed and closed her eyes and, surprisingly, slept.

The following day, having requested some reading matter she was given the Bible and an atlas of the world. She embarked on the first with interest and glanced through the second. During the obligatory hour's exercise in the prison yard she kept her head held high and, as instructed, avoided contact with her fellow prisoners. She managed to keep this up for two whole days without too much pain.

It was around the third day that the excitement faded. It was not until then that she became fully aware of a kind of sour, stale odour seeping through the walls from centuries of poor ventilation and prevailing damp. Her cell was both stuffy and cold. She sensed the presence of something that moved and scuffled. She dare not leave what food she was given on the floor lest her fear of mice and rats became real.

In the exercise yard she observed her fellow detainees with dulled curiosity. Apart from the suffragettes, whom she recognised only vaguely by sight, the women kept their eyes on the ground, and she was struck by the thought that many if not most of them had possibly spent more of their lives in prison than out; that a good half of them were no more than girls, and that there was a kind of resigned doggedness to the way they walked, shoulders slumped, feet dragging, as if tramping mindlessly in a circle was all they knew how to do or would ever do in the future. There were very few outbreaks, or protests; they didn't seem to have the energy.

Back in her cell, alone, Mrs Santenoy continued to wonder about them. How she would have loved to have heard their stories. In her long life she had rarely come across anyone from a background so different from hers, and now, tantalisingly, she was living right among them yet unable to communicate with them. Punishment for a crime committed, for whatever reason and under whatever circumstances, was a crime, in Mrs Santenoy's view, and should be punished accordingly. But if prison did nothing to rehabilitate these women, these girls, what was the point of it? If all they did was to re-offend the moment they were set free only to find themselves back behind bars again, what sort of a life was that? The sadness of it, the waste, was almost more than Mrs Santenoy could bear.

She tried to say as much to the lady wardress. She asked, as a special favour, if she could be allowed to talk to her fellow prisoners, even to teach them. They were probably illiterate, most if not all of them. She could teach them to read and write, as much as she could in her two weeks, it would be doing her a favour as well as them. What was the purpose of keeping them all locked up, alone? At least it would fill the time. At least . . .

The cell door was banged shut in her face. She was on her own, with just the Bible for company and a cell whose walls appeared to shrink with every day she spent inside them.

If she had really known how it would be to be confined to a cell in London's grimmest prison, would she still have joined the crowds marching peacefully from Caxton Hall to the House of Commons? asked Mrs Santenoy of herself. Might she, at the first sign of trouble – from the mounted police mind, not the women – have ducked quietly out of it and gone home? Alternatively, might she, secretly, have agreed to pay the twenty shilling fine and be done with it? Would anyone have found out? Probably not. Except herself.

It was pride and anger that had carried her along Whitehall. That and her fellow protestors. It was pride that got her through the initial shock of being sentenced and transported to prison. At some point in the future suffragettes who had spent time in gaol would be given badges of honour to tell the world how much they had sacrificed for their beliefs. History would venerate them. Families would be proud.

But right now, on her own, Mrs Santenoy sensed the strength that pride had given her literally seeping away. She felt increasingly cold, hungry, weak and unwell. She spent most of the twenty-three hours of the fourteen days of her sentence sitting on the bed and staring at the floor. At night she slept fitfully, listening to the sounds of weeping from a nearby cell and the distant shouts of someone in serious pain.

When there is no one to talk to, or to receive messages from or to send messages to, let alone to see, time no longer means anything. After a while in solitary confinement it is difficult to keep one's wits about one. It's little wonder some prisoners chose to be flogged rather than be forced to spend time alone, day after day after night after sleepless night.

'You can go home now,' said the prison wardress.

It came unexpectedly, even though her two weeks were up.

As Mrs Santenoy regarded her angel of mercy in the guise of the prison wardress she felt a strong surge of pity. She, Katherine, had only had to endure this horror of the building for two weeks, whereas the young woman who faced her, not looking directly at her as if such a thing were way beyond the bounds of intimacy, had to spend her entire working day inside this joyless edifice. And deal with what lay inside it which, for the most part, was women not like Mrs Santenoy. Women whose circumstances outside the prison were often even more grim than they were inside it; women who did not necessarily welcome the words 'You can go home now,' because home, if it existed in the first place, was not a place they wanted to go to.

For her part, home was also not somewhere Katherine wanted to return to immediately. There was a husband to face, and to be interrogated by, especially as to why she refused to allow him to pay her fine. It was hard to explain to a man with traditional views why paying a fine meant she was admitting guilt for a crime not committed. She did not yet have the strength to defend herself against accusations of stupidity or recklessness, of letting the side down and all that. He would become calm again eventually, she knew that. But meanwhile she would stay with a fellow suffragette, for the time being at least.

It was a relief to be in the company of her fellows. The suffragettes like herself who had spent time in prison came out not just with renewed determination for the cause of women's suffrage, but for the cause of women in general and especially those poor souls incarcerated in hellholes like Holloway. Those shouts of pain Katherine had heard came from a woman giving birth, she was told. For her and for others in the suffrage movement prison reform became very much a part of their overall campaign.

In the circumstances one could have forgiven Mrs S for forgetting all about trivia such as *Mrs Morphett's Macaroons*, and her ambitions to tread the boards. A bit of nonsense in the form of a stage play was unlikely to be at the top of her list of priorities.

~

'I am going out today, Meredith,' announced Mme Poulesse. 'I shall be away until around five o'clock. I trust you to mind the shop meanwhile.'

She was examining herself in the mirror as she spoke, adjusting her hat, a smallest twist to the left, a little extra tilt. Meredith watched her dispassionately. For a milliner, at a time when hats, according to Merry's lyrics, formed the most important part of a woman's appearance and told the world all about you, what you yourself chose to place upon your head was pivotal; especially since Madame Poulesse was apparently going to be 'out and about' all day being judged, silently, not for her opinion or her personality, but for her hat. Merry felt a sudden and unexpected pang of pity for her employer.

'Of course, madame,' she said.

She stood by docilely as madame completed her *toilette*, then she opened the door for her and smiled sweetly as the lady sailed through it.

Now.

Merry had continued to work for Mme Poulesse despite knowing about her act of betrayal. She had smiled at the customers and remained on her best and most immaculate behaviour. She had given not the slightest sign that she knew anything of madame's treachery. Volatile she may have been, but even a person like Meredith Martin had to pay the rent and buy food. Morality was one thing to the rich and quite another for the poor.

But Mme Poulesse had grossly underestimated her assistant. Having, as she thought, managed to get away with her grand theft she had continued to take her subordinate's loyalty for granted. She had made the monumental mistake of trusting her, of leaving her now for an entire day in sole charge of several thousand pounds' worth of millinery.

But now Merry's situation was, as she assumed, about to change, she considered she had absolutely nothing to lose. She got to work.

~

'I am sorry,' said Robbie. 'I should never even have suggested it.'

'I just don't see how they would fit in,' said Violet. 'I mean at a pinch they could play two of the minor suffragettes, but – a double act?'

She was looking particularly enchanting today, thought Robbie. Perched in her favourite spot on his chaise longue. Dressed in a purple frock, or maybe it was a jacket and skirt, it was hard to tell. Her neat little head topped by what for these days was a very modest affair with just the smallest bit of net; it suited her perfectly.

'What if you wrote them in as narrators?' said Violet. 'They could stand at the edge of the stage, commenting maybe. Rather like a chorus. And you could give them characters, make full use of . . .'

'You think my play needs narrators?' Robbie asked, not without an edge.

'Or.' Violet thought for a moment. 'How about an intermission entertainment? Not part of the play at all.'

Robbie shook his head. 'That would look decidedly odd.'

'Well then, I don't know,' said Violet. 'I'm simply throwing out ideas, since you are so keen to have the two of them in the show.'

'And you're not.'

'I'm doing my best Robbie,' she huffed.

'I know you are, and I am grateful.'

'I appreciate how talented they are. Believe me this is not personal, not at all.' She sighed and turned to look out of the window. 'Maybe you could write another play for them, as you did for Lolly. Based around them. And find someone else to produce it.'

'Oh dear,' said Robbie.

There followed a prolonged silence, as Violet continued to gaze through the window at nothing in particular and Robbie tried his best not to gaze at her.

He had thought long and hard about the other night, at the music hall. She had had something important to say to him and it had turned out to be nothing more than asking him about theatres for his play, something they could have discussed at any time and in any place.

It occurred to Robbie, perhaps rather late in the day, that business and romance did not make ideal partners.

He liked to consider himself professional enough to keep his personal and his working life separate, but the problem here was that with the one exception of the night at the music hall almost all his get-togethers with Violet had had to do with the play. And even on that one exception he had ended up talking about business.

But wasn't it ironic after all, that he had asked her to produce his piece partly in order to wrest her away from her job in the country and keep her close to him? So he could propose? And now look at them, working partners, and sticky ones at that, and she no nearer to divorcing her husband.

At last Violet, aware of the silence, turned her attention from the window to her companion.

'What are you thinking about?' she asked him.

'You,' he said.

She put on her sternest face, which he never found quite convincing. 'And?'

'You know I want to marry you,' he said.

Her sternest face did not move, not even to voice a reply.

'Please say something,' he said.

'I don't know what to say,' said Violet.

'I need to know what it was you wanted to tell me, the other night, at the music hall. When you began talking about theatres.'

Her face was a disconcerting blank. God, the strain was unbearable.

'I was wanting to ask you to sleep with me,' she said.

'Oh,' said Robbie. 'But you didn't.'

'I lost my nerve.'

There was a pause.

'Why did you want to ask me that?' said Robbie.

'Because I need . . .' she tailed off.

'A divorce, of course. And that means you need to

commit adultery.'

'That is a particularly horrible word,' said Violet.

'Yes, isn't it.'

Robbie leaned forward and placed his elbows on his knees. 'I'll tell you honestly, Vi, I don't want to be your co-respondent.'

'Of course you don't, it was wicked of me to even think it.'

'Not because I don't want to be tied up in your divorce, or to be named, I don't mind any of that, who cares. But I get a distinct feeling that . . .' he hesitated.

'What?' she demanded sharply.

'There you go,' said Robbie. 'That – sharpness. You've changed Vi, to tell the truth I don't know where I am with you any more.

'Oh,' she said. Then, 'Oh dear.'

She looked on the verge of tears.

'There is nothing in the world I wouldn't rather do than marry you. And love you. As you've never been loved before. But all you've done since we've been working together is push me away.'

'Have I?' she croaked.

'When – if – we were to go to bed together, it's because . . .' he cleared his throat, 'we do it for love.'

'Yes. Of course.'

'And I'm not at all sure you love me.'

'Oh,' she said, again. Then after another heady pause she said: 'I think I . . .' she stopped.

'You think you . . .?'

'I think I have lost the wood for the trees. No.' She frowned. 'That's not what I meant.'

'I think – do you mind if I have a go? – what you're trying to say is you are so concerned to prove yourself an efficient and clever theatre producer you've lost sight of the wood because of the trees. How does that sound?'

Violet gazed into her lap, and after a long while she nodded.

~

Acting as her father's dresser cum runner cum personal valet cum servant-slave was not Gigi's idea of fun. It was more like a sentence, a punishment, with no sign of parole. And even though she felt she'd done her penance long ago, there was still the question of a roof over her head, which she was warned in stark terms would no longer be there the moment she decided, as she threatened to do often, to quit.

Gigi's father worked the music halls and right now he was engaged as low-comedian at the Alexandra in Shoreditch, no further than a stroll from Violet's front door, though Gigi was not to know that. At his insistence his daughter attended to him throughout the performance, night after night, two shows on Wednesdays and Saturdays, for no pay, very little respect, and just a 'You brought this on yourself, young lady,' whenever she opened her mouth to complain. If life was so hard, he maintained, she could always get herself an engagement right here in the halls (in the chorus, of course). If not in this show there were plenty of others, where news of her recent shameful behaviour at Daly's would not matter too much. There were moments when Gigi was tempted, if only as a release from the unremitting burden of being at the beck and call of her father night after night.

There had been a time when she would have been happy simply to have watched him from the wings. She had learned so much from him, in particular how to judge an audience, how to vary what he did show after show, fine-tuning all the time, never getting bored, never letting up, never losing his concentration. It had been an object lesson in sheer guts and professionalism. She had admired him then. She had boasted about him to friends and colleagues, that she was the daughter of Jimmy Worth, or 'Worthy' as he was often known. But now, as she watched him making up in the dressing room mirror, all she could see were his wrinkles, and his sad old eyes gazing at himself from his ridiculously over-painted face – paint that may have just passed muster in the old days of gaslight but looked frankly freakish under the glare of electricity.

She had tried to tell him. 'Do you know, Pa, how behind the times you are?'

'What do you mean?'

'No one paints their face like that any more.'

'I don't care what other people do or don't do. I've been in this business long enough not to be told what's what by the likes of you.'

She often joined in with the second sentence of that speech, which didn't help at all.

But now was in a rut with no idea how to climb out of it. Unlike Meredith Martin she did not assume she would be shortly appearing on stage in *Mrs Morphett's Macaroons*, or anywhere else for that matter. She did not want to have to rely on Merry for her future. She did not want to have to rely on anyone. And that was precisely the problem: no actress could exist without relying on other people – to employ them in the first place, to watch them in the second, not to mention the accolades any performer needs to keep them going. Unless she became her own employer, and that was more than she had the energy for. She had got to the stage where she could only think in short sentences.

# 33 Meredith Martin burns her boats

When the Spaniard Hernan Cortes landed on the shores of Mexico in the sixteenth century after a long sea voyage across the Atlantic, he was so confident of the success of his mission he ordered his men to burn their boats so there was no possibility of retreat. So the story goes.

When Meredith Martin decided on her unusual method of revenge against her employer Mme Poulesse she was every bit as confident as Commander Cortes. She took the time to prepare her plan carefully, so when Madame Poulesse told her she would be out for the better part of the day she was ready to implement it immediately.

Such was the depth of her cunning that, while the effects of Merry's plot were almost immediate and complaints arrived at Mme Poulesse's door within days, the source of the problem remained a mystery. This made it very difficult for Madame to be able to point a finger at the probable perpetrator and very easy for Merry to deny all knowledge of and involvement in the near-tragedy that befell the crowning glories of a small group of Madame's most loyal clients.

More ingenious still, the poor lady victims themselves were not immediately able to properly diagnose the problem. Worse, their first suspicion of the cause of the terrible itching in their scalp was not something a respectable person shouted from the rooftops, or even whispered to themselves.

It was Lady Forrester's personal maid who first posited a diagnosis. One can hide the most intimate of physical discomfiture from everyone but one's personal maid. And so it was that Lady F's Sarah, one morning on seeing her mistress scratching away at her scalp with the energy of a wild cat, mentioned head lice. And while Sarah was not a trained nurse she did know something of the horrible little mites from her own childhood.

'*Head lice?*' breathed Lady Forrester.

'Just a suggestion, madam,' said Sarah. 'We had them all the time when I was a youngster, crawling all over the scalp, the little buggers, if you'll pardon the expression. My brother Joey nearly scratched his skin off. They're right little devils to get rid of and all.'

Now it's a well-known fact that a fashionable lady of the time took appalling risks every time she dyed her hair, or used curling tongs, 'rats' or various forms of metal hardware or toxic substances on her hair in order to straighten it, bulk it out or shape it to whatever design caught her fancy. Many went bald as a result. But the itchy scalp suggested something even worse: it implied *uncleanliness* – something the likes of Lady Forrester associated with the slums of the East End. That her personal maid had suffered from tiny creatures which made their nests, and bred, in her hair was bad enough. That those nasty little mites should find their way into her own crowning glory was beyond the pale.

'Not a word of this outside this room,' she told her personal maid. 'What is the cure?'

The word did get out of course, no one quite knows how but the finger must point at Sarah, and in a remarkably short time it became common knowledge, first downstairs and then up, that there was an outbreak of what everyone assumed to be head lice among a small group of ladies of the upper-class and aristocracy. When Lady Forrester's great friend Princess M of G called to say (in confidence) how much she sympathised with Lady F's 'little problem' and how odd it was that she knew of others in a similar predicament, after a good deal of convoluted conversation during which the words 'head lice' were not mentioned once, it transpired that there were to Princess M's knowledge around half a dozen ladies in a similar situation. All of whom, they discovered, after several more minutes of circumlocution during which Lady F still refused to acknowledge she had a problem in the first place, were clients of Mme Poulesse.

So it was that about a week after the problem first manifested itself, Lady F and some of her closer friends paid a joint visit to Mme Poulesse's shop to confront her politely and to ask how it was that her hats were harbouring head lice.

Mme Poulesse was quite naturally beside herself. She began with expostulation and proceeded to disbelief, then denial, followed by a good deal of energetic argument, and winding up eventually with heartfelt apologies and wild attempts to point the finger of blame elsewhere: at the makers, or the men who had transported the goods from the manufacturers to her premises, and finally, at her assistant. Her assistant was so outraged that her unstinting loyalty to her employer should be questioned she resigned on the spot before she could be, as they say, pushed.

At no point did any of the ladies stop to think that since head lice feed off human blood, specifically the blood of human scalp, it was impossible therefore for an inanimate object such as a hat to 'harbour' them. Not one of them suspected the actual cause, which was a form of itching powder readily available to buy at any high street joke shop.

Once again word spread of course, and Mme Poulesse's clients began to dwindle. She spent a small fortune having her premises fumigated and every item in it dry cleaned, by hand, after which no further cases of head lice were reported. But it was too late. Her regular customers would not come near the place. She was compelled first to reduce her prices and then to allow pretty well any Mary, Jane or Julia through her doors, no matter their background or the depth of their pockets. She even contemplated embarking on that dreadful practice called Mass Production, and only managed to avoid it by a whisker. It would be a good year before Mme Poulesse fully regained her status and her reputation and life could continue as normal.

Meanwhile for Merry, revenge was sweeter than she could ever have imagined. Not only was she able to witness first hand the effects of her practical joke on her double-crossing employer, she could wallow in that same lady's doubts as to whether or not it was her assistant who was responsible, or whether she was guilty of wronging Miss Martin not once, but twice.

At the same time however, for Meredith it was what you might call a Pyrrhic vengeance. Her boats were thoroughly burned now, which left her very much in the middle of the ocean with neither boat nor paddle.

# 34 Mrs Santenoy's crusade

'Mrs Santenoy, what an unexpected pleasure!' said Robbie.

She was looking wan, and very frail, and she had the slightly feverish look of a person who's been ill or close to starvation. She entered the room in some haste, clutching at her shawl and her hat, as if she had brought a hurricane in with her.

'I'm so sorry, Mr Robinson, arriving out of the blue like this. I would have written, but I thought . . . what am I interrupting?'

She looked from Robbie to Violet and back to Robbie again.

'You've come at an opportune time, Mrs Santenoy. This,' he gestured at Violet, 'is our producer, Mrs Violet Graham.'

Violet stepped forward and gave Mrs S a little bow. 'I am delighted to meet you, Mrs Santenoy.'

'Mrs Graham came to visit you in Holloway,' said Robbie. 'But they wouldn't allow her to see you. Or to leave a message.'

'Did you?' Mrs S looked quite distressed. 'They never told me! How very kind of you. What was the message?'

'Just to say I had called,' said Violet. 'And to ask if there was anything I could do.'

'Oh my dear, thank you so much.'

'So how are you after your ordeal?' asked Robbie.

As Mrs Santenoy allowed Mrs Woolly to divest her of her cape, but not her hat, she began to jabber. 'I'm a lot thinner and a lot crosser.'

'Crosser?'

'Very cross, as a matter of fact, Mr Robinson. Thank you.' This to the retreating Mrs Woolly. 'And I wanted to talk to you urgently about prison reform.'

'Oh. Well, first of all, sit down, do.'

She looked from one chair to another before she chose the one closest to her. 'It was an ordeal, you are quite right, Mr Robinson. From start to finish. It was only a fortnight but it felt like an eternity. No one to talk to. No books, other than the Bible and – something else, I forget what. One hour's exercise every day with *no* communication with the other prisoners, not even a glance. It was hell on earth, excuse the expression. I couldn't wait to get out and I never want to go through it again.'

She began to sniffle. She dug around in her bag and produced a handkerchief.

'We are bundled in there like common criminals, not even allowed the special privileges for political prisoners, like our own things. There were *rats*, Mr Robinson, in the cells. Not to mention the clothes they make us wear, and the *smell*. Permeating everything – one's clothes, one's food, one's bedding.' She dabbed at her nose. 'I wouldn't wish it on my worst enemy! But that's not why I came here and why I am jabbering on. The point is . . .' She paused for breath.

'Would you like some refreshment, Mrs Santenoy?' asked Violet.

'No, thank you, Mrs Graham. The point is,' Mrs S rushed on, 'your play. This play of yours. What is happening? Is it on yet? I feel so out of touch. And I am so sorry, you have to forgive me, you probably gave up on me. The point is,' she turned to face Robbie directly, 'I want you to include something in your play about prison reform. If it's possible. It is so important. And your play, such a wonderful – what's the word I'm looking for?'

'Mouthpiece?' Robbie suggested.

'What? Oh, yes, I suppose that is what I mean. A wonderful mouthpiece for . . .'

'Propaganda?'

'Well, I wouldn't call it propaganda exactly. That makes it sound as if I'm trying to pull the wool over people's eyes.'

'That's false propaganda,' said Robbie. He glanced briefly at Violet. 'But I think perhaps we need to slow down and take it one step at a time. First of all, are you still interested in being involved in our little venture?'

'Involved? You mean investing? Of course I am, Mr Robinson, all the more so!'

'In that case,' said Robbie gently, 'let's start from the beginning.'

He shifted slightly in his seat. 'We are all set to go, you'll be happy to hear, Mrs Santenoy. We have a theatre, we have our actors, more or less, and we have our script. Which still has a part for you if you wish to tread the boards, as you put it.'

'Oh, I don't care about that,' cried Mrs S. 'What about prison reform?'

'That's . . .' Robbie scratched his head. 'I'm not so sure about that.'

'Those girls!' Mrs S dropped her voice to a near whisper. 'Those poor girls. I'm not talking about the suffragettes now Mr Robinson, I'm talking about poor ordinary girls, convicted of some petty theft, and all because they have nothing. No food, no money, sometimes no home. One of them gave birth inside

Holloway, would you credit it?'

Violet gasped.

'They spend years in there, some of them. In and out, it's the only home they have, in many cases. It's that or the streets. But the *treatment*.' She stopped abruptly and blinked hard. 'As if they were dirt. And you know how it is, if people treat you like the scum of the earth, that is what you become. No respect. No compassion. And I am not blaming the prison officers,' she raised a hand, 'not for a moment. What they have to put up with. I am blaming the Government.'

'Ah, the Government.'

'And if your play concerns women's rights, the right to vote, to be heard, and you want the Government to take notice, then I'd like to include a word or two about prison reform.' Mrs S ground to a halt and stared into her lap.

'Mrs Santenoy,' Robbie spoke very gently. 'I very much understand your point of view, and your strong feelings. They are admirable. As are you, for standing up for what you believe in and sacrificing yourself for your cause. However, at this stage in the proceedings I can't see a way of including anything about prison reform without upsetting what we already have, do you see?' He looked at her anxiously.

'Oh,' said the poor lady.

'I am very sorry to disappoint you, and if there is any other way I can promote your cause I would be only too happy.' Robbie smiled apologetically.

Mrs Santenoy did not reply to this.

'Once a play is complete,' he went on, 'it is very difficult to as it were insert an extra scene into it, about something entirely new.'

'Yes of course,' Mrs S mumbled. 'I should not have asked.' She got slowly to her feet, and Robbie and Violet did likewise.

'Perhaps,' said Violet, 'you would allow us to think about it.' She glanced briefly at Robbie. 'Discuss it between us.'

'Between you? Well, yes, if you like.' Mrs Santenoy smiled weakly, then: 'Perhaps it's best if we left it. Forget I called.'

Violet escorted Mrs S to the front door. 'We will think of something, Mrs Santenoy,' she said. 'I promise you.'

'Thank you, dear,' said Mrs Santenoy. She retrieved her cape, nodded briefly at Violet and left.

'What a woman!' declared Violet as she returned. 'Who would have thought a fragile thing like that could survive two weeks in Holloway?'

'What's all that about discussion?' said Robbie. 'What have you led us into?'

'Calm down,' said Violet. She took her seat again. 'I have an idea. That could well kill two birds with one stone.'

'Which is?' He hovered over her, his hands on his hips.

'And save her investment at the same time.'

'Tell me.'

'And fulfil your desire to include those two troublesome women in your play. That's three birds.'

'Oh?' Robbie's tone softened. He sat down. 'Do tell.'

'Not until I've spoken to them. It may well not work.'

'By "them" you mean . . .'

'Your two favourite ladies. Miss Martin and Miss Worth.'

'Really?' said Robbie.

'Yes, Robbie,' said Violet. 'Leave it with me.'

# 35 A bleak future

Meredith told Gigi about her trickery. In fact Gigi was the only one she felt she could tell as she realised, somewhat to her surprise and dismay, that her so-called friend and rival was what might be considered her best friend. If not her only friend.

Needless to say Gigi found it shriekingly funny. She laughed louder than Merry had seen her laugh before, which was comforting, and a kind of endorsement, as Gigi was not wont to laugh at anything Merry did if she could possibly help it.

'That was clever,' said Gigi, nodding. 'Right clever. You should take it up as a profession.'

'A professional avenger. "Come and get your revenge here!" It is a thought,' said Merry.

They were once again in Merry's bedroom in the house in Lambeth, only this time Merry made sure it was she who was using the bed and her friend the sofa.

'Did you hear anything?' Merry ventured after a considerable time.

'What about?'

'You know.'

'Oh. No.' Gigi lay back in the sofa and considered her feet. 'Did you?'

Merry shook her head. 'I can't understand it. I felt so certain. Even the cards told me as much.'

'What cards?'

'Ma Vlatsky's. Now I can no longer pay the rent,' Merry grimaced at the ceiling, 'I have to suffer her wretched cards. "Let me read your future," she says. And I can hardly refuse. So she does, and she says, "Your future is looking good, Mairie. I see great things ahead".'

'And you believe her?'

Merry shrugged. 'I think I will go to Paris,' she said after a moment. 'They love English girls there, so I'm told.'

'And do what?'

'Whatever they can offer me.'

'Do you speak French?' asked Gigi, though she wasn't really listening for an answer. 'They'll eat you for breakfast.'

Merry sat up in her bed. 'Not me they won't.'

'They'll work you so hard they'll break your spirit. I knew a girl once, they found her backstage, in a corner in some crummy dive, dead as a dodo. She'd been there for days and no one knew she was missing. She died of starvation and exhaustion.'

'I don't believe you.'

'Cross my heart. She was English.'

There followed a quiet moment as each contemplated the startling image of a Paris music hall littered with the bodies of young English *chanteuses*.

'Perhaps we can find somewhere else to do your song,' suggested Gigi.

'What, "The Modern Lady Milliner"? Like where?'

'I can see if the Alexandra will take us on.'

'A music hall! No fear.'

'You just said you wanted to go to Paris to work the music halls there. What is wrong with you?'

'Besides, the milliner song makes no sense unless you're a milliner.'

That was horribly true.

What, thought Meredith, if they had hit their peak? First with Mme Poulesse and her cronies and then at the audition for *Mrs Morphett's Macaroons*? Not to mention their West End appearances at the Haymarket. There has to be a high spot in any performer's life, that by definition she does not recognise until it is long gone. How sad, to peak so early in one's professional life. To know that it is downhill all the way from now on. One might as well slit one's throat and be done with it.

Right now Gigi should have been at the theatre, helping her father. She could picture his face as he hunted all over for her. 'Anyone seen my daughter? Where the hell is she? I will give her what for when I find her, you see if I don't.' His face getting redder and redder. With a bit of luck he'd be so distracted he'd lose his precious timing and his act would go awry. She imagined him now, late for his entrance, his face only half made up, puffing and blowing, losing his props, forgetting his lines. She guffawed.

'What's so funny?'

'Nothing,' she said.

As revenge went it did not rival Merry's, being as it was revenge by default. It was not even intended as revenge as such. True, it was a way to get back at her tyrannical father. Except that the end result would simply be more tyranny when she did eventually return home. If she returned home.

It was not that Gigi liked to triumph over other people's misfortunes, or that she wished misfortune on other people in the first place, not even her father. It was more an indication of her state of mind. It was only when she felt miserable herself that she wished worse misery on other people.

'Maybe Paris ain't such a bad idea,' she said.

Merry did not reply.

'Well?' Gigi looked across to where Merry was laid out on her bed, hands behind her head. 'Did you hear me?'

'Do you speak French?' said Merry. Then, 'I hear they eat English girls for breakfast there.'

'Hmm,' said Gigi.

There came a sudden knock at the door and Mrs Vlatsky entered.

'Mairie, sorry to bother you.' She stared at the figure of Gigi, prone on the sofa, then she spotted Merry flat-out on her bed. 'Ah, there you are. You have a visitor.'

'A visitor?' Merry sat up. 'Who?'

'A young woman, she . . . .' Mrs Vlatsky turned to mutter something to someone just outside the door. 'Her name is Mrs Gram.'

'Gram?' said Merry.

Then: 'Mrs Graham!' Both Gigi and Merry spoke it at once, and both sprang to their feet at once, like the well-synchronised double-act they were. So that when Violet entered the room she found the two women, neither of whom were wearing shoes, standing bolt upright staring at her in identical degrees of shock.

'Hello ladies,' she said.

# 36 First rehearsal

And so came the first day of rehearsals. Everyone on their best behaviour. Eyeing one another nervously and maybe a touch apprehensively. Waiting for someone to take the lead, to set the tone. To perform or not to perform. To simply read the lines in as neutral a voice as possible. Bending over backwards not to look as if they are trying too hard.

Mrs Leonora Heyday was the perfect leading lady. She obviously considered herself the natural matriarch of every company she played with. She regarded her fellow thespians with that gracious, enigmatic, not-quite-superior manner that only true ladies are ever able to master. She waited for someone to open a door for her, or to draw out a chair, and when they did so she bestowed upon them the full gaze of her luminous grey eyes and mouthed a 'thank you.' Once she had taken her seat at the table where the read-through took place she observed each member of the team in turn, over her spectacles, smiling, nodding here and there and even giving a tiny wave at a familiar face.

When everyone was seated and before Robbie had a chance to open his mouth Mrs Heyday took it upon herself to deliver a short speech. She began by thanking everyone for being there (as if she were personally responsible for the fact) and continued by declaring she had no doubt it was going to be a very happy company, that it was a privilege (with her hand to her heart) to be part of the making of a brand new play by a new writer – this with a benign gesture and gracious smile at Robbie – and she looked forward to getting to know each and every of them. That done, she sat back in her chair and looked to Robbie as if to say, 'You may now proceed.'

But it was all quite appropriate. As Mrs Morphett she was perfect casting. She had not attended the audition back at the Criterion Theatre. The Mrs Heydays of this world did not attend auditions. They waited to be asked. They even expected to read the play, or have it read to them, before deciding whether or not to accept the role.

For everyone else meanwhile, the first day of rehearsals was the first time they had set eyes on the full script, with the exception of course of Lolly Mulligan.

Some of the newcomers stumbled over their words. One or two attempted a kind of personation, which they found they had to modify as the full nature of the character they were playing manifested itself. More than a few of them laughed out loud at the jokes and there was even the odd gasp at some of the things Annie, played by Lolly, had to say. And when it came to the finale, when Annie stands up in the House of Commons and announces to her Honourable Member friends that hitherto only women were to be allowed to become members of parliament, one or two of them let out a cheer.

When it was all over the performers leant back in their chairs with a concerted sigh of relief. There was a distinct lightening of the atmosphere. Mrs Heyday gave everyone a gracious round of applause. 'Well done, everyone. Well done, Mr Robinson. Marvellous play. Simply marvellous. So clever.'

And with Mrs Heyday setting the tone of approval, thought Violet, it should be plain sailing all the way. Except for possible and likely disruption from Meredith

Martin and Gaye Worth.

~

When she had arrived at Meredith's door that evening Violet was more anxious than she wanted to be. There was a lot riding on the outcome of her visit. On the one hand there was Mrs Santenoy, whose account of her spell in Holloway Prison had affected Violet deeply. That nervous, twitchy lady who – Violet had to secretly admit – it was so easy to patronise and even to laugh at turned out to have more courage and moral commitment than the rest of them put together. Not in a million years could Violet imagine putting herself through the mental and physical torture of a freezing, damp prison cell with nothing but rats for company. She felt a strong sense of moral obligation to Mrs Santenoy and her fellow suffragettes.

Then there was the business with Robbie. It was no great concern to Violet whether or not they included the two women in his play. But his words to her the other day had struck home. She acknowledged that in order to mask her lack of confidence she had unwittingly turned into somebody she didn't recognise; and it was little wonder Robbie didn't like that person as she didn't like her much either. There was only one way she could immediately think of to make everything right.

On ringing the front doorbell of the nondescript building in Lambeth Violet had been greeted by a lady with very black and slightly unruly  hair – whom she rightly assumed to be the landlady – who told her that yes, Miss 'Mairie' was in and that she had a friend with her. It was with some trepidation that Violet followed Mrs Vlatsky up the dingy staircase to the room on the second floor and found herself confronted by not one, but both nemeses together.

There was a frozen moment as all three women stared at one another in shock, before Violet smiled and said,

'Hello ladies.'

The two women continued to stare at her for a moment longer before they looked away and mumbled, one after the other, 'Hello, Mrs Graham.'

'Could you spare me a minute?' she asked politely.

Meredith motioned Violet to the sofa. There was a short hiatus as first Merry and then Gaye sat down, gingerly, and waited as Violet peeled off her gloves and announced, 'I've come about the play.'

Still they said nothing.

'Needless to say I was surprised to see you at the Criterion the other day,' said Violet.

Merry went to say something but Violet got there first.

'But never mind, you were, and your song was very ingenious. Cleverly written and wonderfully executed. Mr Robinson was most impressed. It's just a shame it has no place in our play.' She laughed merrily, and alone.

'So unfortunately,' she went on, 'much as Mr Robinson was keen to include you in the play we could not think how to fit you in.' She smiled at them in turn. 'We wracked our brains – oh how we tried – I tried. But no matter what I came up with, we simply couldn't think of a thing.'

She paused.

'We could offer you small parts of walking suffragettes of course, but that would hardly achieve the point of the exercise, which is to make use of your . . .' she searched for the appropriate word, 'teamwork'. And you wouldn't be interested in such a thing anyway, I'm sure.'

They were watching her intensely. Gaye was gripping the arms of her chair. Merry was doing her best to look haughtily unimpressed but she was also jiggling her foot, which destroyed the effect somewhat.

'Did you come all this way to tell us we're not wanted?' said Gaye.

'I thought it only right,' said Violet. 'After all your hard work. And I realise Mr Robinson raised your hopes, most unfairly in the circumstances. I felt it only right to tell you the news in person.'

She never stopped smiling the whole time. Gaye stared at her with open hostility. Meredith turned her gaze to her feet.

'Unless, of course,' she said, 'you can think of anything?'

She smiled at them expectantly. Gaye looked grumpily at the floor.

'Ah well.' Violet stood up and started to put on her gloves.

'We could write new words to the song,' said Meredith, still eyeing her feet.

'New words? About what?'

'Anything you like.' Meredith looked up at last. 'Suffragettes.'

'Macaroons,' said Gaye.

'Or how about . . .?' Violet resumed her seat, slowly. She appeared to be thinking hard. 'Prison reform?'

'Prison reform?' they spoke in unison.

Violet then proceeded to relate the conversation she had had with Mrs Santenoy about her experiences in Holloway. She spoke eloquently about those remarkable women who were prepared to spend weeks in total solitude, all in the cause of female suffrage. She described the conditions in Holloway Prison in painstaking detail and ended up with, 'But it's hardly a suitable topic for a comical song, is it?'

'It don't have to be comical,' said Gaye.

'And it doesn't have to be that song,' said Merry. 'Or does it?' She looked at Violet enquiringly.

'I suppose not, if you can think of one that is well known. And loved. I imagine since Mr Gilbert presumably had no objection to 'The Modern Major General' he would happily grant his permission to rewrite the words of another of his songs.'

She did not miss the look that passed between the two women.

'Anyway,' she resumed the putting on of gloves and rose to her feet. 'There we are. If you come up with something let me know. And it would have to be quick, we start rehearsals in two weeks.'

She prepared to leave. 'And of course I'm making no promises,' she said. She opened the door, bade them both goodnight, and went.

As Violet descended the stairs she had to stop herself from laughing out loud. She didn't really care what happened next, she felt vindicated. Childishly so maybe. It had taken them longer to catch on than she expected, but catch on they did, finally. So now the onus was on them to come up with something, and the thought of all the effort she felt sure they would put into it was deeply satisfying.

# 37 Opening night

The tiny Touchstone Theatre was bursting at the seams on the opening night of *Mrs Morphett's Macaroons* in November 1905.

With a cast approaching twenty and three small dressing rooms – one for the boys, one for the girls and one for Mrs Heyday – the actors, and the actresses in particular, had to take it in turns to get ready while the rest hung around in any spare corner they could find: on the staircase, behind the scenery, in the wings or in an over-full green room.

'Has anyone seen . . .?'

'What the blazes, how am I supposed to . . .?'

'Where is my wig?'

Moving swiftly and calmly among them all was the ever-capable Miss Winnie Walters, wardrobe mistress supreme, formerly of Herbert Tree's company, adjusting here, making a tuck there, reassuring everywhere.

One of the younger actresses, a little over-excited, had decided to import a bottle of champagne which she proceeded to open and to swig from, transforming her over-excitement into something approaching hysteria. One of the younger actors pretended, not once, not twice, but four times, that he did not know one dressing room from another and made several forays among the ladies until the door was firmly slammed in his face.

Behind the scenery on stage in a dark corner Meredith Martin and Gaye Ward rehearsed their piece over and over. Robbie Robinson toured the building asking if anyone had seen Mrs Graham. At the top of the stairs Mrs Santenoy paced back and forth practising her one and only line, pausing now and again to jump out of someone's way with a muttered apology.

Mrs Graham was in the prompt corner conferring with Wilfred the stage manager. 'I never saw macaroons like that before,' she said. 'What happened to yesterday's?'

'They got eaten.'

'Oh. Then we will just have to improvise. Do you have a lace handkerchief or something?'

'Anyone got a lace handkerchief?' yelled Wilfred into the darkness.

At precisely the quarter hour the door to Mrs Heyday's dressing room opened and the lady herself emerged, clutching a bunch of roses. She progressed first to the ladies' dressing room where she handed a rose to each of them in turn, holding onto their wrists and whispering, over and over, the very same little blessing: 'It will be a triumph, and you will be magnificent. May God be with us all,' before she advanced, via the overspill of ladies and gentlemen hanging around the corridor to the men's dressing room, where she repeated the procedure.

As Violet emerged at last from the wings she bumped into Robbie.

'I need to talk to you,' he said.

'Yes, what about?'

Just then the plump and surprisingly imposing figure of Felix Overbrand appeared, in full evening dress. Thumbs tucked into his waistcoat he materialised out of the gloom of the corridor as if he owned the place, which of course he did. Clearly, when he was in his element, Mr Overbrand was a different person.

'Mr Author, how are you?' He slapped Robbie heartily on the back and without waiting for an answer he declared, 'I've never known a writer sit through his play from start to finish on opening night. Not ever.'

'Have you not?'

'And Mrs Graham. Your first ever opening night. Or should that be your first first night!' He guffawed.

'Will this do?' The assistant stage manager appeared suddenly in front of Violet clutching a lace handkerchief.

'Yes, perfect,' said she.

'My advice is,' Overbrand placed an avuncular arm around Robbie's shoulders and tried to steer him away from the prompt corner, 'take up position in the back of the dress circle, near the bar. Make full use of the bar and if you find it all too much, escape to the Bolt Hole.'

'What's the Bolt Hole?'

'The Coal Hole public house,' said Overbrand, with a chuckle.

'Thank you, Mr Overbrand,' said Robbie, untangling himself. 'I just need to have a word with . . .'

But Violet had vanished.

'Ah, there are you are, dear,' said Mrs Heyday. She cornered Violet at the top of the stairs, looked deep into her eyes and taking hold of her wrist she presented her with her rose. 'The last one, and the best, of course. For the lady who made it all happen.'

'Well I can't say that . . .'

'I have always believed in beginner's luck.' Mrs H laughed quietly, and melodiously. 'You will never forget your first success. Remember this. Remember every moment. The smell of it,' she closed her eyes and breathed deeply, 'the sound of it, every tiny detail. Remember it all.'

'Thank you Mrs Heyday. And very good luck to you,' said Violet to the gracious lady's back as she glided away and around the corner.

'Violet!' A voice spoke sharply and she turned in surprise.

'What, Robbie?'

'This arrived by post this morning. Do you know anything about it?' He was brandishing a document.

'I am so sorry to interrupt,' came the soft voice of Winnie Walters. She was accompanied by one of the lady suffragettes. 'We seem to be short of a wig, do you think she looks all right as she is?' She was addressing both Robbie and Violet.

'She looks all right to me,' said Robbie.

'Why do we need a wig?' asked Violet.

'I'm playing more than one part,' said the actress. 'And someone, I won't say who, has gone off with my wig, so I'm going to look exactly the same in both roles and no one will guess I am not the same person.'

'Perhaps some hair ornament. Winnie, do you have such a thing?'

'I will find one, Mrs Graham.'

'So sorry Robbie,' said Violet. 'I'll be right back.'

With which the three ladies walked off together in the direction of the wardrobe.

Robbie stood stock still for a complete minute. Then when Violet did not reappear he turned and retraced his steps down the stairs and through the pass door to the front of the house.

~

As first nights go it could not rival Violet's previous experience of the grand opening of Her Majesty's, of course. But she was glad to see that, with several plays opening every week in the West End *Mrs Morphett* had attracted her fair share of dignatories.

As Violet made her way to the front row of the pit (she still refused to occupy the superior seats) she spotted several familiar faces. There was young Olivia Armstrong, accompanied by her mother Lady Armstrong, the bearded and slightly stooping Mr Kapps with his wife Constance. Several of her erstwhile suffragist friends were present, including, to her astonishment, Mrs Fawcett herself. (She'd been invited but never in her wildest dreams did Violet imagine she would actually turn up.)  Then Herbert Tree appeared and proceeded to destroy Violet's anonymity in a stroke by greeting her with a bear hug and talking to her for several minutes.

GBS sat on his own in the centre stalls, staring straight ahead of him. The entire staff of *The Weekly Chronicle* had turned up to mock, jeer and even to review their colleague Robbie Robinson's play. There were other distinguished members of the press, if that is not a contradiction in terms, and even the odd politician. All in all it was quite a turn-out.

Jimmy Worth, his wife by his side, sat in the front row of the gallery, scowling. He had sacrificed a night's pay to attend the performance and he didn't want to have to regret it. On her own in the stalls (her brigadier husband assuming she was dining with friends at her club) sat Mrs Stephenson, estranged mother of Meredith Martin.

Dotted here and there in different parts of the auditorium were several young men, most of them with their wives; their sole (and secret) reason for attending was to witness the West End debut of their one-time lover, for whom the play, it was claimed, had been written.

Last to arrive and most conspicuously was Miss Elizabeth Chester-Bolt. Dressed from head to foot in powder pink satin she floated down the aisle, nodding and waving to left and right like royalty at a wedding, and at maximum inconvenience to her fellow theatregoers she took her seat in the centre of Row H in the stalls, two rows behind GBS.

And at last it was the cue for the curtain to rise.

# 38 The play

Robbie watched the arrivals from a dark corner of the stalls. Then as the auditorium lights dimmed he made his way up the stairs to take his place, as instructed, at the back of the dress circle. He'd give it a few minutes, he thought, until the first laugh, and then he'd repair to The Coal Hole or similar hostelry, again as instructed.

Those first few minutes after the curtain has risen on a play begin with an almost imperceptible murmur of approval – or disappointment – at the set, which establishes in every audience member's mind an expectation of what is to come. Sometimes a particularly elegant setting would get a round of applause, a practice Robbie found bizarre. There was no such applause for Mrs Morphett's drawing room (to Robbie's relief), but there was for Leonora Heyday which, to his dismay, she acknowledged, even encouraged, by turning to the audience with a gracious smile directed in turn to every corner of the auditorium.

And then the play began. The first laugh came quite quickly, and reassuringly, when Mrs Morphett expressed her frustration with the cause of women's suffrage to her maid Annie, who informed her mistress she was 'doing it all wrong, if you don't mind my saying so, madam'; a laugh that, Robbie acknowledged, had as much to do with Mrs Heyday's reaction as it did to Lolly's delivery. When

Annie went on to chide her mistress for being too subtle and altogether too polite, and proceeded by conducting a tutorial on how to communicate with the common people and how 'a bit of vulgarity never did any harm, not if you want to get every Jane and Sally on the street on your side', they laughed again, longer and louder. So much so that Robbie, who had been momentarily distracted by the fact that the eponymous macaroons were not just invisible beneath what looked like a lace handkerchief but that not one of the ladies had actually eaten one, forgot all about them and laughed along with the audience.

The audience! That good-natured, eager group of people, so determined to have a good night out, so easily amused. It would take a lot more than a plate of *papier-mâché* macaroons – or whatever Wilfred the stage manager had managed to cobble together – to upset this audience.

When it came to Annie's front-of-curtain monologue, written solely to cover a scene change, in which she confided to the audience her views on class, and society, and in particular on 'this business of women's suff'rings' – the word was Lolly's invention; Robbie had tried to resist but was out-argued by the rest of the cast – the audience were by then quite ready to eat out of her hand. Lolly had superb comic timing; she knew when and how to hold a pause and when and how to break it with a sudden laugh, or maybe even a skip and jump or, beyond outrageous, a wink. She was playing to the gallery which, Robbie had to admit, was entirely appropriate, for her character and for the play.

He decided to hang on for another scene, when Annie goes out onto the street and tries to waylay passers-by, and in doing so attracts the attention of a young man who, the audience will later discover, is a member of parliament and who will turn out to be the cause of Annie's near-downfall. The drama was heightened by the fact that

Robbie partly suspected the two actors were enjoying an offstage affair, which made the young man's attempted seduction of Lolly/Annie in the following scene that much more, you might say, convincing. At this stage in the proceedings however the audience was taking the man at face value, as Annie herself appeared to be doing. It was not until the end of the scene when he turned to the audience and gave them a look to freeze any smile on any face that their doubts began to creep in.

At this stage Robbie's nerves were definitely beginning to fail him so he ran down the stairs into the street and into the nearest pub, The George, where he immediately ordered and downed a double whisky. Followed by another. At which point he fought and resisted the temptation to disappear into the night.

He returned to his spot at the back of the dress circle, a little light-headed, part-way through the second act. The audience had gone horribly quiet. There came the odd instance of the sound theatre makers most dread: the cough. It was not the genuine choking cough, or even a throat-clearing sort. If you've sat in a theatre as often as Robbie had done as his alter ego Algernon Lightly, theatre critic for *The Weekly Chronicle*, you know an authentic cough from one that signals a mind not altogether engaged in what the eyes are viewing. It is an infectious cough, it spreads with remarkable speed and it tends to manifest itself at crucial moments, masking a word, or worse, killing a joke.

But it was just at this point that there appeared on stage two lady suffragettes. As the music started up and they sang their song so they gradually removed their elegant outer garments to reveal prison uniforms: dark green flannel dresses with a white apron and cap, and the arrows that signified government property. The song went thus:

MERRY & GAYE: Two little maids from Holloway,
    Miserable, lonely and locked away,
    No one to talk to from day to day,
    Two little maids in gaol.

MERRY: Two long weeks in solitude,
GAYE: Nothing to do but sit and brood,
MERRY: My body's wracked
GAYE: And my brain is stewed,
MERRY & GAYE: Two little maids in gaol.

MERRY & GAYE: Two little maids who, all unwary,
    Joined a protest in Parli'ment Square-y,
    Stuck in a poke in solitary,
    Two little maids in gaol,
    Two little maids in gaol.

MERRY: Locked in a cell as cold as ice,
GAYE: Sharing a bed with rats and mice,
MERRY & GAYE: No one should pay such a heavy price
    As two little maids in gaol,
    Two little maids in gaol.

MERRY: One little maid will soon be free,
GAYE: One little maid as well, you'll see,
MERRY & GAYE: Then two little maids'll no longer be
    Two little maids in gaol
    Two little maids in gaol.

MERRY & GAYE: Two little maids, who all unwary,
    Joined a protest in Parli'ment Square-y,
    We'll fight to the death if necessary!
    Two little maids in gaol.
    Two little maids in gaol.

It brought the house down. The applause went on for so long after the girls had left the stage they had to return to give a bow, and then, in response to continuing demand and to Robbie's profound annoyance, an encore.

They had performed the song to perfection, he had to admit. The original was familiar to most of the audience (and in this instance the management had obtained permission from its original writer, Mr Gilbert), and it was delivered with just the right amount of defiant and *faux* innocent pertness by those tricky, clever, objectionable yet perfectly-synchronised ladies called Merry and Gaye.

However it was not what Robbie intended. His comedy satire was beginning to look more and more like a pantomime. The audience were enjoying themselves far too much. He wanted to yell at them to shut up and listen, for God's sake. The problem was after a fallow patch they were all too ready to laugh, and Merry and Gaye had already established themselves, as two squabbling suffragettes, as comic characters. For the first time Robbie understood why the likes of GBS stormed out of the theatre when people laughed at his plays.

He had hesitated over the song. It was fun, but again it made light of the awful business of those courageous women who were prepared to go to gaol for the cause. He didn't think it hit hard enough. Underlying the light-heartedness of the words there was the strangely moving spectacle of watching two stylish women dressing down into prison garb. That was Violet's idea. And the final chord, played on the piano by maestro Mr Dennis as a deliberate discord in order to send a chill into the audience's hearts, was completely drowned out by the applause.

And nobody in the audience clapped louder than Meredith's mother, Mrs Stephenson.

Soon it was time for the final scene.

This was Lolly's crowning moment. She stood upright, on both legs for a change, in the stalls of the make-shift House of Commons, delivering her maiden speech as the first female member of parliament and vowing that, now women had the vote, one day in the not too distant future only women would be permitted to become members. When the House rose in uproar she waited for it to die down and then, in a voice so quiet you strained to hear it, one by one she obliterated her opposition by warning them that she 'had something on them', as she put it.

'You, the Honourable Member for Hendon South, look back to a certain Thursday in May when your wife thought you were still in the House. And you . . .' she turned to face another imaginary MP, 'the Honourable Member for Keswick. What did you have to say to your wife when you arrived home that evening without your hat?' Her voice gradually rose in volume as she rose in authority. 'As for the Honourable Member for Chichester, what would you say if the House demanded to see your tax returns? There is not one member in this House who doesn't have something to hide. There is not one of you who is leading a spotless life. You've had it your own way for far too long, you think you're invincible.' As she spoke she included everyone, on stage and in front of it. The 'House' she referred to was both the Commons and the auditorium itself, and the 'accused' her fellow MPs and the audience. Steadily, firmly, and with total command she sent a charge through the entire place so that when the curtain fell, as it did quite suddenly, to Robbie's joy it did so in complete silence.

The curtain call went on and on. Mrs Heyday, ostensibly the star of the show, made gracious yet ostentatious play of stepping aside and allowing the audience to roar for Lolly. Lolly herself stood on one leg centre stage and grinned like an awkward schoolgirl. As the applause continued she remembered herself. She kissed her hands at the gallery and curtseyed to the boxes. She waved to the people in the pit and gestured wide to the folk in the stalls and the dress circle. She behaved, all in all, like a star.

# 39 After the play was over

The after-show party . . . well, you should have been there, as the newspapers would say.

In one corner see Mrs Millicent Fawcett herself, bedecked in a fur stole, in deep conversation with her stage representative, Leonora Heyday. Mrs Fawcett has a thing or two to say about the play and she is saying it, forcefully. Mrs Heyday listens, head on one side. Then the two ladies laugh.

'I might object to the notion that I do not know how to talk to the common people,' Mrs Fawcett declares, with a smile. 'But it was a neat dramatic device, I quite see that. And as for the depiction of life inside a prison, well, they only have themselves to blame.'

'Who, the suffragettes?'

'Of course. I never held with the idea of civil disobedience, not now and not ever. It is not the way to achieve our goals. But then,' she smiles again, a touch frostily this time, 'it seems my ideas have been superseded.'

In another part of the room Merry and Gaye have linked arms and are laughing rather loudly and drinking rather copiously. Gigi's father, almost the only person in the room who isn't smiling, is giving his daughter the full force of his opinion. 'The song was all right,' he pronounces, nodding. 'But what was all that nonsense with your foot?'

'What nonsense?'

'That – wiggly thing.' He lifts a foot and waves it about by way of demonstration. 'It made no sense.'

'It wasn't meant to make sense. It was meant to get a laugh.'

'That's no way to get a laugh.'

'Well, it worked.' His daughter pouts. 'And you do it all the time.'

'It's cheap,' says Jimmy Worth. 'I always have a reason for what I do. And that silly face you pulled, what was that for?'

'It wasn't *for* anything, Pa!' Gigi is almost shouting now. 'Why can't you say something nice for a change? We got four curtain calls! And an encore!'

'It's not just about the curtain calls, young lady. If you want to . . .'

But he is talking to himself. Gigi, her arm still linked in Merry's, has moved on.

Mrs Stephenson meanwhile has slipped away without announcing her presence to her daughter. She weeps gently all the way home in the cab.

Mrs Santenoy is surrounded by a gaggle of suffragists. Her spell in gaol has given her considerable status.

'Were you really in Holloway?' asks one of them.

'Yes, dear. It was dreadful. Truly dreadful.'

'It was ever such a funny song,' says another.

'It was,' she acknowledges. 'But it was no laughing matter, I assure you.'

'So they're putting us in prison now for demonstrating, are they?' a third voice joins in.

'And when they took off their dresses and there they were in prison garb, well, you could have knocked me down. I didn't know whether to laugh or cry.'

'But what did you think of my performance?' asks the

elderly lady, not without anxiety.

There is silence as the suffragists look at one another in puzzlement.

'Were you in it too?' someone ventures.

'Yes! You didn't notice me? I spoke a line!'

'Well, I'm sure you did it really well.'

'*I* noticed you. You were superb.' This is from Miss Chester-Bolt. She places a hand on Mrs Santenoy's arm. 'We are proud to know you, Mrs Santenoy,' she acknowledges, in a rare moment of honest admiration. Mrs S almost faints with happiness.

Elizabeth Chester-Bolt sails on. Watching her across the room Violet notices she seems to have requisitioned Felix Overbrand. Their arms are linked, and Violet wonders for a split second if she should rescue him. But then Miss C-B turns to say something to Mr O that makes him laugh until his shoulders shake, and he pats her hand and leans towards her until their shoulders are almost touching. Well well, thinks Violet.

Robbie is chatting to his colleagues. There is a good deal of ribaldry and a certain amount of elbow nudging. He realised early on he cannot expect a considered opinion from any of them so he is simply enjoying himself, or trying to. But his laugh is hollower than his friends' and his smile not quite so genuine. He is feeling unexpectedly melancholy.

The play was a resounding success, there is no doubt about it. But GBS walked off without saying a word. And from all the conversations Robbie has been able to eavesdrop, all the audience were talking about was the song, or the part where Annie exposed the wrongdoings of her fellow MPs, or the bit where the young man thought she had fallen for him and she turned the tables on him. And wasn't it funny when . . . and when she did that . . . and he did this . . . As if the sum total of their serious work was no more than a series of comedy turns.

He partly blames Lolly. When you've been working away in a rehearsal room alongside your fellow actors and nobody's laughing at you, that first exposure in front of an audience can do terrible things to an actor. Lolly was experienced enough to know how to milk a joke without killing it. But she did nothing to quell the audience's assumption from the word Go that Annie was a figure of fun. Clever, and more worldly-wise than you might expect from a scullery maid, but nonetheless a comedy character. Each time she came onto the stage you could almost sense the audience gearing up to laugh.

On the other hand, give her her due, the ending did everything Robbie had hoped and dreamed it would do, and that was entirely thanks to the way Lolly delivered her final speech.

It was odd, for a man like Robbie, for whom life always appeared to be a thing not to be taken too seriously, to react this way. He'd written a satirical comedy about a serious subject and all anyone could do was laugh at it. And now, God save us, there are Merry and Gaye in the middle of the room, repeating their whole routine, with Lolly joining in and the rest of the room turning to watch and laughing uproariously.

'Why so glum, Robbie?' comes a voice from close beside him.

Robbie sighs, but doesn't reply.

'Was it because they laughed too much?'

He shakes his head, yet smiles.

'You must be the only writer who hates it when people laugh at his jokes. Apart from GBS, that is.'

'It wasn't the jokes I objected to. The audience was just out to have a good time.'

'Outrageous,' says Violet. 'How dare they?'

Robbie chuckles.

'Just because people laugh doesn't mean the message didn't get through. They'll be telling their friends – There's this grand comedy at the Touchstone, you should go along, you'll have a fine night out. It's about this maid who gets involved in the suffrage movement. - What's that you say? - The suffragists. You know, the women who campaign for the right to vote. You might be surprised, they're not all hooligans who go about breaking windows. Some of them end up in Holloway for their beliefs. You never really gave it much thought before? Well then you should go along, you might learn a thing or two.'

There is another pause. Robbie appears lost in thought. Violet puts her arm through his and squeezes it. 'Dear Robbie, I am sorry you feel so gloomy.'

'I'll get over it.'

They stand and watch the proceedings for a moment.

'Violet, I . . .'

His voice is drowned out by a roar from the middle of the room. It appears Lolly has added some of her own words to the song from *The Mikado* and the three of them have turned Merry and Gaye's routine into a Can-Can.

'Let's get out of here,' says Robbie. He grabs Violet's hand and pulls her out of the door and down the stairs to the street. He leans against the wall, breathing hard.

'Now what?'

'Just a touch of claustrophobia. But look, I received a document in the post today, naming me as co-respondent in the divorce case between Mr and Mrs Anthony Turnip.'

There is a long pause as Violet's mouth, which is hanging open, tries to find something to say.

Then quite unexpectedly Robbie starts to laugh.

'What?'

'After all this time.' He struggles to talk between laughs. 'I am now being accused of doing something I have been resisting for, for who knows how long? As you well know.'

Violet is not quite ready to laugh yet. 'But how?'

Violet is not quite ready to laugh yet.

'Don't you find that hilarious?'

'But how?'

'That's a very good question. It appears there was a witness.'

'A witness to something that never happened?'

'Apparently.'

'Who could that have been?'

'I think it was probably Mrs Woolly.'

'*Mrs Woolly?* But she . . . why would she do such a thing?'

'I imagine someone put her up to it.'

There is another little pause as the two friends gaze at one another in puzzlement.

'And that someone was . . .?'

From upstairs, through the open window right above their heads, comes a shriek from a familiar voice.

'No!' says Violet.

'Who else?'

'Oh my goodness.'

'God bless her,' says Robbie.

It is taking Violet a while to process this information.

'The document was accompanied by a letter claiming that all expenses will be covered by the plaintiff.'

'Yes, just as Ann Veronica said.'

'Who's Ann Veronica?'

'It doesn't matter. But it does mean your name is exposed.'

'So what?'

'So what? Oh, Robbie.'

'Violet Turnip, otherwise known as Violet Graham, will you marry me? Please?'

'Well,' says Violet. She is trying to think of something

witty to say. 'As you say, after all this time, and all Lolly's hard work, and Mrs Woolly. What will you do about Mrs Woolly?'

'I will double her pay.'

'Oh! In that case, I suppose . . .'

The rest is lost in a kiss.

# 40 Keeping on track

The play ran for 140 performances, exactly 20 weeks, which was better than anyone could have expected. The reviews were almost entirely positive: 'One of the most amusing plays to be seen in the West End since . . . ' 'A comic joy . . .' 'Fun and games at the tiny Touchstone Theatre . . .' 'Young Annie the kitchen maid shows every bit as much cunning as the average man, therefore proving the case for women's suffrage . . .'

The only thing the critics took exception to was the ending: 'Preposterous!' they spluttered. 'Too far-far-far-fetched for words!' 'Women,' gasped another, 'running our country? Pass me the smelling salts!' Robbie's favourite went as follows: 'Alas, Mr Playwright shows his inexperience, not to say his immaturity, in the final moments of the play. To suggest a world governed by women takes his otherwise entertaining play into the realms of fairy tale. There is satire, and there is farce, and then there is amateurishness, and Mr Robinson is guilty of all three.'

Robbie was delighted. 'You see?' He waved the newspaper in Violet's face.

'So we were both right,' she said. 'I'm glad you're happy, Robbie.' And she kissed him lightly on the lips.

The word spread very quickly among the suffragettes, who arrived in throngs not just to see one of their colleagues treading the boards of a West End theatre but to bear witness to a play that told their story with such wit and passion and imagination. The generally shy and retiring Mrs Santenoy became positively regal.

Lolly Mulligan meanwhile turned into an instant celebrity. She dined out every night after the show, each time with a different escort. She was seen, and photographed, arm in arm with royalty. She was invited as the guest of honour to the opening of the Piccadilly and Brompton Railway. The newspapers could not get enough of her.

However as the run continued the inevitable was beginning to happen on stage. 'The Gaolbird Song', as it was now known, was growing in length as each verse became punctuated with increasing bits of 'business' on the part of Gaye Worth. Meredith Martin on one occasion actually tried to add a couple of new verses, to the confusion of the conductor and the fury of the playwright. The encore was now a regular feature of every performance. To cap it all, the two ladies had turned the onstage costume change into a kind of bizarre striptease. Robbie was beside himself.

'They have to be stopped!' he muttered. 'They'll kill the whole thing stone dead.'

Violet bit the lip that would have liked to have said 'I could have told you as much.'

'Have you spoken to them?' she enquired.

'Of course I have. It's a waste of time. They claim people are only coming to see the show for their song, which is outrageously arrogant of them.'

'I could try having a word,' said Violet.

'Darling girl, you are an angel. Good luck with it.' He thrust his hands into his pockets and wandered off moodily.

The following night's performance was ten minutes

shorter, despite the fact that the audience, everyone agreed, laughed louder than ever. There was no encore of the gaolbird song, and the two ladies earned more applause in the curtain call than almost anyone else in the company, including Lolly Mulligan and Leonora Heyday.

'What did you say to them?' asked a delighted Robbie after the show.

Violet gave him an enigmatic smile and placed a gentle kiss on his cheek.

~

She had, fortuitously, come upon the two ladies sitting together in the corner of an empty stalls bar between shows. 'Ah, here you are,' she said brightly.

They ceased their conversation and turned to look at her with identical expressions: slightly startled, not particularly welcoming, decidedly suspicious. She took a seat at the table with them and smiled broadly.

'So,' she said. 'How do you suppose it's going?'

'Very well,' said Merry.

Violet nodded. She paused, as if thinking what to say next.

'Would you say, all in all, you are getting more laughs now than you did earlier on in the run?'

The two ladies looked to one another and then back to Violet. They said nothing.

'It's not a trick question,' said Violet, though of course it was.

'Yes,' said Gaye.

'I hadn't noticed,' said Merry, though of course she had.

'I am wondering why the show runs fifteen minutes longer now than it did at the opening night.'

The ladies shrugged.

'Of course, that is in the nature of things,' said Violet, speaking like an old hand. 'If you get a laugh doing one thing you imagine you'll get an even bigger laugh if you do it twice. Do it three times and . . .' She sighed.

The two ladies just stared at her.

'We have a couple of problems, and I need your help,' she continued. She drew a breath. 'Mrs Santenoy. You talked to her, of course you did, so you have an understanding of the dreadful suffering she went through. Your song tells her story perfectly, except that – how can I put this? – for some reason the audience is treating her story as a joke. Which it really isn't.'

She paused again.

'What she went through, Mrs Santenoy and her fellow suffragettes, she did on behalf of all of us women. You, me, everyone in the country. Especially people like us. Working people, clever, talented and ambitious women who do not recognise the limitations the law of the country places upon us.'

'I can't see,' said Gaye, 'as how having the vote has got anything to do with us.'

Violet studied Gaye long enough for the girl to feel distinctly uncomfortable.

'How long were you without work before this play came along?' she asked them.

'Not long,' said Gaye.

'Long enough,' said Merry.

'The theatre is a tough business for actresses,' said Violet. 'Unless you are happy to be part of a chorus of course. There are so few good parts for women. With the exception of Mr Shaw, and Ibsen, you could say women have a pretty poor deal on stage. For the most part all they are required to do is stand around looking pretty and hoping to catch the eye of the dashing young juvenile. Do you remember *Johnson's Retribution*?' She laughed. 'And now, at last, we have a play about women, featuring many more actresses than actors, which is unique on the West

End stage.' She gestured dramatically. 'What opportunities for all of us!'

The ladies were waiting for Violet to get to the point. She did not just wander into the stalls bar for no reason, they independently surmised.

'Do you know why the Great Grimaldi was considered great?' she asked rhetorically. 'Because he knew how to control an audience. He knew how to make them laugh and when to make them stop.' She looked down at her lap for a moment before resuming. 'And there is a story about Richard Burbage, Shakespeare's Burbage, at the Globe Theatre. The audience loved to laugh and heckle the actors at the Globe apparently, even when the piece wasn't funny, and do you know how he put a stop to it? He turned his back on them.'

Still they waited.

'It's a far, far easier thing to make people laugh than to make them think,' she went on eventually. 'Our play is a light-hearted piece about a serious topic. It's a delicate balance. Amid all the "fun and games" as the critics call it, there is a story that the general public are unaware of, that women like Mrs Santenoy are prepared to go to prison for the cause of women's suffrage. Now *that* is no laughing matter, what do you think?'

'Well,' said Gigi, with some defiance, 'if you're saying you can write a comical play about a serious subject then how can it not be a laughing matter?'

'Your words,' this Violet addressed to Merry, 'are perfect. They appear to make light of suffering, and that is why we love the song so much. The problem arises when it becomes a music hall turn, and people forget the story the words are telling us and just enjoy a good laugh at two women playing the fool on stage. Mrs Santenoy is a reticent soul, she would never say a word against it. But what we were hoping for from your song is that it would strike terror into the soul of every woman in the audience. And every man. So you see, when you turn the transforming of your costume into prison garb into a striptease it misses the point. Do you understand?'

'What striptease?' asked Gigi.

'As I said before,' Violet continued steadily, 'it's easy to get a laugh. And you do. But to turn that laugh into something serious,' she paused dramatically, '*that* requires supreme skill. Which of course you have, the two of you.' She looked at them both in turn. 'And the encore. Have you heard of "the law of diminishing returns"?'

Once again Merry nodded and Gigi shook her head. They were neither of them looking Violet in the eye.

'It means the more you do something, the less it means.'

There followed a silence, as Violet waited for some response. Merry appeared to be gazing into the far distance. Gigi was scowling at Violet's right knee.

'Otherwise,' said Violet, after a suitable interval, 'and I would hate to have to do this, but we may have to cut the song altogether.'

'*What?*' Both women looked up, in identical shock.

Violet got to her feet. 'As I said, the show is over-running, we need to tighten it up at the least, or cut it down at the most. And now,' she glanced at the clock on the wall, 'I need keep you no longer, I am sorry to cut into your break like this. Good day to you, ladies.'

And off she went.

Subtlety is all very well, thought Violet as she made her way from the bar through the foyer to the street, not to mention the largely invented history lesson and the half-hearted attempt to appeal to the women's moral principles, which she should have known they did not possess. When it came to these two ladies, there was nothing like the direct threat.

# 41 Finale

On 12 April 1906, the day after the last performance of *Mrs Morphett's Macaroons*, Robbie Robinson and Violet Turnip (née Frogg) were married at St Peter's Church in Giles Street, Bloomsbury.

The reception was held courtesy of Herbert Tree in the ballroom in the Dome of His Majesty's Theatre. It was a considerably larger and more boisterous event than the marriage of Violet Frogg to the dashing Anthony Turnip fourteen years earlier. Mrs Robinson was a picture in a dark green two-piece with a nipped-in jacket edged in cream, with cream cuffs and cream flounces on the skirt, and a cream straw hat with a green ribbon perched coquettishly on the side of her beautifully-coiffed head. The overall effect was of refinement with a distinct touch of frivolity.

The guests included most of the cast and crew of *Mrs Morphett* and one or two members of Herbert Tree's old company at His Majesty's. Lolly Mulligan made an enthusiastic and predictably gushing bridesmaid. Zunker Kapps, blushing and bowing with self-conscious embarrassment, gave Violet away in lieu of her absent father. Reverend Frogg was away on business, he claimed, and his wife had sent her apologies and made excuses to do with chronic dyspepsia. Elizabeth Chester-Bolt, accompanied by Felix Overbrand, uncharacteristically took a figurative back seat in a dress that for once was designed not to show off her best feature. Robbie's fellow reporters on *The Weekly Chronicle* took it in turns to perform the duties of best man.

Suffragettes mixed with actors, aristocrats (Lord and Lady Armstrong and their daughter Olivia) with landladies (Mrs Vlatsky). Mrs Leonora Heyday gave a speech, honouring the bride and groom and reassuring the assembly, at some length, of their long and fruitful life together, adding with a touch of coquetry that she was 'available' for their next production, whenever that might be, the sooner the better, she added coyly.

Then Robbie, with Violet by his side, made a speech. He began by thanking the legendary Herbert Tree, sadly absent due to prior commitments, for bringing them together so many years ago in the very room in which they were now assembled. He told them how his wife disappeared on that same occasion suddenly, on the stroke of midnight, before her carriage turned into a pumpkin, and how she had continued to slip through his fingers time and again, which was why it had taken him nearly ten years to, as he put it, finally corner her.

'She is,' he went on, 'a woman of many parts, as you all know. I have met and come to know and love every one of them.'

Then he (mis)quoted:

'"All the world's a stage, and all us merely players.

We have our exits and our entrances,

And a woman in her time can play many parts."

'When we met,' he went on, 'Mrs Graham, so-called, was a serious and, dare I say it, a reticent young woman. Passionate, when she talked about the theatre. Mysterious about her background. I learned, in time, that she was yearning for something she could not define. Hence the parts, and the lives, and the many names of Violet Frogg,

Turnip, Graham and Humphreys.

'She was on the run, I could see, and I tried to be there, ahead of her, to catch her and hold her. But she ran faster than me and I could not keep up with her.'

There was a ripple of laughter. He turned to look at her.

'The Violet I know now is a different Violet. She is not Frogg, nor Turnip, Graham or Humphreys. Nor is she Violet Robinson, despite what the marriage certificate says. She is just Violet, plain and simple. And yet she is far from either of these. She is, in a shortish phrase, the most tantalising, enigmatic, passionate, contrary, adorable, clever, beautiful woman I have ever met. If there is anything I can be for her, or do for her as her loyal and boringly loving husband until the day I become sans teeth, sans sense and sans everything else, it is to rejoice in the person she is. Just Violet.'

He turned to the assembled guests. 'Ladies and gentlemen, please would you raise a glass.'

'To Just Violet!' said the assembled guests in chorus.

There were sniffles, and applause, and the odd cheer.

Robbie finished by promising that their union would continue to be both a personal and a professional one, and that together they would light up the skies over the West End, words which drew shouts of approval from the thespians present.

Meredith Martin and Gigi Worth stood side by side looking on. Gigi sniffed into her handkerchief.

'Are you crying?' barked her friend.

'Not really.' Gigi gave her nose a hearty swipe and stuffed her handkerchief into her bag. 'I was just thinking.'

'That makes a change.'

'How as it is possible to get married without losing your – you know.'

'If you mean what I think you mean most of us lost it

long ago.'

'Your whatdyacallit. Freedom.'

'Freedom?'

'To keep on doing what you want to do. You can have the best of all possible worlds.'

'You're strangely philosophical today, little Gigi.' Meredith looked down at her diminutive friend with a kindly smile.

'I feel ashamed. Sort of. Don't you?'

'Of what?'

'What we did, all those years ago.'

'Water under the bridge.' Meredith reached out to grab another glass of champagne from a passing waiter.

'And after all we did to her, she gave us the biggest break of our lives.'

'That's true.'

'And we never even apologised.'

'I think we made up for it. Don't you?'

Gigi thought for a moment. 'You never know, do you?' she said at last. 'At the time. Who's going up, who's on their way down.'

'Where the next engagement's going to come from.'

'Who you can be rude to and who you can't.'

'There's a moral here somewhere,' said Merry. 'If I could find it.'

Gigi exhaled deeply.

'Was that a sigh?' Merry demanded.

Gigi nodded. She was watching the happy couple. They were dancing, or rather shuffling slowly, alone, in the centre of the room, while guests stood in a circle around them looking on with the kind of benign smile reserved only for couples in love and newborn babies: a mixture of affection and tenderness tinged with longing and a touch of envy. She had never seen two people so absorbed in one another that they were completely oblivious to their surroundings. They were talking animatedly, and laughing, never taking their eyes off one another. At one point Violet laughed so much at something Robbie said she laid her head momentarily on his chest, at which he point he drew her into a close embrace, and the shuffle-dance effectively shuffled to a halt.

Gigi stood with her mouth open. She tucked her hand into Merry's arm, and this time she sighed audibly and deliberately, and this time her friend did not admonish her.

The embracing couple untangled and gestured for their friends to join them on the dance floor. The band, sensing a change in mood, upped the pace as one by one other couples took to the floor. Leading them was Veronica Ann and her husband Cecil, followed by Zunker and Constance Kapps, Lolly and Patrick, her actor colleague and current lover, Elizabeth Chester-Bolt and Felix Overbrand, and so on, until the space was full.

Gigi and Merry continued to look on from the sidelines, arms still linked.

'What now?' said Gigi.

Merry squeezed the arm of her friend and rival. 'Who knows?' she said. 'Something will come up, I can feel it.'

'I hope you're right,' said Gigi.

Then, 'Let's dance,' said Merry. She moved onto the dance floor, dragging Gigi with her. And as their fellow guests looked on in amusement they swirled around the floor to the music of – what else? – *The Merry Widow Waltz*.

# Historical note

As the sharp-eyed among you may have noticed, I have played around with the timing a little. *The Merry Widow* did not appear on stage at Daly's until 1907. As for the suffragettes, while the first to be gaoled for protesting – Mrs Pankhurst's daughter Cristobel and Annie Kenney (a miner's daughter and Robbie's model for Annie Addeley) – were given short sentences in October 1905, longer sentences were not handed out regularly to suffragettes in general until later, when Mrs Pankhurst's policy of direct action began to truly take off.

Details of the House of Commons debate in chapter 7 are taken from Hansard, 12 May 1905.

# Acknowledgments

Once again, a huge thank you to Joan Deitch for her copy editing, and for her encouragement, discernment and knowledge.

Many thanks also to Jane Dixon-Smith for the cover design and to Anna de Polnay for her illustrations.

§

If you enjoyed this book I would be very grateful if you could post a review on the platform you bought it from. Thank you,

And if you would like a free copy of my short story anthology *All We Need Is Love* and to subscribe to my occasional newsletter for behind-the-scenes snippets about my novels, please visit my website at https://patsytrench.com

# Author biography

Patsy Trench has spent her life working in the theatre. She was an actress for twenty years in theatre and television in the UK and Australia. She has written scripts for stage and (TV) screen and co-founded *The Children's Musical Theatre of London,* creating original musicals with primary school children. She is the author of three non-fiction books about colonial Australia based on her own family history and four novels about women breaking the mould in times past. *Mrs Morphett's Macaroons* is book four in her 'Modern Women: Entertaining Edwardians' series and is set in the world she knows and loves best. When she is not writing books she teaches theatre part-time and organises theatre trips for overseas students.

She lives in London. She has two children and so far one grandson.

Social media

Facebook: PatsyTrenchWriting
Twitter: @PatsyTrench
Instagram: claudiafaraday1920
Website: www.patsytrench.com

# Bibliography

Among the several dozens of books I consumed in order to immerse myself in the Edwardian theatre and music hall scene, the following I found particularly useful and entertaining.


Arliss, George, *On The Stage*, John Murray, London, 1928

Bailey, Peter, ed, *Music Hall, The Business of Pleasure*, Open University, Milton Keynes, 1986

Baker, Michael, *The Rise of the Victorian actor*, Croom Helm, London, 1978

John Betjeman, *Victorian and Edwardian London from Old Photographs*, Batsford, London 1969

Bingham, Madeleine, *The Great Lover: Life and Art of Herbert Beerbohm Tree*, Hamish Hamilton, London, 1978

Calvert, Mrs Charles, *Sixty-eight Years on the Stage*, Mills & Boon, 1911

Colette, *The Collected Stories of Colette*, Farrar, Straus, Giroux, New York, 1983

Collier, Constance, *Harlequinade: The Story of My Life*, John Lane the Bodley Head, London, 1929

Courtneidge, Robert, *I Was An Actor Once*, Hutchinson & Co., London, 1930

Fawcett, Millicent, *Women's Suffrage*, T C & E C. Jack, London, 1912

Fawcett, Millicent, *What I Remember*, T Fisher Unwin, London, 1924

Graham, Joe, *An Old Stock Actor's Memories*, John Murray, London, 1913

Griffith, Allen Ayrault, *Lessons in Elocution*, Adams, Blackmer & Lyon, Chicago, 1865

Grossmith, George, *A Society Clown*, Arrowsmith, London & Bristol, 1888

Jerome, Jerome K, *On the Stage and off*, Field & Tuer, London, 1885

Kingston, Gertrude, *Curtsey While You're Thinking*, Williams & Norgate, London, 1937.

Pearson, Hesketh, *Beerbohm Tree*, Methuen & Co., London, 1956

Pope, W Macqueen, *Carriages at Eleven*, Hutchinson & Co. Ltd., London, 1947

Priestley, J B, *The Edwardians*, Heinemann, London, 1970

Trewin, J C, *The Edwardian Theatre*, Blackwell, Oxford, 1976

www.ingramcontent.com/pod-product-compliance
Lightning Source LLC
Chambersburg PA
CBHW031944110726
47902CB00001B/288